ANGEL'S VENGEANCE

A PARANORMAL ANGEL ROMANCE

ELEMENTAL ANGELS

AIMEE ROBINSON

AMR PUBLISHING LLC

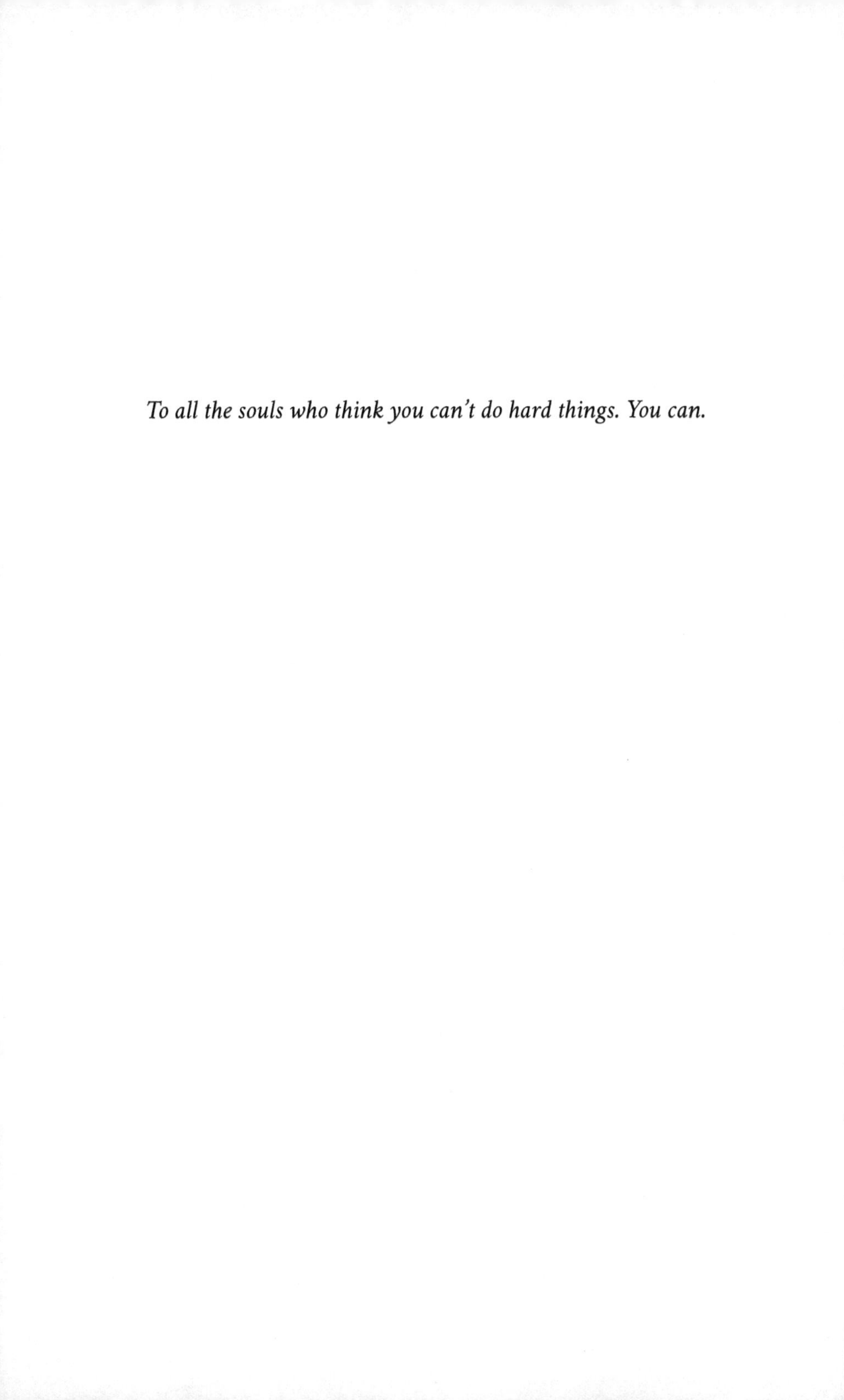

To all the souls who think you can't do hard things. You can.

ELEMENTAL ANGELS

Angel's Target

Angel's Duty

Angel's Devotion

Angel's Light

Angel's Temper

Angel's Conquest

Angel's Vengeance

Angel's Smoke

CHAPTER 1

Misting snowflakes danced in the streetlights below but would be too puny to cushion Rhode when he finally—really, *any* minute now—hurled himself off the roof.

January in New Hampshire brought with it shorter days and, therefore, shorter attention spans on the photocells in the outdoor lighting tasked with illuminating all of Aurora's small-town charm. It was a handy feature most of the time, especially when darkness frequently descended before the mortals' dinner bells chimed.

For Rhode, however, the little streetlamps' enthusiasm for the job was sorely underappreciated. After all, when a fallen angel of the Empyrean was about to test his flight ability for the first time since he was freed from eons-long enemy captivity, spotlights weren't necessarily in the *pro* column. Knocking off the rust was one thing. Lighting up the show for any potential audience was another thing entirely.

Rhode pressed the toes of his boots farther over the edge of the mechanic's garage until his steel-toed tips hovered above the still-leaf-leaden gutter. It was a directional focus of sorts and aimed his body where he hoped to land—*hoped* being the operative phrasing.

He squared his shoulders back and called forth his wings, again grateful that he was alone. The shiver that licked up his spine every time they appeared should have been second nature, something as normal as breathing for a seraph.

And then his ever-so-unhelpful brain chose that moment to remind him that even breathing could be strenuous given the wrong environment.

Rhode chased the memory away and recentered himself. Then translucent flaps of energy unfurled from between his shoulder blades, lengthening and solidifying through his outerwear until Rhode's back muscles strained with the pseudo-familiar weight.

Familiar but still strangely foreign.

He imagined the sensation was much like what Drea, his caregiver and soul bond to his sentinel brother Chrome, had once described to him as phantom limb pain. She'd mentioned it casually during one of their physical therapy sessions in those early weeks following his rescue. Mortals who had lost a limb often still experienced the sensations of having it: physical aching, itching, lingering spatial awareness, even temperature and vibrations.

The concept had intrigued him almost as much as the fact that mortals could still function so completely without their limbs.

In the end, though mortal physicians still hardly had a handle on the whys and wherefores of the phenomenon, they likely boiled the cause of the phantom sensation down to a miscommunication between the mind and the body. The central nervous system sending signals to the brain and spine to tell that part of the anatomy to move, despite it no longer being there.

Commands issued to parts of themselves that were long dead.

His muscles had connected with the explanation long before Drea had finished describing it, with Rhode having experienced the very same thing but in reverse. Despite what he'd endured, his body was still willing. His mind, on the other hand . . . .

It had been so long since he'd called forth his wings that he wasn't even sure whether he still could. His brothers—sentinel angels who had fallen to the mortal realm in a bid to protect the Empyrean, Heaven's highest realm, and were now stuck there—had not pushed him in his recovery, a fact he was grateful for despite how heavily it weighed on everyone.

No, only *he* could push himself to heal, though he doubted such a mundane word could even apply.

Bodies were far easier to mend than minds, and yet he found himself on a roof convincing his scrambled senses that some part of him still remembered how to fly.

Because if he could fly, he could fight. And if he could fight, he could find the demon responsible and pay him back a thousandfold for the lifetimes that had been stolen from him.

For *all* that had been stolen from him and done to him.

The mechanic's garage he was perched on wasn't particularly high, maybe twenty or thirty feet off the ground. The building was a modest automotive shop that serviced the New England tourist town's residents with basic repair, towing, and oil change options. Two bays. A parking lot with ten spaces. No gas pumps. A sign on the side of the road boasting what Rhode had to guess was a clever play on the word *lube*. And most suitable for his purposes on that particular evening: operational hours that did not include Sundays.

With the sun having just shuttered its drapes over what was left of the weekend, there was not a single mortal, or well-meaning angel, in sight.

Once again, Rhode had retreated to the solitude that had

been his long-constant companion. What he'd fought to escape for so long and what he always found himself coming back to despite the sentinels' many attempts at reviving that once-affable side of him.

But frozen tundras were frozen for a reason. Permafrost didn't take a vacation, regardless of whether it wanted to.

Rhode stretched his arms and wings wide. With the moon at his back, the condor-length curtains had taken shape and crept their heavy shadows above his shoulders and farther over the edge of the flat roof until the dark silhouettes of his flight feathers taunted him from the pavement below. He tightened his abdominals, which had strengthened beyond what he'd once known them capable of, and puffed out a soft grunt.

By the mages, his back muscles were tight. Despite the consistent training regimen he'd adhered to, some parts of the body were hard to work when the action they were designed for hadn't been available to them in some time.

Still, he managed to hold his wings out as wide as he could, relishing the strain. From that high above, the shadows of his wings didn't look any different than what he'd remembered of them before his captivity.

Before he had turned into a shriveled shell of the seraphim commander he'd once been.

His eyes immediately landed on his wings' curvature, but surprisingly, he didn't flinch at what the contours revealed. They were the same. Exactly the same as he remembered them, even the left one, which had always crested just slightly higher than the right.

He swallowed around a thick wad of emotion and squinted through the lightly falling snow. Hell, he was a damned fool if he thought he was prepared for this.

"How do they look exactly the same?" he whispered to the wind, an air of disappointment coloring his words, as if seeing an unrecognizable image of his own shadow would have made his course any clearer.

As if he needed further evidence of the mutilations that had been committed upon him or justification for what he'd do to avenge them.

Before he could think better of it, he whipped his head to the side, lifted his lip in a snarl, and examined the abomination of what was attached to him.

The reflective surface winking back caused a tight fist to curl in his gut. Seraph and sentinel wings had been cast from the prime mages' pearlescent energy when the races were created. They contained powerful remnants of the Eternal Flame, the source of all light and life in the realms. Once that energy abated and the wings took form, the appendages were soft but strong, swift, brutally sharp, and always efficient.

They were not metal. At least, not his.

The wind picked up and turned from chilly to biting. Almost icy. It was an apropos change to accompany the glacial sheets of feathers that sat shingled and poised for his command. The silky sheen of his natural-born wings was gone, carved away, and mutated into something wholly dark and other.

Yet one more thing that had been taken.

Rhode extended his fingers toward the latest part of him that had also been irrevocably changed. The list, it seemed, was never ending.

Rhode cursed softly under his breath as he brushed his fingertips up and down the smooth rows of metallic feathers. Mages, what he wouldn't give for a day with no surprises. A day where he could wake up and *not* discover some new horrible realization about how the body he was in was no longer his own. Or whether there were any parts of him left to recognize at all.

"Metal," he whispered into the cold night air, his breath fogging against his wings.

He cleared his throat and shifted his feet farther over the lip of the gutter. Then, with a shift of his muscles, he flung his wings high and wide. The movement was quick and comforting, like an old friend waiting to be called into service, albeit armed with a different weapon.

His wings were warm, just like those of Chrome, Tungsten, Titan, and all the other sentinels. Those angels, too, had been altered when they'd fallen to the mortal realm, with metal claiming more than its fair share of who they used to be. And that was before the sentinels had plucked him from hell and enfolded him into an embrace so loving and vibrant he'd likely never find such warmth again.

Except he had, hadn't he? It was in the very heat of his new wings and the newfound power that pumped furiously through every tightened muscle.

It was a different sort of heat, one that had only been coaxed out of him in the quiet reprieves from Cyro's . . . attentions. When Rhode's soiled cell was a blessing because starved solitude meant safety.

Safety and perhaps a certain spark that had been blooming in its vengeful intensity over the past year and a half since his rescue.

Rhode scanned the parking lot below, assessing where to land. Already, his wings were primed and pumping back the early winter's chill in great gusts around him. Surprisingly, they were neither lighter nor heavier than what he remembered. They just *were*.

He'd take it, for what choice do he have?

The only vehicle in the parking lot was a hook-and-chain tow truck tucked next to a row of trees that separated the mechanic's shop from the wooded area fanning out around it. No life. No movement. Not even a dusting of snow yet to cover the ground.

Perfect.

Rhode crouched low and smiled back against the strain in his thighs. It was a welcome, powerful tension that his muscles embraced with open arms. An inaugural flight that would be the final skill he'd have to master anew before his focus would shift and the tides would change. Before he could finally aim his ire in the direction of who deserved it most.

Cyro. The demon ruler. His captor. His current mark.

And soon, the first to feel the full force of Rhode's true vengeance.

Smiling at what the future promised, he readied himself to leap, to take the first flight since he'd been captured, when a shadowy figure sprang out from among the trees.

Rhode quickly pivoted and sank back on his heels. *Shit.* Then he recalled his wings and shivered as the metal faded into translucent energy and his wings were reabsorbed into his body.

"No one is supposed to be here," he ground out as he stared daggers at the intruder down below. "Damn mortals."

But the figure didn't keep running across the parking lot as Rhode had hoped. Instead, the person slowed when they reached the edge of the pavement and looked around through the thin veil of snow that had begun to increase. The white winter coat's hood did a hell of a job staying in place, surprisingly, as its wearer whipped their head in every direction imaginable until finally stalling out on the tow truck.

Rhode had often thought many things about mortal behavior were odd, but living among the sentinels' mortal mates had taught him to keep those observations to himself. Still, questions were questions, and as he sat hunched on top of the roof, those puppies began to pile up. Engaging with mortals was the literal last thing he had any interest in, but that didn't mean his curiosity needed to be ignored. Besides, the sooner he learned what was going on down below, the sooner he could get back to throwing himself off a building in the name of recovery.

He was just getting comfortable when the mortal walked back a few paces, then charged at the truck and slammed a shoulder against the driver's side window.

A single bored brow arched up Rhode's forehead. "Really?"

Then a sharp cry rang out as the mortal threw their head back and clutched their shoulder. The hood finally fell away, along with what remained of Rhode's meager interest in the caper. But right as he was about to retreat, riotous golden curls captured his attention as they escaped their confines and settled around the mortal's shoulders.

Her shoulders.

Whatever curious humor that had glued Rhode in place fled on the next breath when he connected the woman's actions with the object of her vandalism. "A thief, are you?"

He watched on as the woman, chest heaving, looked around her feet, then picked up a rock, took a few steps back, and heaved the thing at the window.

Rhode leaned forward, becoming more invested than he cared to admit. "That won't work the way you think it will, though it's far better than your shoulder."

The glass didn't shatter, as he predicted, but then his celestial senses snagged on a curious sound and pulled his ear closer to the scene below. A subtle snap.

"Ah," he murmured with recognition. The glass had been cracked. Moderate progress, he supposed. She grabbed another rock, aimed at the same fractured point, and threw it again.

Then Rhode's interest went the way of the dodo. While stealing a vehicle wasn't exactly petty theft, the act was equally uninspiring. Though he had been living among the mortals for the past year and a half since his rescue and had witnessed many wondrous things, larceny wasn't one of them. It was one thing for a mortal to steal for survival, to do what they had to do, but this woman? He narrowed his eyes and was immediately—well, he wouldn't say saddened. Disappointed perhaps, for her clothes were certainly fine enough to suggest that the crime she was engaging in was not one of dire necessity. Crisp blue jeans hugged a well-fed frame, the winter coat's bright white hue didn't carry so much as a smudge, and her boots were still nicely soled. Her face was turned away from him, though, but even from behind, her hair boasted a vibrancy that came with easy access to clean water, regular bathing, and sanitary supplies.

"Oh, little miss, stealing is never the answer."

Should he say something? Do something? Mortals' affairs were not his. Never were. The mages knew he had other things to occupy his thoughts, even when he so desperately might wish for a reprieve from them.

But this was an active theft by someone who, all things considered, should damn well know better.

The glass had yet to shatter, but the woman kept trying. At this rate, Rhode would be lucky if he could jump off this roof and get a flight in before spring. Still, there was no rush. He had to remind himself of that. Even in his recovery, when his body had pushed past its once-familiar strength into a physical territory Rhode had never explored before, he forced himself to slow down. He was an immortal angel. Time, as had been unfortunately proven, was immaterial. So, if that meant waiting out a thief while the more tender parts of him risked frostbite as he perched on a rooftop during a New England snowfall, then that was what he would do—

A depressed whine, one barely audible but still ominous, pierced through the quiet winter calm. Every muscle in Rhode's body tightened with a honed reaction. That tumultuous heat in his core rose up, churning in defense of what the sound meant.

Rhode ducked low and scrambled across the roofline, trying to get a better vantage point of the trees. His stomach bottomed out right as the low hum of vibrations began to build on the scant piercing wail. Then, like clockwork, the dark magic came.

Green lightning lit up the falling snow, providing a shimmering curtain behind which a portal opened and exploded into the night with a roar. One by one, a group of three males—all pale, bald, tattooed with teal and gold swirls, and draped in black tactical gear—filed out. As soon as the last bootheel left the threshold, the portal winked out of existence and a black SUV screeched into the mechanic's parking lot, blocking the exit. Another three males dressed in the same manner flew out of the doors before the tires stopped rolling and aimed some sort of firearm at the woman, though it didn't look like any gun Rhode had ever seen. The muzzles gave way to a funnel attachment, with the large end of the cone facing the woman. Then the men took a step forward, and that meager streetlight caught the reflection of two gold bands rimming the males' throats.

Charmers. Two bands signified them as elite class. Cyro's warrior demons.

One of the charmers who had come through the portal was running toward the woman but gestured at the closer males with weapons. "Grab her! Grab her now!"

Grab her?

Rhode's body seized up at the sight of his enemy, even while he struggled to make sense of what was happening. Why would the charmers go after a mortal woman? Had she inadvertently stolen from them? She couldn't know what they were. That was out of the question. Charmers frequently took the appearances of mortals when interacting with them and were almost indistinguishable from the real deal.

Except for now.

So then why…?

The woman turned back toward the approaching charmers, and whatever questions remained floating in Rhode's head solidified into cold brutal intentions.

Her shimmering eyes were stretched wide. Nostrils flared.

Eyebrows arched. Confident movements from a moment ago had turned stilted.

Fear. This woman was in fear. The signs were etched across every one of her body's curves and contours, even the ones dimmed by shadows.

She wasn't a thief. She was a victim. One running for her life from the very demons who'd ruined his.

Rhode rose, retreated a few steps from the lip of the roof, unfurled his wings, and roared. A few running strides later, he was airborne.

CHAPTER 2

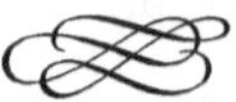

Neela could explain the fear that had her slammed against the tow truck, sure. The tears, on the other hand? Those were a big fat surprise, given the circumstances. She had such little experience with the occurrence.

Then again, what about her current situation *did* she have experience with? She'd never been caught before.

The puffer coat was a bonehead move. An impulse purchase that half a dozen of her favorite fashion content creators *swore* was one of that season's quintessential New England necessities. Sure, that was all well and good for the perma-camera-ready waifs who didn't already come preinstalled with a hefty amount of lower body lining and unfairly proportioned curves. For all of the coat's smooth lines and precision stitching, it was absolute shit in the stretchy-enough-to-run-for-your-life department. And the insulation sucked to boot. Might as well have been a mosquito net for all the good it did keeping out the chill from the frozen slab of steel at her back. Or blocking the scorching ire from the firing squad to her front.

Shit. How the hell did they find me?

Too late to figure that out now.

She swallowed back the acrid taste of desperation that threatened to clog her throat. She'd made it too damn far only to be dragged back like some pet who had absentmindedly wandered off when trying to find a spot to relieve itself.

She was no pet, not anymore, but if she didn't find a way out of this, the cage she knew all too well was exactly where she'd end up. Again.

Neela dug deep to find the voice she'd carefully honed in private. The one fueled by rage, indignation, and the possibilities of a world she'd only ever been allowed to peek through the window at. The voice she imagined a stronger version of herself using time and time again as naturally as a bird would use its song to greet each new day.

Or maybe a raptor.

Before she could heft that voice high and scream its release, a thunderous cry stopped her heart and stole her breath.

Then the first gun went off.

A strange web jettisoned and twisted through the night air before smacking her in the face. It took her all of half a second to realize the cage that had landed on her. A trapper's net.

One-inch mesh pulled against her skin, wrapping her body in a tightly coiled prison. Neela flailed and screamed like any animal would and tried to kick out of it, but she only succeeded in hitting the ground that much faster. Another pop rang out, then the weight surrounding her doubled as a second net anchored her more fully to the blacktop. Her legs were caught under her, and she roared out in pain when she twisted harshly and her knees crunched against the frozen asphalt. Wetness obscured what little she could see through the holes in the cargo net, but she managed to make out yet another goddamn funnel pointed toward her.

A third net. A surefire capture.

Then that strong voice inside her soul had gone silent with

the cold stillness of a death row inmate the second after the injection had been administered. With nothing left to fight with, she closed her eyes and tucked herself as tightly as she could before the launcher was fired and the net imprisoned her for good.

I can't go back. I just can't.

The gun went off, and she braced for the impact, but something entirely different assaulted her instead. A roar. No, a bellow. One she thought she'd heard bouncing off the parking lot right before the nets took her to the ground.

Only when her muscles could no longer take the strain of the tension did she crack an eyelid and nose around until she found a clear opening through the net. Her brain almost shorted out as it struggled to make sense of what her eyes were tracking.

"What the . . . ?"

Wings. Two silvery-white wings blurred beneath the moonlight and shredded the approaching net in midair like a falcon diving for its prey. Then the blurs turned into a strange duel of sorts, or maybe a dance. One commanded by something—a creature?—that slashed and spun around the netting, until bits of nylon confetti fell from the sky, peppering Neela's hair and blanketing the rest of her. Neela clenched her teeth and managed to reposition herself to take in more of what was happening, but that only led to more questions.

The wings were attached to a *man*—a man carved in brutal shadows who hovered above the ground and held two sickle-like weapons. A man with a face so calm and silently ruthless that it made her grateful for the netted barrier between them.

A chilly awareness speared through her gut.

The others who had scrambled from the tree line were running toward them at full force, unsheathing weapons, but the winged man paid them no mind. Did the dude not hear them, or was he too focused on ratatouille-ing the net? God, he was like some gladiator who was so focused on carving his name in the sand that he had zero time or interest in the lion about to rip his head off. Though, to be fair, if she had his power —or any power, for that matter—she couldn't say she'd feel any different.

Neela squeezed her eyes and shook off the fantasy of what-ifs. They'd never done anything for her, and they sure as hell weren't about to here.

Instead of swinging his attention to the three running for him, however, the winged man dove toward the three armed attackers closest to her and hooked the muzzles of two guns into the nook of his unusual weapons. With barely a tug from him, the firearms were sliced in half, while the third gun met a similar fate before the flying man's boots had even touched the ground.

Heavy grunts grew louder behind her.

"Look out! There are more coming!" she cried, still trying to free herself, but the mesh was so heavy and her limbs were pinned at such harsh angles, it was like trying to shrug out of a coffin.

The man ignored her, and as he continued to fight, it made sense why. Short of a nuclear bomb, Neela didn't think there was anything that could distract him. She'd even bet her latest morning glory night blooms that pediatric neurosurgeons had less focus than he did. His combat movements on the ground were a seamless extension of what he wrought in the air. Though Neela never thought such a concept would make sense, there was a definite beauty to his brutality, so much so that she couldn't look away even if she wanted to. He may have been outnumbered, but his size and strength alone were unmatched. His arms whirled around in seasoned swipes, but never in the same direction. He was too fast, too efficient for his opponents to pick up on his routines. When one kicked right, he would duck and arc left, slicing through highly open and way-too-vulnerable ribs. The contact and gruesome sounds would have made her cringe if there'd been enough space beneath the net to do so.

Trapped and alone, she could only lie there and watch as the winged man swirled in and out of shadows, hacking away at the others like a machete-wielding survivor in the rainforest trying to reach the one and only helicopter back to civilization.

She should have been grateful. She *was* grateful, but something about the man sparked an entirely different set of warning bells to start jingling.

Behind her, the others' approaches grew louder, and her heart kicked into her throat. Then she remembered her position, just who was chasing her, and why.

Shit. She needed to get the hell out of there. Fast.

She tried twisting in her bonds when an arc of blue flames flew across the parking lot and pierced the forehead of the small triad's leader. Electric fire kindled upon impact, then quickly churned across the rest of the flesh, devouring all that healthy muscle and tissue like cancer. He fell flat on his back and, with arms and legs flailing and cries being choked off by flames, dissolved into a pile of ash before her eyes.

Fear clogged her throat, paralyzing her. "Holy—"

Three sets of boots touched down in the parking lot. Boots belonging to men with, yup, more metallic wings. Wings and flaming-blue weapons.

Neela tracked her eyes up and up and up . . . God, they were the largest men she'd ever seen! Despite all their wings being similar to the first man's who'd swooped into the fight, only two looked like, well, men. She had to blink a few times to call her certainty to the surface, but when she narrowed her eyes on the final man in front of her, the only explanation for what she saw had no choice but to solidify.

The third one was most definitely and completely covered in metal, from the charcoal-gray hair pulled back in a bun to the wide gleaming cuffs encircling each meaty wrist. Never mind the dangling mace and battle ax coated in a blue fire that never seemed to burn him or any of the others.

Yeah, the dude was metal all right. With every small glimpse Neela managed through the netting, men with wings seemingly made from various types of elemental alloys assaulted both her senses and her attackers.

The rest of the parking lot fell away into some form of an arsonist's wet dream. Electric blue flames arced across bodies in a dazzling display of horror. Even the falling snow seemed to read the warning on these men's faces, wisely jumping out of the way of the flames.

Then there was a slight tug at the corner of the netting holding her head down. Before she could turn around fully, that strange sickle-shaped blade flashed in her periphery and the rest of the mesh fell away.

"Run. Touch nothing."

Neela kicked the remainder of the nets free and was about to bolt when the voice by her ear nearly stopped her heart.

That voice.

Somewhere, primary parts of her picked out the bits of timbre that made sense, the notes that rang with a gentle familiarity, while moving to the side the parts that didn't.

The hint of a tenor's raspy whisper. Vowels that almost fell away from the tentpoles of stronger consonants. Fragments. Nothing but the essentials. Urgency. All of that floated to the surface, far above the foreign darkness that seemed to coat what, for so long, had been spoken with a haunted sort of tenderness.

It can't be . . .

Neela scrambled to her knees and spun to find the man with blindingly white-silver wings holding that sickle-shaped weapon in one hand and a shredded net in the other.

And that was when the rest of the pieces clicked into place. It had been too dark before, the streetlights too dim and her vision too obscured. Up close, however, yes, she could see it. Though her brain had to work overtime, it managed to slowly morph the gaunt lines and haunted angles of the man from her memory into the powerful package before her. Through the haze of the past, the scraggly beard had fallen away, revealing a rough-hewn jaw hardened with tension. Strength compounded on strength as he squatted before her, with his muscular thighs hugged by black denim supporting a frame that didn't make sense with the one her mind called forward.

He'd been sick. Close to death. Not . . .

Then those umber eyes searched out hers, and she nearly fell back on her ass.

Many things could change about a person. Hell, she could write a freaking ten-book anthology on that subject. What never changed, however, was their soul, no matter how much one wanted it to. She'd been alive long enough to know that. And beneath the perfectly cut body capable of not only freeing her but also, apparently, flying, that same soul held out a direct line to her own.

"Axtar," she breathed.

Recognition flashed briefly in the depths of those carob-colored eyes, along with something she couldn't quite place. Fear? Confusion? He opened his mouth to speak—

A bullet exploded through his tucked wing and pierced clean through his right shoulder. Blood peppered the air, misting Neela's white coat with its gruesome spray. The man roared in pain, clutched his shoulder, and tried to turn around to see who had fired at him. Horror seized the last breath from her lungs as he faltered, his legs giving out beneath him. He toppled forward, and she caught him as best she could. Though he still tried to use his right arm to prevent himself from crushing her, the effort was largely worthless. If any part of her was still uncertain about the amount of strength he wielded, it was quickly jettisoned from the ship. All two-hundred-plus pounds of the man fell on top of her, effectively pinning her against the side of the tow truck.

"Rhode!" The largest of the winged men, the one who had been in a metallic form but was now flesh and bone like the others, sliced his ax through the only remaining body that hadn't yet been reduced to ashes. The final head separated from its owner, and blue flames had gotten to work eating away at the rest of it—including a hand that held yet another gun she hadn't seen before. A gun that was still smoking.

Rhode? Who's Rhode?

Neela stretched her arms wide around the man's broad shoulders and did her best to roll him over and lay him flat on the blacktop. Her thighs burned with the effort, but she eventually had him supine enough that she could inspect the wound.

Wounds, at least, she could handle.

"Go . . ." The hoarse whisper that fell from his full lips was nothing like the demand from earlier. All confidence had been stripped away, only to reveal a sad desperation that offered hints of something far sadder.

Did he . . . ? No, he couldn't want this, could he?

"No, I'm not going to leave you," she said as she shrugged out of her coat. "Help! Someone help me!"

Heavy footsteps pounded the pavement around her, but she didn't bother to look up. Because by the time she'd wadded up her coat enough to place it against the bullet wound in his shoulder, her hands stilled.

Several buttons had been lost on the silk shirt he wore, allowing for the edges of the garment to fall free in relief to expose the wound left behind.

A wound that no longer seeped blood, as Neela expected, but one that had turned all the skin around it into large crumbling flakes of rust and was spreading nearly as fast as that blue fire from earlier.

Nothing. There was nothing in her arsenal of wound care

knowledge that could even come close to explaining away what she was seeing. And she knew the moment he realized it, too. *That* was why his sadness was so permeating, why the finality of the word he'd spoken to her betrayed the regret they both felt.

Because he'd lost hope.

His lids dipped, providing a final shroud of dignity to shield the haziness of his last moments while the rust crept higher over his chest and up his neck. His throat bobbed quickly, and his gasping breaths faded into rattled wheezes.

"Move. Out of the way. Now!" The large male with the man bun grabbed her by the shoulders, knocking her off-balance. Neela tried to catch herself but fell forward, bracing her hand on the shriveling bare chest of the man who'd saved her.

None of them were prepared for the eruption of white light that enveloped both her and the man whose heart had, a second ago, stopped beating beneath her fingertips.

CHAPTER 3

Flecks of Rhode's awareness flirted with the familiar bite of excruciating pain. Ever the fighter, for better or worse, his mind still tried to bob to the surface, while his body resigned itself to the agony of torture.

There was something he was leaving behind, though. Something his memory recognized, even through the blanketing acid that sizzled across his skin. Something he didn't want to leave quite yet. Something curious . . .

He tried to reach for the memory, for whatever it was that felt elementally wrong to abandon, but every time his brain would snag on a loose thread of comprehension, Cyro's magical warfare would burn hotter, heavier.

Rhode's body fell away from him then. No sensation, no movement. No pain, even. Just nothing.

He'd never been so lucky, no matter how many times he'd wished for the prime mages to grant him oblivion. It was fitting, he supposed, that now, when something was gnawing at him, a clue finally offered after eons of searching, it was snatched away like any great danger should be.

And then it all came rushing back to him a thousandfold.

Searing light flared behind his closed eyelids. A gentle weight pressed into his chest, molding against him, bringing with it the faint aroma of hyssop, freshly tilled earth, and *life*.

The fire that exploded on its heels incinerated it all. Through the din that erupted around him, he heard muffled shouts of "Grab her!" and "Off! Now!" Then a different sort of pain roiled through him, one that both burned for and cried out against the weight being lifted off him. A sharper pain filled in the depression left by that comforting heaviness, instead tumbling within his core and dispersing throughout every muscle in his body. Limbs stiffened, balls tightened, and teeth gnashed together as the brilliant white light receded bit by bit, leaving healthy skin and tissue and awesome power in its wake.

Flames. Blue electric flames exploded from his core and arced down every part of his body. He could feel them, but . . . not. There was no longer heat, nor any scorching pain. There was only power. Power he'd solely witnessed in battles long ago but never wielded himself.

Angel fire.

"Back up. Everyone back the fuck up *right now*! Jesus Christ, how is this happening?"

As soon as Rhode registered the speaker's voice, the fire around him retreated, shuttling into a ball of banked embers deep within his soul's depths.

"Chrome?" Rhode whispered hoarsely.

"Right here, brother. I'm right here." Strong arms gripped him behind his back and gently sat him upright. On any other day in the life of an Empyrean warrior, the picture that solidified around him would have made perfect sense. Piles of dead charmer ashes turning cold enough to gather a thin layer of snow. His sentinel brethren solid and hale, fresh from a victory.

What had yet to make sense was the breathy inhale of the woman standing next to a tow truck.

"I didn't know you had wings," she said through a stifled sob.

Then his body nearly exploded again.

Never had he seen such breathtaking abundance as what stood before him. From the rooftop, he'd only been able to make out bits and pieces of the thief. The bare-bones basics afforded by any aerial view. But up close?

She was a blessed bounty.

A vibrantly coiled corona of gold spun down to her elbows, only parting from her full breasts in so far as to hug them, framing them as an offering beneath a bed of cashmere that extended past her generous hips. Her hands were balled up into worried fists beneath her delicate chin, which quivered slightly, likely from the cold, for the outerwear he'd first spied her in sat in a heap on top of him.

The past few minutes came back to him in a rush. The attempted robbery. The charmers. Nets firing from cannons. The woman trapped, lashing out beneath the mesh. The pain. The fire.

Her scent.

And then a collection of words that made some semblance of sense on their own but none whatsoever in the context of who had spoken them. *I didn't know you had wings.*

Rhode tossed her coat aside, shrugged off Chrome's hold, and then, much to the angel's colorful protestations, got to his feet. Iron and Steel, two of the other sentinels, stepped forward, a shared concern passing across their tense features.

Instantly, Rhode's stomach seized up, and he fought against the familiar disdain that always threatened to pull him under whenever he saw those expressions painted on his kin's faces. Damn, how he hated those looks. Hated them ever since he'd been plucked from Cyro's grotto and thrown into a different sort of hell. They were looks of limitless possibilities and resources, kinship and community, renewed purpose and responsibility.

All things one had little use for when they'd been robbed of as much as he had been. And yet, there they were, stoic reminders baked into the forms of his loyal brethren who looked at him through the lens of their singular shocked and shared emotion: hurt.

Rhode tried to clear away the sentiments that had gathered in his throat and silently pleaded to four different sets of eyes for any explanations for what had just happened to him. He'd do far better to get answers to his own questions first than face the painful ones poised behind everybody's lips.

Steel was the first to step forward and flicked a discerning gaze between the woman and Rhode. "You two know each other?"

"No—" Rhode answered.

"Kinda—" the woman responded over him.

Rhode pinned her with a warning. "Do not tell tales with these men. You will not like the outcome."

"I-I'm not. I wouldn't," she rushed to clarify. "I just mean that I didn't know you with wings."

"You didn't know me with—"

"Wings. That makes the boatload of us, apparently." A simmering crackle disrupted the night's stillness and ushered in the earthy sweetness of Chrome's choice Nicaraguan cigar. After the angel took a drag and freed the blue smoke to dance with the snow, he circled the butt end at Rhode and threw all his misguided authority into the gesture. "Just when in the hell were you going to tell us that you've been able to call out your wings again? Was this a recent development or did you figure it out somewhere around month six or so but concluded it was none of our damn business, so what the hell, you'd just keep your mouth shut about it for another fucking year?"

Rhode gritted his teeth. "I am not discussing this right now," he seethed, then curled his fingers and caged them to gesture over his exposed chest. "What I want to know is what the hell just happened to me!"

Steel's icy glare softened with concern. "You called forth angel fire."

"Impossible!" Rhode slashed his hand through the air.

"Yes, it should be," he acknowledged, dragging a hand through his short blond hair and shaking his head. "But it happened regardless." Then his frosty stare settled on the woman with a questing sort of sadness.

Her soft voice rose up among those of the arguing angels. "What was that white light?" Honeyed eyes flicked to Rhode. "What happened when I touched you?"

He paused in his seething just long enough to eye her in disbelief. "You . . . you touched me?"

She nodded. "When you were"—she lowered her gaze and squeezed her fists beneath her chin again—"dying, I think. Parts of you were crumbling away. Whole patches of skin were turning to rust and just flaking off you like you were an old car bumper or something. I didn't know what to do. Your friend screamed at me to get off you, but when he pulled me away, I lost my balance and fell forward." When she lifted her eyes again, a silent sincerity lit her features with a desperate honesty that would have made his heart smile once upon a time.

Now, it only made his soul scream.

"I landed on your chest, and that's when the white pulsing light flared out. I felt it. In here." She tapped the collar of her sweater, which was just high enough to force his eyes away from what had commanded his attention earlier.

So that had been her. The soft weight he'd felt blanketing him, molding him back together in some elemental way. *That* was what his soul had thrown itself at as whatever it was had stitched him back together. That delicious heaviness was the anchor that the roaring parts of him had been able to cling to as the rest of his body felt like it was being melted down into new molecules with a new mission.

Rhode shook his head in abject bewilderment.

Then a plume of smoke wafted across his periphery. "Lot of people I know would have begun leaking out of both ends and turned tail if they saw a man start losing chunks of himself like that, yet you're still here." Chrome narrowed his eyes at the woman and shifted the cigar to the other side of his mouth. "Why aren't you running, lady?"

"And I'd like to know just how you know so much about him." Iron adjusted a leather bracer and tightened his fist on the handle of his mace.

Steel spread his arms out in a placating motion. "Easy, guys. Look, it's clear we all have questions—"

Rhode's kamas were out and under Chrome's and Iron's throats before either of them had taken their next inhale. The cigar tumbled from Chrome's mouth, while some of the hairs on Iron's beard separated at the root and slid down the curve of Rhode's blade. He couldn't say what propelled him to act, if only that *not* acting, even against his own, was like a strike against his soul. Rhode growled into the angels' faces. "No threats. You hear me? You will *not* threaten her."

"Oh?" Chrome barked, sticking his neck out closer against the bite of the blade. Molten metallic flames swirled in his former intelligence master's eyes. "Does that mean you're happy to threaten us? You finally feeling up to talking to us after *almost dying?*"

"I had no say in this night!"

"Bullshit. You had a say, you just chose to keep your mouth shut. Every fucking night since I pulled you out of that grotto, you've had a choice. And I've given you your space, dammit, because it was my fault you were taken in the first place." A heavy silence settled over the parking lot but did nothing to quell the rage amplifying the moment. "I thought you needed time. I knew you had stuff to work through, and I thought that as long as I gave you time, however much you required, that you'd eventually come and find me. Trust in me again. But instead, I pick up on the scent of charmers, follow it here, and what do I see? My former seraphim commander, who barely looks me in the eye anymore, let alone talks to me, slicing up the enemy with his wings out, blades out, like the past year and a half just didn't happen. Like I hadn't been *begging* Drea, my own fucking soul bond, to lie to me and tell me that everything will be okay with you, with us. That tomorrow would be the day you'd finally talk to me about what Cyro did, because I don't believe for a second you don't remember."

"Cyro? You know him?"

If any words in the mortal realm could have broken through the rage coating Rhode's vision, those were it. All four angels turned toward the woman in unison as Rhode lowered his blades.

"What do you know of that name?" he asked.

Those golden eyes of hers widened, but thank the blessed mages, she still answered him. "He's my sire."

And his fists promptly hardened around his weapons once more.

Chrome coughed in disbelief. "Come again?"

"My sire," she repeated.

Steel and Rhode stood there, mouths agape.

Then Iron shook his head, his motions jerky, and extended a finger toward her. "Then you're—"

"A charmer."

CHAPTER 4

Neela had heard of neutral zones. On nights when the grotto had been quiet and the rhythmic lull of her suite's twinkle lights and salt lamp had to work overtime to chase away the reality of just *why* Cyro's camp was so quiet, she'd sometimes catch a west coast hockey or football game on TV. Her frame of reference for the neutral-zone concept had been embarrassingly basic, but she'd always resonated with the gist of it: a precious space that couldn't be encroached upon by either team. A mutually agreed-upon no-touchy-no-takey area. Essential and literal line-drawn boundaries within which peace could be kept.

They'd always sounded so idyllic and so very different from the world she knew. But now, as she sat in her very own form of a neutral zone, with her butt enjoying far more cushioning than a padded wicker restaurant chair had any right to offer, there was something bitingly uncomfortable about the space.

The announcers on TV never warned her about how thick the tension was within those imaginary walls.

After the ashes in the parking lot had floated away and the snow decided to start making up for lost time in earnest, the blond man—Steel, she'd learned—had thrown himself between the other heated men and suggested they continue their *conversation* in a more hospitable location.

No one missed the elephant-sized emphasis he'd thrown on top of that word.

And that was how Neela found herself gripping a steaming mug of spiked hot chocolate, staring down an obscene amount of New England charm, and hating the fact that her first time in a real mortal restaurant had her eyeing the door like the thing had betrayed her by letting her enter in the first place.

The proprietress of the restaurant, Molly, grabbed a bottle of bourbon from beneath a counter and, after plopping herself in the seat across from Neela, unscrewed the thing and poured two *more* healthy glugs into Neela's cocoa. Then, with all the flair of someone short of patience and long on foresight, brought the bottle to her lips and knocked back a few swigs of her own.

It would have been impressive if Neela couldn't escape the fact of why the stuff was needed at all.

"Whatever you're thinking, know that I'm not." Molly's kind eyes twinkled beneath the dim glow of the eatery's soothing lights, and her words were delivered with an encouragement that had Neela blinking through a veneer of disbelief. Not only was she sitting across from a mortal who was actually speaking to her but she also couldn't keep herself from side-eyeing the very man who'd saved her life.

And the very man she never thought she'd see again.

"How do you know what I'm thinking?" Neela asked, though her attention was only half on the bright-eyed brunette.

"Because that gaggle of guys over there can be intimidating to even the most confident of onlookers, but only slightly more than the majority of the brothers can claim to have a level head at the moment." Then she leaned forward conspiratorially. "My soul bond included. He's the auburn-haired one with the close crop who won't turn his back away from our table." She winked. "His name's Brass, and he's a bit testy when it comes to unprovoked rage, so until Rhode, Chrome, and the others all manage to have a little kumbaya moment, I doubt he'll let any of them get too close to you."

"Too close to *me*?"

"Well, you *and* me. And since I don't believe for a second in judging someone until they show their ass and give me a reason to, I'm just going to hang close to you, if that's okay. You're not exactly giving off *slay the world* vibes, despite what any of them might be inclined to think. Besides, you look like you could use a properly infused warm-up after what happened, rather than having unfounded accusations slung at your face." Molly nodded toward Neela's mug. "Drink up. No one's going to hurt you here. They all know I just had the floors waxed. No way are any of them that stupid as to mess up my hardwood during peak winter tourist season." The stink eye that bounced from Molly's eyes to the men, who still had yet to acknowledge Neela, was sharp enough to cut glass.

Or cut off body parts.

Neela smiled her thanks, at both Molly's kindness and the increasingly effective way the drink warmed her cheeks and her doubts, and buried her face in her cup. Unfortunately, the thing gave her precious few of the answers her mind was clamoring after, so she shifted her gaze to the prominent back of the man nearest her and the only one who hadn't moved from his self-appointed post since they'd all gotten there.

Brass—and Molly's soul bond, as she'd described it. A sentinel angel. One of several, apparently. All of whom had fallen to the mortal realm fighting the sins of her sire.

Angels.

That's what Axtar was. A fallen angel.

But the wings they'd all wielded earlier were only one of the many, *many* things that Neela had yet to wrap her head around.

Beneath her lashes, she covertly inspected Brass's back. While his crossed arms made the large slabs of muscles flare out in prominence, and the clear tension in his demeanor left zero room for give when it came to his spine's flexibility at that moment, nothing about his physique screamed *wings*.

But she'd seen them for herself on some of the others, and Molly had explained the ins and outs of their appearances. The way they'd morph and stretch from the angels' bodies in a translucent skein of energy, then solidify into the harsh planks of aerodynamic metal Neela had seen earlier.

Each pair molded into the specific metal the angels' commanded. All different. All not without their own powers and capabilities.

Neela stole a glance again at the group huddled in the opposite corner of the restaurant's dining room. The shades were drawn, and actual working shutters on the building's brick facade—which would have looked ridiculous on any other establishment but worked design-related wonders on the space —were sealed up tight. There was nothing to give the outside world the barest hint of a suggestion that a small-scale atomic bomb was simultaneously being detonated and diffused.

Axtar.

No. Rhode. That was what he'd called himself. He'd thrown that moniker out with such surety that it made her question whether she was wrong about him. Had she confused him for someone else? Her heart had fluttered an insistent beat when he'd stood before her, until he flinched when she'd said the name—flinched like those adults did in mortal movies when they came across a seemingly irrelevant object and it triggered some childhood flashback.

Except this was anything but a movie, and wherever Axtar/Rhode/whoever went when she'd mentioned the name and caused his eyes to tighten was clearly nowhere she had any business urging him to revisit.

Intellectually, she'd known that and would never forget the hellish circumstances of their encounters, if she could even call them mere encounters.

So then why did she secretly wish he'd remember her regardless?

At the far wall, joined by even *more* men with equally and impossibly wide shoulders, was Rhode, engaged in some sort of heated conversation with the other angels who she'd met earlier. Chrome and Iron, if she recalled correctly. However, after taking another look at the way Chrome was pushing through the other bodies around him to jab a finger beneath Rhode's chin, she might have to amend her use of the word *heated*.

Whatever the discussion, it had blown past *heated* a while ago and was firmly set to *broiling*.

The men were fuming, that much was clear, even though very little of what they were talking about was coherent. She got the gist, though. Didn't need an advanced degree to read anger right.

Neela's stomach twisted, and the hot chocolate threatened to curdle in her gut. Rhode's face, even draped in fury, was such a beautiful terror only made more breathtaking by the powerful and icy stillness of his frame, one she still couldn't look away from or reconcile with the images her memory kept calling forth. His mien was such a contrast to that of the men around him, Chrome in particular, who was a veritable inferno to Rhode's imposing glacier.

And then, like any silently resentful glacier, it splintered.

Rhode grabbed the nearest chair and raised it high above Chrome's head. But before he slammed it down on the angel's skull, bright blue flames erupted down Rhode's arm and incinerated the chair into ashes. Like the snow from earlier, black flecks tumbled around the men, coating everyone in the remains of Rhode's quiet rage.

Molly roared up out of her seat. "Hey, what did I say about keeping the floors clean? And you owe me for that chair! That was hand-braided wicker!"

But her screams were barricaded behind Brass's immovable back as the angel threw himself in front of his raging mate. Others hollered, and a few of the angels tried to grab Chrome and Rhode by the arms, but neither were having it.

Chrome shrugged out of their hold, blinked away his confusion, then snarled. "Did you just try to attack me?"

The flames licking around Rhode's arms extinguished. "That is the wrong question."

"Oh, really? Because I think it's the perfect fucking question. Or is this what your repayment truly looks like?"

Rhode seethed. "Does your care come with strings attached? Is that why you pulled me out of that hell? So I might one day drop to my feet and praise you to finally assuage your own guilt?"

Fire crackled behind Chrome's eyes as his jaw tightened. "You know it doesn't."

If Neela thought the tension was thick before, it morphed into something downright impenetrable. She tried to look to Molly for answers, but all she got was a patient Brass holding the woman back as his mate kicked out and cursed at every male her death-ray stare zeroed in on.

Then Rhode unexpectedly swung his arm in Neela's direction and leveled a finger right at her. "The *right* question, the *only* question I want to know the answer to is what the hell that woman has done to me." White-hot flames swirled among irises that a moment ago were an earthy, familiar brown. "And why is she still breathing?"

CHAPTER 5

It had been some time since Rhode had been scooped out so hollow to the point where very little was up for discussion when it came to his faculties. It wasn't a foreign feeling by any means, just one he blessedly hadn't had an opportunity to visit since he'd been topside. But now that he was no longer on his back on top of a stone slab with chains weighing down his dignity, the true terror of that vacuum slammed into him like a Mack truck.

Logic, emotion, and even that damn fire he'd somehow managed to wield were all ejected from his body and overall consciousness. Because in what world would he have ever raised a weapon, let alone one laced with a power seraphim had no history or capacity of brandishing, to Chrome? His former intelligence master, who had been at one time his truest brother in every sense of the word that mattered?

The answer to that and all of his torments, as it had been for so many agonizing years of his life, always—*always*—began and ended with the same singular group of beings.

Charmers.

No sooner had the chair's ashes fallen at his feet than his

finger found its next target. It was the only thing that his trembling body and addled brain could make sense of. Not the roar of angels around him, nor the strong arms that yanked on his shoulders, pulling him away from whichever of Chrome's responses was liable to lead to the destruction of far more than a single wicker chair. Rhode heard nothing, saw nothing, felt nothing, except the magnetic pull toward the woman across the room whose very presence urged his insides to riot and rage.

Through the shouting and mélange of muscles, one very large, very imposing figure broke free and placed his barrel chest right in front of Rhode's outstretched finger. Tungsten—the prime sentinel, with his shoulder-length mane of golden hair vibrant enough to equal, if not outshine, the hair of the very woman he was blocking Rhode's view of—pushed forward until Rhode's finger had no choice but to bend at an angle that had it backing down. It wasn't long before Titan, Tung's second, and Iron had flanked their leader, choking off any view of the female entirely.

And then, with one swift jerk of his chin, Tung commanded what was left of Rhode's beyond-divided attention. "We are going to have a conversation. And you are going to sit down and be a part of it."

"In front of that thing over there?" Rhode flicked his chin toward whatever part of that demon was still on the other side of the mountain of angels blocking his view.

It had been the exact wrong thing to say.

Tung's eyes grew stormy with pewter flames, and the banked fury of the prime sentinel caused Rhode to take a step back until he had no choice but to plop onto the nearest hard surface that would support him. "Listen well, *Axtar*."

Rhode gritted his teeth. "Don't call me that."

"Then give me a reason to call you otherwise, because right now, you have not earned any right to keep your own name or head, let alone make demands of me. You attacked one of your own, one of *my* sentinels, your own goddamn brother, and damaged our hostess's property."

Rhode snapped to his feet and shrugged off Titan when he tried to urge him back down. "He's not my brother!" Rhode raged, no longer able to quell the fire or keep from screaming what his heart had longed to rail into the world. "*I* am not your brother," he said, pounding his chest. "I am a seraph. *Was* a seraph. We are different as much as we are the same, and you of all beings know you cannot be forced into a mold by sheer will or association alone. Or should we ask Tamara her thoughts on the subject?"

Every single voice in the room was snuffed into silence. Shouts collapsed into shattered sighs of disappointment, while other words were choked off by sucked-in breaths.

Tamara, or Tammy, was Tungsten's soul bond and twin sister to Titan's soul bond, Rose. Like Rhode, she too had been abducted by charmers, but that was where the similarities in their experiences ended, for unlike Rhode's eternal imprisonment, she had been rescued after six months.

He, on the other hand, well . . .

Only he knew what parts of him had truly made it out alive, which was why the blow he'd just dealt was the kind reserved only if you wanted to make damn certain there were no bridges left to burn.

Tammy's relationship with Tung had been one of intense turmoil, with each one fighting against fate to secure their own form of self-preservation.

As Rhode had been told, it had been a miserable time for the prime sentinel, as well as the others.

And he'd just ripped open that bag and poured it all out for everyone to get a fresh view of, spoiled parts and all.

Including the curious woman who still sat silently at the far table, professing not to only be a demon charmer but the offspring of the very one who could claim credit for innumerable suffering souls, the least of which, though still living, crowded out the restaurant's small dining room.

Tungsten bared his teeth, giving Rhode a raw glimpse of the quiet rage that had the best chance to match his.

Good. Parts of him, the portions that had grown in bulk without cause or direction, screamed for a fight, for anything to tear into so they might feast on something else's suffering for a change.

As Rhode stared at the prime sentinel, the leader of the Empyrean's eternal guards, for the first time, he wondered . . .

Would the angel truly do it? Would Tung take that next step? Mages knew Rhode had given him every reason to do so, even as his gaze traced the lines of the one angel who everyone thought truly had boundless patience.

But did that theory extend to what Rhode had become? And why the hell did he wish to test it so?

Rhode sank into the prime sentinel's stare and searched for the answers hidden in the swirling depths of eyes that once held such compassion and understanding. Figured it was about time he chased that away, too.

A cascading crash resounded through the back hallway. "Fuck him, and fuck this. I'm done!" Chrome swept an arm out wide, and another rack of drinking glasses met their end in shards at the angel's feet.

Brass stepped in before the others and swept a fuming Molly out the front door right as Bronze and Steel managed to muscle Chrome into the back hallway that led out to the alley.

Through the cages of their arms, his former intelligence master found Rhode and shouted, "We're done. You hear me? Whatever's going on in your head can fucking spin itself out on its own. No one needs this shit, Rhode. Not me, not Drea, and sure as hell not the rest of us. Got that? No one needs *you*! So have a nice goddamn life, 'cause I'm done having you take up such a huge part of mine."

Both doors slammed shut, simultaneously sealing him in with the consequences of his actions.

The heavy silence that pressed in around them moved through the air like sludge through a sewer, and some quiet part of Rhode knew that he'd never breathe freely ever again. It wasn't that he expected Chrome to behave in such a way, but . . . well, what *was* the expectation, exactly? How did one tell their oldest friend that the past was nothing more than a collection of memories for those lucky enough to still recall them? And luck had never cast its favor on Rhode for all the years he'd begged for it. Screamed for it.

No, what few memories he had were nothing short of sensory imprints, but they were more than enough to put even night terrors to shame.

At least night terrors ended eventually.

Rhode whirled away from Tung and slammed his fist into the wall, pulverizing a patch of decorative hand-pressed lavender that had been caged into something against its will. "Dammit!" But when his forehead settled against the cool surface of the drywall, the relief, like always, was promptly wicked away.

"For what it's worth, I'm Neela, not a *thing.*"

Shit. He'd forgotten about her. The demon. *Wonderful.*

But for the first time since Rhode had decided to leap off a building, he wasn't entirely ungrateful for the others' presence. Well, those who'd stuck around, anyway.

Tungsten, ever the damn diplomat, would soon take over. Any moment, the prime sentinel would ask Iron and Titan to seize the woman, then they'd finally be able to have that little conversation with her that Tung had alluded to earlier, one that would involve no shortage of cross-examination and angel fire.

Slowly, the gnawing tension fled from his shoulders, and the hard surface against his forehead started to register more suggestive pressure than pounding pain. Thank the mages for small mercies.

Yes, there was at least one disaster Rhode would be able to get to the bottom of, the least of which would be finding out just how the hell a female charmer existed in the first place, let alone one who claimed to be an heir to Cyro. What had she been doing in that parking lot? If she was truly who she insisted to be, why on earth would other charmers be chasing her, never mind trying to apprehend her?

And most importantly, just what the hell did she do to him?

With each question unraveling from the tightly coiled yarn ball of neural synapses in Rhode's mind, more of that collective calm settled into his muscles, easing that strange burning in his core where the alien angel fire from earlier seemed to originate. The flames were gone, barely a simmer in the pit of his soul. Whatever had erupted out of him had thankfully been depleted. He felt almost normal, familiar, with that same hollowness returning to settle low in his gut and weigh his conscience down.

He never thought he'd be so happy to feel so dead inside. But dead was good. He could work with dead.

Instead, Iron and Titan took up residence at each of his sides, neither of the angels touching him but also strategically blocking the sole avenues to the exits.

And just like that, his muscles twitched with unrestrained warning. When Rhode slowly turned around, the scene was not one of a prisoner being apprehended, nor of a demon being threatened with a fire-fueled dagger at its throat. Any of those would have made sense.

What he saw, however, had his hands flying for his kamas. All they caught was air.

"Nope. None of that." Titan held up the bundle of weapons in his fist and leveled a sad *this is why some people can't have nice things* glare at him. "It's a safe bet that Brass is going to melt these puppies down after the shit you just started in Molly's dining room. Either that or he'll give 'em to Molly so she can take a swing at you. Whatever the case, consider them on probation."

Rhode heard the angel's words, but while his brain was slowly processing the repercussions of his earlier actions, it had no juice left to make sense of what Tungsten was doing across the room.

The prime sentinel grabbed a chair, placed it next to the wide-eyed woman, carefully settled his bulk into it, and said, "Before we speak further regarding the circumstances of tonight, it is incumbent upon me to inform you that no harm will come to you here, by my hand or any of my angels."

Rhode blinked through a shock that did a stellar job of stealing his words. Once he'd found them again, he said, "What? How can you say that?"

Tungsten's expression was equal parts grim and illuminating, the kind of face a head coach adopted when she had to inform her Olympic competitor that they had just won a place on the podium—but for a bronze medal. Then the prime sentinel hoisted every ounce of karma into his heated stare and promptly blew Rhode's world apart.

"Because no Empyrean warrior shall ever harm a soul bond of our brethren, whether that angel be sentinel . . . or seraph."

CHAPTER 6

There was a reason Neela always, *always* had background noise playing in her suite at home, be it music, TV, or, more often than not, YouTube—even while she was sleeping or when she wasn't there. That was why her low-light-thriving spider plant had the absolute biggest, fattest flowers any underground self-professed plant whisperer had ever grown.

It was also because she knew far too well just how swiftly silence could kill. Stillness often came with far more oppressive and damaging repercussions.

So, yeah, her mouth might have run away with her when Tungsten finally finished his spiel.

"I'm going to stop you right there, big guy." Neela whipped out her hand. "You're saying a whole lot of words that don't mean what I think they mean. Can we backtrack a sec here?" Then she spun her hand in a circle and shut her eyes, as if that would make the redelivery of his message any more palatable. "The fire stuff. Go over that again but slower, please."

A corner of his lips lifted. "All beings of the Empyrean, like my angels, contain a spark of the Eternal Flame within them, which is the source of all light and life in the realms. When two halves of the same spark come in contact with each other, a soul bond connection is formed, one that links two souls together for all time. The mortals have had many phrases for this concept over the years, but the most current one in Western cultures, I believe, is soulmates."

Cue suffocating silence.

"Soulmates," she repeated in a whisper of disbelief. And let the record show she tried *so damn hard* not to flick her eyes toward who she newly dubbed the Looming Male of Murderous Intent.

Yeah, no dice there. While *he* was doing an excellent job of pretending the air around her was miraculously converting into carbon dioxide all on its own, she couldn't stop stealing glances and wondering whether his incessant pacing was a frustrated habit or one war commanders used to intimidate the enemy.

Because the odds were an even split on that one.

Mated. To a seraphim commander. Of all the things she knew about him, which was pretty close to bupkis, *that* little fact had been one of the biggest surprises among many.

He was a powerful seraph. A war general. A commander of an entire legion of spies. A prisoner of war.

And now, he shared a connection with her that, according to Tungsten, wasn't just permanent but eternal. After what her sire had done to him.

If the reality of the situation wasn't so nauseating, she'd try to laugh it off, except her facial muscles hadn't been able to do anything except wince through one harrowing experience after another since the sun went down. But they somehow got with the program right quick, as they always seemed to do whenever Rhode's voice fired up a room. That time, however, it wasn't amusement that had her jaw hanging open but shock.

"Absolutely absurd. Impossible," Rhode sneered at Tungsten.

"Is it? What other explanation do you have for why you, of all angels, can suddenly command angel fire?"

Then that thick and aggressively pokey finger swung in her direction again. Man, she had gotten *so good* at not flinching. Too bad her outward efforts did little to calm her inward nerves whenever she found herself the object of Rhode's attention.

"She did something to me. Something else. She's a demon. Trust me, Tungsten, she is more than capable of crimes you couldn't conceive of."

She was . . . What did he just say? Had he just…?

Neela shot to her feet. "I am not!"

With a voice that brooked no argument, Tungsten offered his ever-so-levelheaded two cents. "We will sit, and we will talk. No one is accusing you of anything, Neela," he clarified. But once she settled back in her seat, the prime sentinel's tone changed to something altogether darker as he addressed Rhode. "And if I have to weld your ass to a chair and have Iron and Titan hold you down, you know that is what I will do. Now, I have a theory, and you will hear it whether you want to or not. The facts of the matter suggest it's not solely conjecture but truth. A truth you need to, at the very least, understand, for I know acceptance is out of the question."

The gravity of Tungsten's words urged Neela to hold her tongue, but Rhode continued to pace a trench into Molly's newly waxed hardwood.

"While the Empyrean houses many types of celestial beings, including the seraphim, who make up our soldier and spy legions, there are only seven sentinels. We are the elite guard of Heaven and command her armies by virtue of one unique power: our angel fire. As a seraph, Rhode does not innately possess such a power. And neither is a seraph healed by the manner in which he was once you touched him, which leads me to believe two things."

"What?" Neela asked, while Rhode's silence let her question hang suspended for longer than she would have liked.

"I believe that when you touched Rhode for the first time, the soul bond connection was initiated, lending its healing force to Rhode."

"He's right." Titan stepped forward and ran his knuckles under his neat beard in contemplation. "Saw the same thing happen with Rose the first time we met. She's patched me up more times than I can count, and the power she gives off sounds exactly like what the others told me they saw in front of the mechanic's garage."

"Ridiculous," Rhode added. "And it still doesn't explain the fire."

"Which brings me to the second truth." Tungsten leveled his heavy stare at Neela, and she knew that whatever tumbled out of this angel's mouth was something she wouldn't be able to escape from. "I also believe that you, Miss Neela, are something more than a mere charmer, and Rhode, though we all wish differently, may no longer be a simple seraph."

Neela fidgeted in her chair, doing her best to both avoid and make sense of what Tungsten was saying. But when the prime sentinel's accusatory tone shifted in the direction of Rhode, she didn't know whether to be grateful for the reprieve or worried about what it meant.

"You've said you have no memories of what was done to you. Is that still the case?"

Rhode halted his pacing, and the other two angels stiffened, with neither appearing eager to bear witness to whatever was coming next.

No memories? Was that true? How could he have no memories from before?

She carefully tried to reconcile that possibility, but every time she attempted it, a sinking feeling rose up to drown out all the other far more hopeful scenarios.

The slight spark of unknown awareness when he'd first met her.

The even quicker cooldown and about-face once he'd learned who she was.

The silent coldness and hostility that, would they have been alone, she suspected would have been far more brutal.

The conclusion was a rock-hard kick to her more tender parts, chief among them being the simpering organ in her chest that had only ever cared for her plants until recently.

He remembers. He just wishes he didn't.

"Yes." Rhode's solemn response had broken through her hazy thoughts, and she had to remember whose accusation he was addressing. The disappointment at his dubious dishonesty struck a sour chord within her, though the precise explanation why still eluded her.

"Then I shall now ask Neela to enlighten us a bit further." Tungsten's pewter eyes pinned her to the floor. "Tell us how it is that Rhode came to find you, for it will no doubt prove useful in understanding why a commander of an Empyrean spy legion now finds himself bound to a demon."

RHODE KEPT his body absolutely still while he waited for the charmer, Neela, to speak. During that time, he raked his ruthless internal assessments over her form for the dozenth time. Despite the difference in her outward appearance and the obvious peculiarity of her gender, he couldn't ignore the sensory markers of her race that were indeed buried below.

Deep beneath the hyssop and earthy aromas that seemed to carry across the room and envelop him whenever she adjusted her mass of hair, the underlying essence of the shadow realm still coated her makeup, like the smoke ring hidden among the most succulent cut of meat.

Neela was a charmer. There was no mistaking it, which meant he had no true reason to discount her story or her origins. And didn't that just rankle him all the more?

In truth, the simple fact that she even had a name surprised him to the point of borderline intrigue. In all his time in the demon camps and grottos, never once had he recalled any of the other charmers being named. Names were personal—or, in his case, had been at one time. The only thing *personal* about the charmers was their unique delight in others' misery.

But this one had a name. Neela.

He'd heard all but a handful of sentences from her and was repulsed to discover that he wanted—*needed*—to hear more. If she kept talking, maybe his mind would cease the relentless spinning. However, the longer he stood there, trapped within the four walls of the increasingly cramped restaurant, the longer he feared he'd already gone insane and the anticipation was just another way for his brain to roll out the red carpet, bypass the coming attractions, and welcome him into the fresh hell that was the feature presentation.

"We have never met a female charmer before, so forgive us if we appear skeptical," Tungsten offered as a way of encouragement. As if getting her to talk would make anything about Rhode's current circumstances more palatable.

"It's true that I'm the only female, but you are *so* wrong if you think I have any sort of power to wield against you. In fact, I shouldn't have been able to manage magic at all, let alone whatever healing hooey happened in front of that mechanic's garage."

"Why is that?" Iron asked.

The woman shifted the cloud of golden curls off one shoulder and arranged it on the other, looking for all the world like she'd rather be eating her shoe than subjecting herself to the proverbial firing squad. "Because I'm a mistake."

Titan's brows shot up, along with those of the other angels. "Pardon?"

That *did* cause Rhode to bristle, though not for a reason he'd ever admit. It wasn't an accident that he'd kept his back largely to her, despite every cell of his training ordering him to maintain the enemy in his sights at all costs.

Laughable, really. He'd already paid the cost, hadn't he? So what was one breach in procedure when facing her would only highlight his very real and very concerning mistake?

Even with his back to her, his muscles pulled in taut stretches of tension, as if his body was revolting against not keeping its prey within its sights.

But he couldn't look at her. Couldn't stand to allow even his eyes to touch upon her fine features for more than was necessary before he lost the battle of not only drinking in her presence but drowning in it.

Mages dammit, but she looked nothing like a charmer, and his body thickened with the memory of it. Of all the infuriating things he could claim a photographic recollection of, why was *she* not only at the top of the list but the sole occupant of the roster? There were no angles to her form except for those that freely plunged his gaze off the cliff of her curves before carrying it down a wealth of seductive slopes. Delicate, yet plentiful from every riotous curl to flaring fit, she was a mouthwatering vision.

And the embodiment of all his nightmares.

Rhode clenched his fists, his face blazing, and tried to hold on to the sole truth of Tungsten's words as salvation for his body's traitorous reactions.

The soul bond. If Rhode required more proof of the prime sentinel's supposition, he needn't look any further than his attraction. It was as she said, a mistake, for the mages only knew he'd never choose this fate willingly.

And he was a prisoner to it once again.

The soft breath Neela sucked in tickled the hairs at his nape even from across the room, so he looked over his shoulder as the demon stole his attention anew, and he braced himself for more of the universe's surprises.

"Cyro is our sire. All of us. Each charmer is birthed from a part of him, literal pieces of himself that he hacks off and combines with dark magic to create the race."

"Pieces of himself?" Titan asked.

"Yes. I don't like to think about it too much, but I doubt mortals like to dwell on the logistics of how they were born either. In any case, each sect of charmer is spawned from a different part of our sire. For mystics, the magic users, they are created from fingernails. Our elite, the warriors, stem from drops of our sire's sweat. And the apexes, Cyro's most powerful class of charmers, are cast from his fangs."

The information she'd just revealed swirled heavily among the sentinels, while still remaining just out of reach. Furtive glances spoke of how quickly the wheels in their minds were spinning and ultimately coming to the same abrupt halt as Rhode's own.

Vital intelligence but ultimately useless.

Neela, seemingly unaware of the silent analysis, simply took a sip of her drink and continued. "Cyro regenerates whatever parts of himself he uses and can create an army of charmers in no time at all at this point." A penetrating silence filled the room with the implications of her statement, and Rhode's hand instinctively drifted toward the empty holsters of his kamas. Then Neela took a deep breath. "But that wasn't always the case. Before he figured out his current MO, there was me."

At that, Rhode shifted and lifted a brow at her. "MO? Really? Is Cyro teaching his minions Latin now?"

She bristled. "Modus operandi," she fired back with the air of a teenager who, rather than intending to bridge a generation gap, preferred to blow it up instead. "Was something I said unclear?"

"No. Simply that you don't speak like they do."

Neela straightened her back, the maneuver offering up further distractions than Rhode had the patience for. "And you don't get to tell my story."

A silent challenge flitted through those honey-gold irises, so like those of every charmer he'd ever known, and yet . . . not. Before he threw himself across the room to do mages knew what—Grab her? Kill her?—he locked his knees and nodded for her to continue.

"He never told me the whole tale, but Cyro has always had a goal to breach the gates of the Empyrean, though once he learned I was a failed attempt at achieving that goal and wasn't able to help him in that regard, he largely kept me segregated from the meat of his plans."

"Why didn't he just kill you?" Rhode asked.

There. He'd said it. Whether it was a calculated wish on his part or a genuine curiosity, he couldn't say, but it didn't stop him from reveling in the slightest bit of enjoyment at the discomfort thickening the air.

Good. At least I'm not the only one knee-deep in this shit.

A flicker of surprise—or was it something like hurt?—tightened Neela's features. "Because he can't." She paused, and damn if he didn't see an inferno to rival what the mortals thought of hell burning in her eyes. "As I said, his goal was to get into the Empyrean, but as a being of the shadow realm, he can't abide by any light, be it celestial, solar, or otherwise. So, he needed something, or someone, who could do both. During one of the earlier conflicts with I'm guessing your kind, he acquired an item from the battlefield. I never knew what it was, but the story goes that he fused that, along with a part of himself, into the dark magic he cast to create me."

She lifted a lock of her shockingly golden, tightly coiled hair. "But I didn't come out looking like he intended. Whatever that item was that he found, well, it didn't agree with his powers or plans, apparently. While it's true that I can go out in light where other charmers can't, that's where the extent of my abilities ends. I have no powers, and magic doesn't work on me. I have no gifts of the mystics, no innate strength of the elite, and certainly no skills that would be of use to the apex's order. My sire had one shot with whatever he'd procured on that battle-field, and in the end, all it got him was a powerless immortal demon whose only talents are her abilities to sunbathe and serve as Cyro's constant reminder of what he could have had and lost." A tightness settled around her shoulders before she lifted her chin. "But don't worry. He's since perfected the formula."

"And he can't kill you because only angel fire can truly destroy a charmer." The words left Rhode's lips before he could think of their ramifications. It wasn't until the other angels all rose from their places and flashed warning looks that he real-ized his misstep.

He didn't want to kill her, at least not yet, but hell if they knew that.

Hell if he truly did, too.

"Yes," Neela answered, acting for all the world like Rhode hadn't just poured a bucket of chum on her in a sea of hungry sharks. "So I finally ran away."

That had his ears perking up.

Iron took a step forward but never let Rhode wander too far into his periphery. "You ran away, and I take it Daddy noticed when you didn't show up for dinner on time."

She scoffed. "More like I ran away because I saw something I shouldn't have, decided I wanted zero part of it, and thought it was time I took my chances among the mortals. And let me be perfectly clear about something." Her gaze snapped to Rhode's, and he had no choice but to listen. "Just because Cyro and his band of merry assholes can't kill me doesn't mean I can't be hurt."

Two thoughts slammed into his mind simultaneously. The first was the regrettable lament that, of all the beings in existence, he'd somehow bonded with one whose colorful vocabulary could rival Chrome's. The second, and far more concerning, was the tunnel of terror that her words scraped through his chest.

. . . can't kill me doesn't mean I can't be hurt.

Had she been hurt?

Was she hurt like me?

All at once, his mind spun out of control, whirling through the bevy of blurs that made up his core memories, the ones he had trained himself to stay far away from lest his mind revert to what he'd worked so hard to escape.

Violence roared in his ears, and those sputtering flames of angel fire tried to punch through his veins, but without their fuel, they could only wail at his insides until his head threatened to explode. Around him, words were said, dialogue exchanged, some murmurs that rang vaguely of agreements in *we'll continue this tomorrow* tones.

". . . he's got another item, something he calls a relic . . . trying to pull the same shit as he did with me, but this time, he's convinced he's figured it out."

The din in Rhode's mind sputtered to a halt, but his muscles only tightened further.

"No," he whispered through clenched teeth.

But the others didn't hear him. They were too focused on Neela and the gavel her final words struck them all with.

"The relic is a piece of the Empyrean's gates. Cyro believes that, once he casts the dark magic needed to fuse parts of himself with a part that contains verified celestial magic, he'll be able to create a new race of charmers, one that is no longer subjected to the dark alone, is just as powerful as he is, and can enter the heavenly realm once and for all."

CHAPTER 7

If there was one thing Rhode never quite managed to get used to, it was the infuriatingly perfect temperature of the angels' underground den. Chalk it up to years of living in a petri dish that would make even the most flourishing of mold spore colonies turn their noses up, but temperature-controlled climates still made him itchy. Hidden beneath New Hampshire's White Mountains, the den was a veritable cavern-turned-fortress that was a marvel of geothermal and solar energy engineering. Hot water reservoirs, floor-to-ceiling generators, underground turbines, and a matrix of exhaust pipes made it so that, despite the granite around them, every room was a perfect ambient temperature.

And that was less than ideal when all you wanted to do was torch the first thing in sight and let the stifling air choke off the screams threatening to punch through your chest.

"Yup. Okay. See you in the morning, then." Titan pocketed his phone and grabbed a beer from the fridge. "Brass is at Molly's place with Neela. She'll be staying in the guest room at the apartment for the time being. Bronze and Steel will be patrolling the grounds for the rest of the night in case any more charmers show up. Neela felt pretty certain they'd continue to look for her, but without those other ones you guys smoked being able to get a message back to home base, she doesn't see how they could find her easily. We should be good for a bit."

The *tsss* of the can tab popping open echoed off the stone walls, but it only served to rattle Rhode's nerves even further. Even the rhythmic rise and fall of Titan's throat as the beer slid down the angel's gullet felt like an oily caress over Rhode's skin.

Titan lowered the can and extended a finger. "You want to know what's weird?"

Iron swept his arm in front of him. "You mean weirder than the shitstorm that was the last few hours?"

"Funny." Titan tossed a beer to Iron, who caught it and opened it up one-handed. "But yeah, weirder than that. Turns out, Neela didn't have a game plan beyond getting the heck out of Dodge."

Tungsten folded his arms over his chest. "You're certain?"

"Yup. She mentioned to Brass and Molly how her main goal had been to get away and that she didn't want to figure out her second step until she'd managed to take the first one because that was hard enough. Didn't go into details about that ordeal, though. From what Molly said, the woman's beat and went to bed as soon as they showed her a mattress." He laughed softly to himself. "I think we all can appreciate that kind of exhaustion."

Rhode walked over to the bar and poured himself two fingers of whatever amber liquid happened to be closest. He was going for the burn, not the bouquet. "I can't believe Brass allowed her into his home, a space he shares with his soul bond, no less." Rhode knocked back the liquid, but the stuff did little to mimic the banked fire that still sat unsettled in his core.

Fucking hell, he wanted to punch something, if for the sole reason to have a controlled action to be responsible for. His muscles still obeyed him. His precision, strength, focus, all of it had slowly come back under his command during the labored months of physical therapy with Drea and then were honed with the grueling training he'd run through on the mats. The relief and utter internal elation at his body not only responding to his requests but carrying them out with relish and a newfound purpose was a win he'd never thought himself capable of achieving again.

And then, with a single leap off a building, it'd all come crashing down before him. His work, his time and attention, his fucking *plans*, all blown apart by *her*. Cyro's get. Who he was inexplicably linked to.

Once again, he was afforded no choice, no option, no allies or prime mages to turn to. There was no help for him whatsoever.

In so many ways, he was right back where he damn well started, wasn't he?

He was just about to pour himself another drink when Chrome's charged voice boomed through the great hall, threatening to shatter the glass in Rhode's hand. "As long as we're talking about what should and shouldn't be allowed, why don't we open up the floor, huh? I'm in a learning mood. And you know what they say: 'When you're green, you're growing. When you're ripe, you rot.'"

Iron lifted a brow. "Did you just quote the McDonald's dude?"

"You bet your ass I did, and as always, it's applicable. Timeless, even. And speaking of time . . ." Chrome sauntered into the cavernous space as if the profundity of his words was owed entirely to the sheer quantity of firearms strapped to his body.

His one-time brother, within the safety of their sanctuary, was dressed for battle, and the arrogant asshole was making it perfectly clear to all the sentinels that Rhode was the one who had given him the reason to armor up.

If Rhode had any remorse left to offer, he'd have burned off the tattooed seal of the seraphim commander adorning his forearm that Chrome had placed there.

But regret had been shown the door long ago, and something much darker had moved in instead. Something that had grown far too wild to tame, despite all the love he had for every single sentinel, as well as their mates.

That wild thing clawed at the cage, and Rhode had to remember just why the hell it was best to keep his mouth shut.

Chrome held up a small jar with a shard of what looked like metal trapped inside. "I could give a flying fuck whether you choose to share or not share what we risked our lives to free you from, but that doesn't mean *I* have to keep quiet. You see, us *sentinels*"—the sneer encasing the word might as well have been a brand for the hiss Rhode's fire recoiled with—"have been living on this rock for too fucking long not to take precautions. This right here?" He rattled the jar. "It's a missing puzzle piece with a mouth that's bigger than mine."

Tungsten pointed a finger between the angels. "I will have civility or so help me mages, I will throw you both into the nearest volcano and let the fires sort it out. My soul bond is here, sleeping not far from this room."

The sizzling threat lingered in the air, making the atmosphere even more stifling, but Chrome barely flinched.

"If we're talking rip-roaring fires, then Rhode and I should be evenly matched, as both of our metals have similar melting points. See, it'd be fun for the whole family!"

Titan and Tung fell silent while Iron lowered his beer from his mouth and said, "Metal? What metal? Rhode doesn't command any."

And that was when Rhode realized that, during the fight, none of the angels had truly seen his wings up close.

Rhode ignored Iron, then bared his teeth at Chrome through the shocked stillness of the room. "Shut. Up."

"Nah, I don't think I will, unless *you* want to finally tell the good people what your wings are made of. You know, since you finally decided to reveal them at all." The dusty silver in Chrome's stare was a challenge that Rhode's fire responded to with all the ferocity of a lion cub roaring in the face of a very adult, very male lion.

Trapped. Again, Rhode was trapped. In the absence of any true power and surrounded by a group of angels who would have him on his ass faster than he could inhale, he held his tongue while Chrome's motormouth drove them both off a cliff.

"Thought I was seeing things when this little puppy winked back at me from one of the ash piles in the parking lot earlier. A single sliver of metal that had been left behind. It didn't look like one of our metals, and I got worried the charmers were doing tests on metal manipulation again, so I swiped it and did a little chemical analysis." Chrome shook his head. "The color's off, far too bright to be from Tung, Steel, Titan, or myself, and Steel and I are the only ones with metals close enough in color who had actually been at the fight regardless. But then I took a second look at your lovely wings, and things started to connect. The metals panel I ran finished off the picture for me." Then he slammed the jar down on the table. "This is rhodium. Hard. Durable. Unaffected by air and water, except at temps that don't support mortal life anyway. Inert against corrosion and most aggressive chemicals. And oddly enough, it has the exact same silvery-white patina as that of your brand-new set of wings."

Then Chrome reached into his back pocket and popped a square of peppermint gum into his mouth as though he hadn't just lit Rhode's world on fire. "I'm willing to bet that dear old Cyro worked some prime mages-level magic and tried to make you his little super soldier, an angel of the Empyrean who can command the one metal that would withstand whatever corrosive shit Cyro could cook up that would take the rest of us down." Those silver eyes narrowed, and every ounce of hatred came dripping off Chrome's words—words of smug pride fired with wounding precision. "And I'm also willing to bet that, given the similarities, that fucked-up mix of mutated power and the Eternal Flame's spark gave you our angel fire but put it on probation like it did with the rest of us before we soul bonded with our mates. But unlike the rest of us," Chrome added, "we had a family to work through it with."

The implications of his words arced through Rhode so deeply, his muscles couldn't even work up the time to form a protective barrier around the darker depths of his soul. The parts that, in another life, during another era, might have truly cried out for anything other than gnawing vengeance.

Instead, he let his former intelligence master rage on and watched the confusion on his once-brothers' faces as it morphed from disbelief to wariness to full-blown mistrust.

Fucking perfect.

"Let me make this perfectly clear," Chrome added, as if his performance hadn't already brought down the damn house. "There is zero room for lone rangers in this war, especially for ones who straddle the line because they don't trust their own."

Chrome strode for the door before Rhode's fury even had a chance to formulate a plan. By the time Rhode had pushed off from the bar and Iron and the others had stepped in front of him, Chrome's parting shot over his shoulder was an echo within the trapped cavern of Rhode's mind.

"It sucks having the world ripped out from under you, doesn't it? Especially when the ones who built your fucking foundations are left holding nothing but empty supports."

CHAPTER 8

Iron slid the bottle of scotch across the farmhouse table until the glass bumped up against Rhode's knuckles, offering a nudge that could mean any number of things—none of which Rhode overly cared about at that moment. "You know, for what it's worth, I wouldn't have blamed you if you decked him."

Rhode didn't lift his gaze to those mismatched eyes. Couldn't take the censure or the comfort. It was bad enough the bastard refused to leave him alone while the others wisely went to contain the raging, far more urgent fire that was Chrome's temper. Instead of uselessly pining for solitude, however, Rhode focused on the swirling letters of the bottle's label. The loops and dips were so nonsensical, so meaninglessly elaborate that, for a brief moment, it felt kind of good to get lost in the silliness of the mundane.

Getting lost in anything was a far better alternative than obsessing over his current situation.

"Also, for what it's worth, I don't blame you for keeping things to yourself."

Rhode snorted. "I'm a liar."

"You're a spy. Those are different."

"Doesn't matter."

"It sure as shit does. Otherwise, Tung and Titan wouldn't have left to oversee damage control and make sure Chrome didn't vaporize half of Aurora because he's having a bad day."

"He's right to hate me."

Iron shrugged. "Maybe."

Rhode leaned forward but still refused to meet his stare. "Maybe? Try absolutely. You don't know what—"

"Happened to you? Yeah, you're right. And honestly, it's none of my fucking business. You know why? Because the only thing I care about is getting off this rock. Let me tell you, there have been nights when the right choice didn't seem so right and the wrong choice happened to sport a bit more luster around its edges, you feel me?"

Rhode risked the glance then, and boy, did he wish he hadn't. Of all the sentinels who'd served at the mercy of the celestial mages' will and for the good of the Empyrean, Iron was the most lethal for a reason.

A reason that even Rhode, with his own haunts chasing him nightly, knew better than to scratch at. If he ever wondered about curiosity's dire effects, well, he needn't look any further than the shitstorm that had just erupted a few hours ago, did he? As well as what the temptations of a dark mind can fall victim to when the urge to carve out one's curiosity becomes a very vivid, very real nightmare.

But then the sentinel's mismatched eyes offered up something deeper than simple pity or anger. Rhode hadn't the word for it exactly, but if he had to put a name to it, the closest he could come up with was calculating compassion.

It was as equally unnerving as it was intriguing, so he grabbed the scotch and gave his hands something to do that didn't involve arming himself.

Spell broken, Iron sat back in the chair, forcing the old oak legs to groan against his shift in wait. "Chrome will get over it, but he's not the one we need to talk about."

"Chrome gets over nothing. He forgets nothing."

"I'm not concerned about where his head's at. He'll do what he has to when the time comes, as he always has. The past is a dangerous place to live in, and while most of us would give our left nut to sublet that part of our lives out to anyone foolish enough to take on that lease, it doesn't change what still needs doing and what we need to move forward with." Iron gestured toward Rhode, or more specifically, the vacant space behind his shoulders where his wings would occupy if he had them out. "Like how your new wings and powers might work to our advantage if we can get Neela on board."

Rhode's head shot up, his stomach already souring at the mention of the charmer's name. "What does she have to do with any of this?"

"Like it or not, she's not only the key to unlocking your full use of celestial angel fire but we now have someone with front-fucking-door access to Cyro himself. Hate her all you want, but the woman knows where the asshole's at, what he's planning, and, bonus for us, wants nothing to do with him." Then those two-toned eyes flashed varying shades of topaz as angel fire swirled beneath his features. "If you can convince Neela to get on board, then we can infiltrate his hideaway, grab the relic, and use it to find our way back to the Empyrean while destroying whatever abomination of an army he's cooking up. We can end this finally. No more souls lost, no more toiling away with mortal bullshit." Iron leaned closer until the heat of his words nearly choked off Rhode's objections. "The others, they have their soul bonds. I don't know what decisions they'll make when the time comes, but I'm not willing to forgo the opportunity to at least give them that choice."

"Why? Why me?" Rhode asked, hating how the desperation

squeaked through uninvited. "You have no idea what's changed, no idea what you're asking me to—"

"As I said, I don't care. Bronze tried to get another relic once, and he couldn't deliver. By the time you told him about the relic's other half and its power being nearby in the lycan lands, he'd already mated with Clara, and whatever juice had been in that shard of the Empyrean's gates had been used up. But from what Neela said, Cyro's still got the other half of the relic and hasn't spent its power yet." Then Iron did something Rhode had never seen the angel do in the eons he'd known him. Iron's thick hand reached across the table and grabbed Rhode's wrist. One squeeze. That was it. One firm impression that could never put into words all that Iron was asking of him. "We've got one shot. Talk to Neela. Convince her to ride with Team Angel for a bit. Then it's game over, one way or the other."

Game over.

How many times had the very same concept drifted into Rhode's semi-conscious mind over the years? Sometimes about what was being done to him, sometimes about things at large. It was always an untouchable ideology. A nice thought that often danced through other delusions that would visit him. Words and sounds and feelings that hung around even when they had no reason to.

Kind of like a broken seraph among suped-up sentinels.

And then there was Neela. A golden-haired embodiment of all he'd lost and hated, the proverbial push off the cliff to the jagged rocks below, even if the hands doing the pushing weren't hers.

A death knell wrapped in silks and sensuality and . . . something else.

"She knows me," he murmured, recalling how she'd used his celestial name when they first met.

Iron sat back. "How?"

Rhode shook his head, hating that another charmer had

again owned intelligence over him. But it didn't need to be that way any longer, did it? Not truly. As he turned Iron's words over in his head, analyzing them for traps and pitfalls, a new course of action started to crystalize.

Iron was right in his methodology. If Rhode could reach the relic in time, it *would* give them a way back to the Empyrean, a place the other sentinels had not seen since they'd enacted the Sealing, which closed off the realm's gates to Cyro's advancing armies, as well as themselves, and fell to the mortal realm.

But Rhode was never going back home. He'd been barred from that avenue long ago after he'd been captured. Most nights, he doubted he was even an angel anymore, let alone one who would be welcome to walk among the court of celestial mages and the other beings of the Empyrean.

No, his was a different path, one that would only ever be a one-way trip. After all, vengeance didn't burn that hot without a reason, and once it erupted around its intended target, there was never anything left to salvage, including the one who detonated it.

Rhode slid the bottle back to Iron and stood. "I don't know how she recognized me, but I intend to find out before I make her take me to Cyro."

CHAPTER 9

Neela had heard about thread counts. There was some sort of metric associated with them, right? The higher, the better if she had to guess, but how high was the best? As she extended her arms above her and stretched every muscle to the farthest reaches of Molly's guest bed, she figured the sheets surrounding her had to be somewhere north of average but just shy of too-fancy-to-be-comfortable. Whatever they were, they freaking rocked.

God, she'd miss this. For however long she had left in this bed, she'd take meticulous mental notes on not only the sheets but every mortal marvel around her—of which there were many.

The modest guest room was nowhere near as large as she'd seen other mortal content creators lounge around in. Often, they had king-size beds, walk-in closets, attached full bathrooms, and more sunlight than she'd ever seen in her life.

Not that she'd seen much.

But this—*this* was a bedroom she could melt into and surround with no shortage of sun-loving and completely pot-friendly plants. The fresh morning rays pouring in through the window left no amount of bookshelf unkissed. She smiled, mentally replacing every cookbook tome weighing down the particleboard with imaginary pots of early spring violets and pansies that would do just fine if she kept the temperature right. Or maybe even a bit of lavender.

The fantasy was the warm hug that gave her the courage to finally straighten her spine and crawl out of bed. A glance at the alarm clock told her she had roughly ten hours of daylight on her side before she had to worry about her sire sending any more charmers after her.

And he would. There was no question about that.

"Up and at 'em, lazy girl."

By the time she was dressed in her clothes from the day before and had tamed her hair enough to the point of a well-conditioned lion's mane, she made her way out to the living room and nearly slammed into the back of the loveseat in front of her. Or, more accurately, nearly flipped over the cushions and sucked face with the buttery leatherette.

Across the living room, another set of couch cushions cried out in protest as they struggled to support the massive bulk of Iron and Rhode, who'd just been handed coffee by Molly. Brass, meanwhile, stood in front of the door, sipping from a travel mug and acting for all the world like one warning look from him was enough to keep anything and everything on the other side of said door.

But it was Rhode who stole the immediate words from her throat.

He was the first to stand but not the first to address her.

Crap.

Somehow, in the morning light, everything about him seemed so different, almost foreign, as if he didn't so much as move through the sunlight but rather *it* moved around *him.* The effect was beyond eerie and so . . . wrong. His stance, his movements, none of them fit his powerful frame comfortably, and she wondered whether, like her, he was far more comfortable draped in shadows than sunlight.

"Hey! Did you sleep okay?" Molly rushed out of the kitchen, a piping-hot mug declaring *Don't forget, it all started with Smurfette* in one hand and a bottle of some indiscernible dairy product in the other.

"Yeah, it was amazing. Thank you."

"I'm so glad. And you know what else I'm so glad about?" Molly cast the stink eye to end all stink eyes in Rhode's direction. "That Brass has *assured* me Rhode won't go destroying any more of my stuff if I let him talk to you while my mate drives me to work. Right, honey?"

The auburn-haired angel's stiff nod spoke volumes.

"Good. You're all lucky it's Monday and we're closed to customers today. I've got a bunch of stuff to prep for tomorrow and, apparently, new chairs and glasses to order." Then she leveled her finger at Rhode. "I'm serious. You're still on the hook for that furniture."

"Understood," Rhode agreed.

"Wonderful. Neela, Brass will be back in about twenty minutes, and then he can help get you anything else you might need. Clothes, food, what have you."

"Um. Thanks. Sure."

The front door snicked closed about a nanosecond before whatever interrogation she was apparently in for began. Great. She hadn't even gotten one cup of coffee in her yet, and from the sour pusses on the angels' faces, she'd need a whole lot more than the drip stuff to get her through whatever she'd just been set up to deal with.

Because no matter what they had to say to her, it most certainly would be something that needed to be *dealt with*.

"You don't speak like them," Rhode observed.

"You've said that already."

"And you've yet to address it."

Neela put her hand on her hip. "Why does my speech bother you so much? What about it needs addressing, exactly?"

Iron placed a hand on Rhode's shoulder while he gestured for Neela to have a seat. "I think what Rhode's trying to say is the charmers we're familiar with don't have a knack for a lot of the common mortal vernacular. They tend to learn what they need to in order to acclimate among mortals but not enough to blend smoothly into conversations for extended periods of time. You talk to one of them for longer than twenty minutes in one shot, and you start to notice something's off—"

"Like yourself," Rhode interjected before taking his own seat.

"Thanks? I don't know whether that's a compliment or an insult." Neela tucked a wad of hair behind her ear, only to have her shoulders sink when the heavy stuff broke free despite her feeble efforts to tame it.

Rhode tracked her hand but immediately snapped back to business. "We're not here to offer either."

"Obviously." When neither of them elaborated, clearly waiting for her to explain once again the anomaly that she was, she sighed and took a bracing sip of coffee. *Mmm. French vanilla creamer.* At least she wasn't so different from Molly that they couldn't share the same taste in chemically altered and artificially flavored questionable dairy products. "You'd be surprised at the number of perks that come with being Cyro's only aberration offspring who he can't kill and who can also enjoy the light. I'll just say that I'm not lacking comfort. I have my own suite of rooms hidden belowground, decked out with all the things any woman would want: high-speed Internet, streaming services, jetted tub, plenty of shelves for my plants and gaming consoles..."

"Gaming consoles?" Iron asked.

"Well, yeah, I can't play Baldur's Gate with Sars Love if I don't have access to his server. Sometimes I'll tune in on Twitch if I catch him live, but he can drone on a bit. Editing is important, am I right? Oh, and just outside my apartment is my greenhouse. Technically, it only has night-blooming plants because it's underground, but I still call it that nonetheless."

Iron finally plopped onto the couch. "You have a . . . okay, what?"

"A greenhouse. I used the old indoor ice rink from the Lake Placid Olympics and turned its foundation into a footprint for where I wanted to house my plants. It worked out perfectly, minus the ice, of course. The square footage was exactly what I was looking for."

The two angels exchanged a look, and Neela worried whether she'd gone off course again, whether her elation at having someone to ramble to would scare away the intended audience.

Then Iron shook his head. "As far as I know, the Lake Placid Olympic Center is still standing. The 1980 games weren't that long ago. How did the mortals not notice a missing ice rink, especially the one from the famous Miracle on Ice game between the Soviet Union and the US?"

Neela smiled into her mug. "I wasn't talking about the rink from *those* games. God, how would anyone even nab that? Isn't it, like, a major tourist attraction in the area?" She took another sip of coffee. "I meant the ice rink from the *other* Lake Placid Olympics. The ones held in 1932."

"Holy fuck." Iron dropped his head into his hands, and Neela almost felt sorry for the guy. Almost.

"How?" Rhode's question was almost accusatory. "How can you live among the mortals so freely, all while living underground?"

Then it was Neela's turn to clam up. "I-I don't."

He quirked a silvery blond brow but said nothing.

"Cyro keeps me in comfort and gives me anything I want because he can't kill me. But I'm also a prisoner as much as I am a charmer. The fact that I can go out in the light while he and the others can't pisses him off more than anything else. So, I get to pay the price for his misery. Because I'm the only one who can handle the exposure, over the years, I've built my prison to accommodate my interests. It all changed when the Internet came into being, though. Since then, I've created countless online profiles, interacted with so many content creators, learned the ins and outs of every influencer, and, yeah, kind of acted like I was one of them."

A sharp pain hitched within her chest. "You have no idea what that sort of connection means for someone who never hoped to have any. My entire existence has been one of shame, degradation, and extreme isolation. My plants, my online peeps, they're all . . . Well, they *were* wonderful before I left, but they were only surface-level interactions. Essentially, faceless chats with binary codes. I never used a camera or microphone or anything like that. Couldn't risk Cyro finding out I was connecting to the outside world in some fashion. So, yeah, while I can't say I know mortals, I definitely know *of* them, if that makes sense. I doubt they give out honorary badges for being known by association, but I guess that's why I come across more human than not."

Holy hell, she'd never spoken any of that out loud, least of all to real living, breathing beings who could see her facial expressions and talk back. She couldn't even blame her racing heart on the admittedly awesome coffee.

"Iron, leave us."

A heavy beat passed between them. "You sure?"

Rhode's stare held all the heat from the night before, when he was losing his shit in the restaurant, but was tinged with a bit more reserve, as if some sort of deal had been made in exchange for him to speak civilly toward her and he'd relented. "Yes."

"Five minutes."

After Iron left the apartment, Neela didn't know whether to start up a conversation or wait for Rhode to say whatever the hell he had on his mind. Seriously, the secrecy was a bit too dramatic for the early hour, and if she wasn't careful, she'd waste away all her available sunlight drinking in the man before her instead of hightailing it as far away from Cyro as possible.

"Did you live with Cyro?"

Neela blinked. Talk about direct. "No. My suite was not far from his holdings, but it wasn't connected. He had charmers keep tabs on me because I'm immune to magic so he couldn't use it to contain or detect me. I had a regular patrol cover my perimeter, though. That's why I was able to finally sneak out. One of the guards was late to his shift."

"But you know where his home base is located."

"Yes . . ." Oh, she did not like this line of questioning. Not one bit.

Rhode stood, and Neela forgot just how breathtaking the full measure of this man truly was. Dark eyes and powerful muscles framed by steely contours were wrapped up in a silk shirt and dress slacks. He was the picture of seductive stealth, and her heart ached with joy to see him standing so tall.

"Can you access it?" he asked.

"I can . . . Why are you asking, though?"

"Can you move freely throughout his property?"

Then it was her turn to ask the questions. Neela abandoned the coffee on the table and shot up. "Okay, what's all this about? I just broke free from that asshole. I'm not about to run back there."

Rhode stepped forward. "You can, and you will." The heat from his words thickened the air between them. "I need that relic, and I need you to get me close to it."

"What? Are you insane?"

"As much as it pains me to admit, you and I share a common goal: Cyro's destruction. If I can gain that relic, the sentinels and I will finally be able to return to the Empyrean and stop him from creating an army capable of invading Heaven's highest realm and snuffing out all life as we know it."

Neela shook her head. "That's a literal suicide mission."

"Not if you're with me." Then he leaned forward, and her muscles tightened with that strange tickling energy from when she'd touched him last. "Besides, I have a feeling you know more than you're letting on."

"I don't know what you're talking about."

"You do." His deep eyes swirled with a dark promise, which quickly faded to the pearlescent silver of the wings she'd seen earlier. "Because you have seen me before, Neela. Somehow, you know me, and I intend to find out how."

Her throat clogged with undue tension, but she gritted her teeth through it regardless. "I am *not* going back there. I can't. Do you understand me? I *can't* go back to that life."

Rhode straightened, and an unreadable expression danced across his features. "How about an exchange?"

She regarded him and, dammit, hated that she was so intrigued, both by what he might offer and to keep listening to him talk. "What sort of exchange?"

"A story for a story." His shiny black loafers made their way across the carpet until their heels clapped out a slow rhythm on the galley kitchen's linoleum. On top of the windowsill sat a small aloe plant Neela had learned that Molly used for cooking burns. She'd snip off the tips of its leaves to source the cooling gel within as needed. Neela feared for the poor plant as Rhode caressed one shiny pointed leaf between his fingers, taking its sensory measure as one would a bolt of fabric. "You have a fondness for plants."

"Yes."

"There is an arboretum not far from here. Do you know what that is?"

"Of course I know what an arboretum is," she rushed out

before her limbic brain could settle her excitement. *Be cool, Neela. Be. Cool.*

"I will take you there in the daytime—today, even, while there is no threat of Cyro finding you."

An arboretum. A botanical garden full of trees, shrubs, and other woodsy plants she could never hope to harbor in her small night-blooming greenhouse. To have one in New Hampshire that was still open in the winter was more than her frazzled mind could handle. Was he seriously offering to take her there? To see it *in person*?

"I believe there is a year-round greenhouse there as well."

Hot tears stung her eyes at the enormity of what he was offering her. "You would take me there? Really?"

"Yes. I will let the plants and wildlife share with you the story of this land, these mortals, and why their souls are worth saving. In exchange for a story of your own," he added pointedly.

"And what kind of story do you want to hear from me?"

A sharp knock on the door nearly shook the apartment. The sound was only mildly louder than Iron's booming voice. "Brass is back. You guys ready to go?"

"What do the mortals call it these days?" Rhode mused. "An origin story?"

"Origins of what? I already told you all about me."

Oh, she did not like the way he looked at her, as if any of his remaining emotions got sucked into a frozen zone with no hope of or interest in retrieving them.

Then he fired that Arctic chill right at her, and she, as usual, was powerless to stop it.

"The origins of how you know me."

CHAPTER 10

As far as mortal tourist attractions went, the North Woods Arboretum was as unassuming as they came. Rhode and Neela had agreed to kick off their outing during a common lunch hour. Though expansive in their own right, the grounds were not far from the town's main drag that offered up food fare for the daytime workers. If Rhode had to spend the afternoon among mortals *and* a demon, he'd at least do it when the majority of onlookers were stuffing their faces during their barely thirty-minute lunch breaks.

And these people thought paranormal creatures were the supposed heathens.

Wrought-iron arches welcomed them into a world that was both serene and mysteriously haunting. Neatly manicured trails escorted them farther among arboreal sleeping giants who had been tucked in beneath thick blankets of snow and ice from winter's earlier leavings. Every few steps, they'd pass by a placard describing the various genera of each shrub, berry, and infernal pine cone.

To be sure, there was immense beauty around him. Vastly scaled cypress and blue spruce trees were a few of the basics he'd recognized, but none of them commanded his attention like the bright white puffer coat in front of him that had been newly cleaned and was darting from sign to sign along with its owner like a child in a candy store fretting over which chocolate bar to choose before the store closed.

"Oh my God, I can't believe it! An emerald sentinel juniper! Oh, and look, it even has berries. They're so blue and pretty nestled in their green little needles. Kind of looks like a bird's nest, don't you think? It's so stinking picture-perfect, I can't even!"

Rhode begrudgingly joined her in front of the shrubbery bed. "Can't even what?" While the plant was certainly alluring, he had a hard time seeing what about it would warrant her ear-piercing squeal that had nearly ruptured his eardrum.

The look Neela threw at him contained equal parts embarrassed teenager and impatient government employee. "I was saying that the plants are incredible."

"Why don't you just say that?"

Neela zipped her coat higher up her neck and leered at him. "I just did."

He snorted. "Forgive me, but I have not had the opportunity to learn the plethora of languages the other angels have."

"It's not a language. It's common vern— Oh, whatever."

After summarily dismissing him, Neela continued to flit through the manicured forest, marveling over things he had to remind himself that he had once taken for granted. Dappled snow clinging to far-too-thin branches. The musk of earthy pine dampening down the subtle crispness of the cold air.

Cold air in general.

But he could hardly focus on it for long. Every time Neela danced from one patch of flora to the next, her trailing scent made him question his decision to hover so closely. Even among so much greenery, those earthy hyssop notes seemed to flare behind her every time that hypnotic riot of curls whipped in front of him.

Though he hadn't developed much of a taste for the mortal food in New Hampshire, with the sole exception being Molly's cooking, he *had* learned that licorice was not a flavor he wanted anything to do with. And yet, this woman carried with her a gentle mintiness that enveloped the harsher edges of the more abrasive hyssop scents he'd experienced. And he didn't hate it.

Which was ridiculous. How could anything about the golden whirlwind before him, who was straining over a railing in an attempt to plunge what seemed like the more vital parts of her face into some other cypress' similar golden foliage, spark anything but disgust?

The question had been slamming around his mind for the better part of their excursion and only fueled his frustrations at having so many damn loose threads to begin with.

And he, an Empyrean spy, for god's sake.

Despite his unease, he had little interest in worsening his already precarious circumstances. So, when her remaining foot lifted off the ground, he pushed off the railing and called her away from the needle pit of whatever she was willingly throwing herself in.

"Walk with me," Rhode remarked. "There's a path up ahead that takes us through a more wooded area, away from the main gate and office. The privacy will allow you to speak freely."

He was only slightly surprised when he heard her foot land back on the pavement, followed by both heels trailing quickly behind him as he headed toward the path.

"Okay, I guess we're doing this, then." Neela's voice had dimmed so much from the brightness it held earlier, and he begrudgingly cursed himself for it. Clearly, he'd snuffed out all the wonderment that had kindled a new luminosity in her resplendent features only a moment ago.

Damn, but this whole outing was supposed to facilitate a

trade, wasn't it? Information for information. He'd let her roam the grounds wildly for an entire hour, after all. It didn't matter that a part of him warmed just a little at how easy it was to give her the delight fueling each one of those dashes across the walkway.

They had business to discuss, and the sooner they got down to it, the sooner he could find a way to cut whatever ties had been established between them.

But then he caught her bottom lip jutting out, despite the frown weighing the rest of her smile down, and a new level of annoyance slammed into him. Oh, fucking hell.

It was such a small ask, wasn't it? To meander through plants she'd not seen in the sunlight before? Even he was not so callous as to refute the simple pleasures he recalled upon regaining his freedom. Sunlight on skin. Clean clothes. Cool rain.

He lifted his eyes to the sky, asking for patience from mages knew whom, and sighed. "We can return."

When she didn't say anything immediately, he risked a glance at her and was pleased to see that she had taken up stride next to him.

He was even more pleased to see that full lower lip twitching as she fought for how to react to his offer. Was there a smile struggling to break free?

And more distressingly . . . Why the hell did he care?

His chest contracted with a strange sense of pride at the success of his tactic. Yes, it was his method for getting her to do as he wanted that pleased him. *That* fit, even if his logic didn't entirely feel as right as it used to. Still, he had to remind himself why they were there and what real success would mean for him and the others.

Neela took a deep breath. "Okay, so . . . origin story. Well, for as long as I can remember, I've always lived underground, like the rest of my kind. And for most of that time, I viewed it more as a sanctuary than a restriction. Wherever Cyro and the others migrated to, it always came with a special secluded area just for me. I didn't know any different, you know? Despite the circumstances of our living arrangements, whether they were prolific or sparse, I always had spacious accommodations with free-roaming access to any parts of the hideaway that I wished. But after a while, things just felt . . . weird. I began to question why there were no others like me. No females, I mean. I even wondered why I didn't share any of the features common among the male charmers, outside of my eye color, that is, and even that is a shade or two off from the rest of my kind."

Rhode nodded. "I noticed as much."

"Yeah, kind of hard to miss." She unzipped the upper part of her coat and exposed the bare column of her throat. "No gold bands either. Or swirling gold and dark teal tattoos covering every inch of my skin. And let's not forget"—Neela grabbed a fistful of her curls—"I ain't bald."

A sharp traitorous chuckle pushed against the seal of his lips, but he managed to swallow it down. "No, you are not."

"My conversations with the other charmers were always minimal at best. I got the sense they tolerated me as much as anyone who was forced to interact with neighbors in the same apartment building. But the relationships always just kind of hung there, you know? Real surface-level stuff. Still, I didn't mind so much. We all had the same goals, the same understanding, the same way of life, for the most part."

"You make it sound like some sort of nomadic colony."

"In a way, it sort of was, I guess, except I didn't have the same tasks as the others, nor was I treated the same. I never knew why. And then, one day, Cyro called for me."

Rhode's footing faltered, but he quickly caught himself and hid the misstep under the guise of adjusting his posture.

"It was not long after my inception that he wanted to speak with me."

"Inception?"

"What you would call our birth. I would say it was about a year or so after that."

"He waited that long to speak with you? As in, *ever* speaking to you?"

"We're not a particularly chatty crew. Our existence is more utilitarian than that of the mortals. Don't get me wrong, we conversed when needed to accomplish tasks or convey information, but beyond that, things were pretty quiet. Some charmers, however, show signs of disease in that first year following inception. We don't know why, but not everyone makes it to their first or second year of life. Perhaps it has something to do with the part of himself Cyro chooses to create us from or the strength of the dark magic he uses during the casting. Who knows? But a year is kind of a big deal for us. So, shortly after I made it through my first year, he called for me."

Neela stopped in front of a tall maple tree and ran her fingers over its brown and tan bark. The particular genus wasn't one Rhode could even easily pronounce, but she seemed to recognize it instantly. "Cyro handed me a stone and instructed me to portal to the surface and place it at the base of the nearest tree. That was all. Once I did that, I was supposed to open a portal and return." An errant piece of bark had begun to peel from the trunk, and she swiped a thumb over it, trying to reunite it with its home. "I couldn't portal. I tried, in addition to other charmers helping me, along with Cyro himself, but none of us could get the magic to work on me. When he finally ordered me to take the stairs to the surface instead, I was elated because at least *this* was a task I could do. If I couldn't portal, I could sure as hell climb some freaking stairs. So I scrambled up the stone steps, eager as anything, flung the door open, and immediately screamed my head off at the shock of it all." She took a deep breath. When her voice returned, it resonated with heavy pain. "It was pure daylight outside. Before either of us knew my capabilities, he sent me into the heat of the sun with no warning, no explanation for how he expected me to complete this task without succumbing to the light or why I was even called upon to do so in the first place. None."

Rhode's jaw ticked. "He was grooming you."

"You could say that, yeah." Then she turned her back to the tree and let the great maple support her. "But at the time, I was just so eager to be useful, I couldn't see beyond my sire's disappointment or the disappointment of the others." A flicker of hurt crinkled the corners of her eyes. "Then he tried to kill me."

Rhode's muscles stiffened. "What?"

"Over and over again." The ghost of something harshly familiar danced within her eyes, but she blinked it away before he could identify it fully. "I've been set on fire, drowned, electrocuted, all by his dark magic. Charmers I knew my whole life were tasked with holding me down, forcing me to drink all manner of vile potions, you name it. At one point, he even tried to dissolve me particle by particle by placing me in some magical chamber."

Somehow, even the forest knew to quell its tranquility, though Rhode hadn't realized a thing was possible. The birds winter hadn't yet managed to chase away even choked off their subtle squawks. It was as if no sound existed . . . except the thundering blood pounding a war drum in his ears.

"But my sire isn't a fool and doesn't tolerate failure for long. He figured out that something in my inception process had been different. Whatever object he'd nabbed from that battlefield and used to create me didn't give him the end result he desired. He'd also learned, through lots of fucking trial and error, that not only was I not what he was hoping for but that I also couldn't be killed, in the sunlight or otherwise."

Rhode clenched his fists and stuffed them in his coat pockets. He would *not* say anything. He would *not* ask the thousand questions lighting his tongue on fire.

"It was determined that, ultimately, I wasn't just power*less*, but power didn't work on me in general. No magic, no spells, nothing. But because celestial angel fire is the only thing that can truly destroy a charmer, as you so helpfully pointed out earlier, and it's not like Cyro can touch the stuff or even have access to it without torching himself, he was left with a wonderfully immortal and utterly worthless creation. Something that reminded him on the daily how much of a failure his highest hope had been. So, what does anyone do with their skeletons? They build a huge state-of-the-art decked-out closet for the suckers and shove them in there good and tight. And over time, if those skeletons are lucky and quiet and promise not to disrupt anything or get in the way, they're given bits of freedom around the grounds but never more than that. I'm allowed to be helpful, so long as I never remind him of just how harmful I truly am."

"Why?" Rhode breathed out, though he wasn't entirely sure what he was asking. *Why did you stay? Why didn't you fight back? Why are you truly telling me all of this, despite my asking you to? You could lie. I'd know if you lied.* And then . . . Please *fucking lie to me.*

Thankfully, Neela seemed to read his scattered thoughts. "I stayed because, even with my limited freedom, I still had my plants. Growing, breathing things that relied on me to keep going each day. When some would overgrow their pots, they needed me to transplant them into an environment they'd flourish in. When some branches or leaves would show evidence of disease, they needed me to prune away the pestilence for their flowers to bloom. To them, I was useful. I wasn't some grand mistake that didn't deserve to take up space. I was vital in a way, and to me, that feeling went both ways." Her throat worked on a swallow, and his eyes snapped to the slender column that she hadn't yet zipped back up from the elements. Tiny goose bumps dotted her delicate flesh, and his nostrils flared.

She took a deep breath, one that sobered as well as strengthened. "It took an eternity, but eventually, once Cyro realized I wasn't going anywhere and, likewise, couldn't interfere with his plans in any meaningful way, I begged him to let me care for something else, something that brought me a new type of joy that tending to my plants couldn't quite achieve." Then she flicked those golden eyes to him, and her attention struck him so hard, he had to take a step back. "Not something else, exactly, but some*one* else."

His celestial senses roared within the cage of his body, shouting warning signs of a danger he could neither see nor hear.

Then she took a step closer, and, damn coward that he was, he couldn't help but retreat a step farther.

"Have you ever cared for anything so deeply before, something where you know you're the only being alive who could help the other in some way?"

Memories of his final mission with Chrome rose unbidden from the recesses of his mind. The night before the Sealing, his insistence on hunting down the cause of their intelligence breach, one that had resulted in his entire legion of seraphim scouts returning from Cyro's camp in pieces.

Send me, brother. I will not fail you.

How many times had he turned that final phrase over in his thoughts, when other far more pressing matters pounded on his mental door for attention? Chief among them breathing, screaming, crying. Bleeding.

It was the last time he had truly called Chrome by the name of brother, despite the angel's status as a sentinel and role as intelligence master.

They had been as one back then. Two sides of the same mind. Tyrus, as Chrome was known in the Empyrean, and Axtar. The officer and the spy.

But like any ancient civilization whose great enlightenment had stunned the world, only to fall barren to time and consequence, demise was imminent and guaranteed. Always. And sometimes, it needed to be so.

"Have you?" Neela asked again when his silence stretched on too long. "Cared for anyone like that?"

Yes.

"No."

Neela narrowed her eyes. "What about your brothers? Don't you care for—"

"They are *not* my brothers," he seethed, pushing forward on his hips. "They are sentinels, guardians of the Empyrean. I am a seraph. We are not the same."

"And what about the soul bond? Why was that the first bit of magic I've ever been able to wield?"

"It's a connection in name only, one that solely has celestial significance," he remarked, dismissing her with a wave of his hand. "Nothing more. Outside of me accessing the power of angel fire as a result of that connection, it means nothing."

Neela put her hands on her generous hips, and Rhode had to lift his chin to remember what truly governed his anger in the moment.

"What am I, then? Some kind of celestial battery?"

Then he sneered at her. "You're a demon."

The barb landed before he had a chance to adjust his aim. He'd only meant to warn her off, to frighten her enough so that she'd stop scratching at his wounds, for god's sake. The shock-turned-retribution on her face was, unfortunately, one he was well familiar with—and one he was in no way prepared for.

"If I'm such a demon, why did I bother keeping you alive at all?"

Stunned, Rhode shook his head, convinced he hadn't heard her right. "What are you talking about?"

But holy hell, was there a metric ton of immovable resolution carved into those captivating features. And like an explosion, he couldn't look away. Self-preservation had gone out the window. All he could do was brace himself for the slice of the blade careening toward him.

"That's right. The thing I was caring for in Cyro's grotto? It was you, *Axtar*."

The thunder in his ears ricocheted down his limbs until every muscle vibrated with an uncontrollable rage that was equal parts shock and petrification.

No. It's not possible.

Brittle cracking broke through the silence, followed by heavy thuds of something wet, weighty, and abundant. Above, a giant and regrettably barren tree branch from a nearby oak snapped off the trunk a good ninety feet in the air. Coated in ice and burdened by dense snow, the branch plummeted to the forest floor—right above Neela.

CHAPTER 11

It was an unnerving feeling to have your voice be the sole thing to fill the silence one moment and, the next moment, have it choked off by the elements around you. Thick, heavy snow bounded down on Neela's shoulders and head, but it was nothing compared to the weight of Rhode's body as he threw her to the ground. Uncoordinated hands grasped for each other, but only his succeeded in finding their mark. Flat on her back, head pounding and eyes blinking overtime to shake the snow from her vision, she could see the enormous iced-over tree branch hurtling toward them.

"Rhode! Move!" Neela tried to squirm her way out from under him, but the bastard likely weighed more than the maple she'd been marveling over earlier.

The angel gritted his teeth, then a sharp slice ripped through the chilly air. Wings. Two gleaming pale silver wings shot from his back, and terror gripped her heart at what he was intending to do.

She'd seen those wings before and, amid the tossing and turning that plagued her last night, put the pieces together of what exactly they were made of, what she knew Cyro had done to him—and how truly brittle his metal could be.

"No!"

The impact scattered every remaining raptor in the trees and smashed Rhode's forehead into the ground next to her ear. His grunts and strangled breaths provided the soundtrack for the snow cascading around them. Then the cage of Rhode's arms extended, cowered, then extended again as he struggled to support the huge branch flattening the two of them into the packed snow.

Bruising pain assaulted her as her limbs mingled with Rhode's, pressing into each other at sharp angles. Owing to the meager padding of her winter coat, her back had been some-what spared the worst of the impact, but that meant nothing for the straining angel above her, whose every ragged breath inter-laced with her frightened ones.

It all ended as soon as it started. The falling wet snow settled around them, its heavy cascade no longer pattering on the shield of Rhode's wings.

Neela squinted for what meager light she could access within the shadowy cage of his wings. Over Rhode's shoulders, a mighty oak branch glinted back at her as it stuck out several feet on each side beyond Rhode's already condor-length wing-span. Breath somehow rushed into her compressed lungs, which were so tightly flushed against his deep chest.

And that was a pity, because her panic didn't make her nearly as helpful as she'd hoped.

"Holy shit! There's a tree on your back!"

"I'm . . . aware . . ."

"No, you don't understand. With the age of that oak and the length of the branch—it's a good fifteen feet long at least. Add on the ice encrusting it and the diameter of the wood, how wet the core will be owing to the season, that's got to be a good thousand pounds!"

Rhode's shoulders threatened to burst the seams of his coat as he tried to push the weight off them as much as he could. His eyes were squeezed shut, his brow creased in what she had to imagine was both pain and concentration. "Got that."

"But your metal! It's—"

"Dammit, woman, I fucking know, all right?"

Sweat beaded across his forehead as his hips swerved, then steadied with the weight of the rocking branch. Holy hell, he wasn't just keeping the thing from crushing her but *balancing* it as well. The man was banking his body so the limb—a limb the size of many mature trees—wouldn't roll over his head and flatten hers.

"Are you hurt?" he grunted out as he held a plank above her while a tree held its own plank on his back.

"I'm fine. But how can we—"

"Need to shift."

"No. Rhodium's too breakable. It doesn't have the tensile strength to—"

Hot breath tickled her ear and brushed across her nose as he tried to push up and look at her. "If you have a better idea, I'm all ears."

That silver fire swirled in his eyes again, pinning her impossibly further beneath the weight of his stare. Then she sucked in a sharp breath as his hip flexors chiseled out a hard path along her inner thigh. He groaned and tried to tilt his lower body away from her, but he only succeeded in widening his legs a bit to redistribute the weight.

Which put a whole lot more of him front and center against her.

"Fuck, this branch is too heavy."

"What will happen? If you shift?" The question was her only acquiescence to the inevitable transformation and the only option that would separate their two quickly fusing bodies.

Rhode's voice softened to a nearly inaudible whisper. "I need my fire. Can't access it like this. Not yet. Need to incinerate the wood."

"Why can't you access it yet?"

He looked away and took that vibrant stare with him.

"Oh."

The soul bond. Molly and Brass had given her more of the rundown on what happened when a celestial angel connected with their mate, and the reality made her all sorts of worried. In Brass's case, and that of the other sentinels, their fire was trapped inside them, only to slowly be set free when physical contact with their soul bond increased over time.

There was a great significance to it, as she understood things, one with lasting consequences.

One of those consequences being that the angel could finally access their full fire power, albeit briefly, until the full bond snapped into place.

The wheels were turning over faster in her mind when they stopped in front of a line she'd never considered crossing before.

She had powers, too, didn't she? Or at least, something like it? What if . . . ?

"What if I touch you? As your soul bond. Would that help fuel your fire?"

Shifting wouldn't work. They both knew that. There was a reason Cyro's experimentations involved rhodium and not some stronger metal. Already, Rhode's wings were struggling, his right one beginning to dip and bend below the left. Another minute or so and she didn't have the confidence he'd be able to bear the weight any longer.

The branch could be destroyed with angel fire, quickly and succinctly. And if they really were soul bonds, there was only one way to call it forth at that early stage of the connection.

They were as up, close, and personal as two people could get, sure, but it wasn't like they were skin to skin or anything. If

Neela had to, she could wiggle her hand up from where it was pinned and touch the side of his face or something. It was workable, doable. Useful.

But the way his eyes slashed back toward hers told her everything she needed to know about her little proposition.

He'd let the tree crush him first before he let her touch him, and would happily do so.

That truth filled the already infinitesimal space between them, choking out her shorter breaths, even as his breathing changed to keep pace with hers. She couldn't be sure whether it was the inevitability of her suggestion or the brutal revealed honesty from earlier, but somehow a weight far greater than that of the tree branch seemed to settle around them.

The silence wasn't helping. With so many of her senses cut off, the lesser-used ones flared to life with the boom of a starting pistol. Rhode's wide chest not only flattened her into the snow but pushed against her breasts until each of their syncopated breaths lifted them higher above her coat's open zipper. There was no reprieve from the contact, no place for her nipples to search out a less abrasive respite.

There was only his strength lying flush against her from his sharp collarbones to his warm thighs firmly bracketing hers. They were so close that if she dared to look up again, her lashes would brush against his jawline. Would the skin there pebble the way hers did whenever his breath kissed her nose or her cheek?

Would he hate her more for wanting to find out?

Then his hips shifted, and that singular hardness from earlier pressed into her more ardently, pulsing against her thigh with an insistent warning. Crap.

No, don't think of it. Do not think of it. He can't control his body any more than you can at the moment.

Neela was flustered and at a loss for what to do, what to manage. Instinctually, she leaped for what she could latch onto, which so happened to be the spun silk of his shirt where it tucked into his chiseled waistband. His open overcoat's brushed wool welcomed her touch as it cradled her hands closer to his sides—sides that heaved with a different kind of exertion than what had originally thrown them together.

"I'm sorry," she breathed, though she wasn't entirely sure what she was apologizing for. Touching him when he so clearly didn't want her to? Breathing in his air when the sweat on his brow begged for what little fresh oxygen was available? For lying to him about recognizing who he was and not having told him sooner?

It was the dealer's choice on that front.

"For what it's worth, I never touched you when you were in Cyro's grotto. Others did, but I wasn't one of them. I refused."

The option of escape had been taken from them both. The walls around them were only as strong as whatever faltering power remained in the impressive male blanketing her from the world. But somehow, that penetrating stare returned and swung back with a force that she wasn't entirely sure was the lesser of two evils.

And then both of their breaths quickened, setting a rhythm that ebbed and flowed with the unspoken understanding between them.

"Do it," he snarled, lifting his head so his mouth inched a tad closer to hers. "Fuck, do it quickly."

"What? Do what quickly? Touch your face?"

A harsh swallow rode the length of his throat, which was close enough for her to feel in her body. Her fingers tightened against his hips, and to her great surprise, he didn't canter away.

He moved *closer*.

"It needs to be a kiss," he said, closing his eyes again. The pain in his words was an audible blow to her heart. "For fuck's sake, it needs to be a kiss, all right? A simple touch on the face won't do it at this point. My power, whatever remains of it, is too depleted. The soul bond connection isn't strong enough yet." Then he looked at her again, and anger, hot and brutal and as violent as she'd ever seen, lashed out at her from those fiery eyes. "Just do it, and let's be done with this."

There was no ounce of compromise in his stare. No acquiescence to their circumstances or acknowledgment of Plan F trumping Plan A. There was only the heated fury she sadly recognized every time one of her kind had been called in to administer more of his *treatments* when he was a captive and she was a naïve onlooker.

It was a fury he needed in order to break through the pain of having another charmer touch him. Pain he always knew would come but which he had never known if or when it would relent.

Whether it was her touch or another of her kind, it was all the same to him. It was all repulsive.

A sharp tear pricked at her eye, but she refused to let it fall. She wasn't entirely sure what had been wounded most keenly. Her dignity? Her spirit? Or more embarrassingly, the fluttering urges of attraction that had parts of her trembling just as much as the body above hers?

The branch creaked its warning, leaving no time for her discomfort or sadness to settle in for the sulk they longed for. Instead, she lifted her chin to be level with his, a true task given how harshly he'd begun to shake. "I'm not the monster you think I am, and I'll prove it by taking you to Cyro. I'll show you I am not like him."

"Just shut up and kiss me already, would you?" he bit out, eyes clenched shut once more.

Resigned to the task, she lifted her lips to his and let the tear fall. She no longer cared what other parts of her chose to separate themselves from her as well.

CHAPTER 12

There were a lot more words Rhode wanted to say, *should* have said, but those were robbed from him as he melded his trembling lips with hers. It wasn't a sweet meeting of mouths or a passionate tangle, nor was it a curious wonder, with trails traversed and layouts learned.

No, it was a violent mashing that had a job to do. One very singular, very fucking important job.

And by the mages, it worked.

Rhode's body responded instantly as the fire within his core received the kickstart it needed. Rolling waves of power spread through every muscle in his body, blooming them to capacities he'd not known before. His already taxed muscles strained inexplicably further with each lick of electric blue flames that consumed him.

Dammit all, but Neela was right. He wouldn't have been able to risk a shift.

So it had to be this. Her. Against him. Touching him.

The scope of his new reality was the final spark of ignition his power needed. Flames erupted all around them, lashing out to the tips of his wings and curling around the branch like the legs of a black widow's deadly embrace. Cracks and pops hissed above him, followed by the acrid smell of charred wood. The load lightened bit by bit, but each sway of relief his muscles adapted to brought more comfort and reassurance than he'd ever imagined. Soon, his flames began to lessen, and nothing was kissing his shoulders except the delicate sprinkles of ash.

Which was a massive fucking problem because it left him with no other recourse but to address the softness beneath him.

And what softness it was.

He hadn't known what to brace himself for, not really. He never truly did. But something about this, about her, was so entirely different, he almost didn't know what to do with the shock of it all.

Everything, from her mouth to her middle to where her thighs cushioned the strength of his, was an assault on senses that had only ever known just that. But this? This was . . .

A respite.

His muscles slackened into the sensation before his mind could think better of it. Rhode's elbows met the ground and accidentally tipped his mouth farther against Neela's, unintentionally shifting his bottom lip in the process to taste more of hers.

The sensation seized his body.

Holy mages, she was sweet.

A sugared decadence moved across his mouth and arrested him in a way he'd never thought possible. Owing to no logic whatsoever, he brushed his lips against hers once more, savoring the pillowy enchantment that was both a distraction and the focus of whatever mess he'd found himself in.

Rhode dimly recalled what he'd tried to fortify himself against when he'd told Neela that it had to be a kiss. Even as taxed as he was, the bulk of him had known the fucking drill by that point and tensed as needed in miserable anticipation.

But Rhode had known misery. Holy hell, had he known it. And this . . .

Only in the quiet recesses of his mind could he admit to himself that kissing Neela was unimaginable bliss. A bliss he had no right seeking out, but damned if he could ignore what he'd so long been denied.

And it wasn't just her mouth that tempted him to seek out more. It was every aching curve that met his muscled ridges. Her lush body was a welcome cradle to all he had suffered, and his brain was threatening to short-circuit with the reconciliation of it. She was a charmer. A get of his tormentor. A soul bond by circumstance.

But beneath him, with his eyes closed and no one but his mind's eye to judge or blame him, she was wholly and completely female.

The flames around him had yet to douse fully, and he welcomed the strange sensation with a need just as alien as his situation. Adrenaline that wasn't ordinarily there controlled his maneuvers. And as long as the flames still simmered down their bodies, a part of him could make the argument that his actions were not truly his own. In the quiet cocoon of the steps needed to ensure their survival, Rhode wasn't entirely in the driver's seat, and neither was Neela. They were yet again victims of celestial circumstance, though this time a circumstance that came with far more intrigue than injury.

And that was when the moan reverberated through his lungs and pushed past his claimed lips into hers. It stunned him before it slayed him, and he couldn't for the life of him name the flavors bursting across his senses that had dragged the unexpected sound out of him. They were far more than his escaping vocabulary could describe and entirely nothing like what he'd ever associate with a charmer. Still, he couldn't help but try to name them for fear that, when it was all over, he'd never recall the delights of such a cocktail ever again.

By the mages, she tasted like life, like some vital indulgence his tongue couldn't help but dart out to steal more of. The impulse curled his gut, but not in the way he'd planned when he resigned himself to letting a charmer get so close to him again. With Neela, it was as if every muscle and tendon in his frame, despite being as strung out as they were, had somehow found a gear they'd not been able to access before.

A very greedy, impatient gear.

His breath hitched when her lithe fingers tightened at his waist before falling lower to claim his hips in a bracketing embrace that only fused them impossibly closer.

Was she . . . Did she actually *like* this? His mouth exploring hers? His body providing a shell of protection that, for any sane female, should have been viewed more as a cell than a sanctuary?

But those questing fingers traveled lower still, curiously circling the outside of his thighs. Then, they froze, as if they'd forgotten their place, and quickly spirited away back to their normal handholds.

And he'd never regretted the retreat more in his life.

"No," he growled into her mouth. "More."

Rhode had no earthly idea what to do with his hands, but he sure as hell couldn't keep them fisted at the sides of Neela's head any longer. Missing the feel of her on his thighs, he grabbed one of hers and settled it on the outside of his hip, anchoring it there with his large hand.

It was all the encouragement both of them needed to bask in whatever reprieve the mages were offering them for a little while longer. Once the flames died out and Rhode had to open his eyes to the carnage that was and always would be his reality, this wouldn't be allowed to happen again.

Things always looked different in daylight, didn't they? Even being starved of the stuff for so long, he knew what the illumination always revealed. Ugly cracks and raw crevices that made perfect homes for any manner of nightmares to settle in and fester.

Terrors didn't need spacious living accommodations, after all. They only needed one single opening.

But not here. Not now.

Neela shifted her head and, to Rhode's great delight, sheepishly searched out more of him with her tongue, embarking on a quiet answering expedition. Somewhere beneath the fire, their unspoken dance had flourished beneath a grand orchestration. There was a hesitant intent, a slow and steady drip that harmonized their movements.

A marvel, really, considering that Neela was engulfed by his fire as well. That was what happened among soul-bonded pairs in the beginning, before the fire was firmly under the sole control of the angel wielding it.

The mate was the one who had to first ignite it, and the experience was far different for mortals than other beings, as he'd been told. Human central nervous systems initially used their pain receptors to conceptualize the fire around them, even though they were never actually being burned. It was a shock type reaction.

Not so with others. Still, the possibility of Neela in pain, however unlikely, snuck its way into their intimacy and stung him with a brutal sharpness. Was she hurt? Was he harming her? Why he cared at all was a question that had been drowned out by action.

Rhode lifted off her with a growl. But as soon as he flung his eyes wide, a different sort of worried wonder greeted him.

A halo.

Neela lay beneath him, her lips kiss-swollen and her eyes bright with a pleased shock that he had put there. But beyond her brilliant eyes was another sort of brilliance. All that finely coiled hair that seemed to claim everything it touched was adorned with the final wisps of angel fire. *His* angel fire. A gift that their oddity of a connection had, for reasons he had yet to discover, made him the only seraph able to command the power.

Able to command it because of her and only once she called it forth.

"Are you all right?" His eyes thirsted over her, timing each flutter of her lashes to the dying licks of the flames that had begun to extinguish.

"I'm breathing. That's a plus."

"Yes," he acknowledged.

She cleared her throat but made no move to rise. "I think I was on fire."

"You called it forth. Of course you were on fire."

"You told me to."

Yes, he had told her to do that, hadn't he? The words made sense in so much as they didn't.

"You should get up," he said, still focusing on the flames.

"Um. You need to get off me first."

Rhode blinked, barely hearing her words. He was far too busy tracking the last line of blue embers as they outlined the farthest tendrils above her head. Mages, her hair was lovely, adorned in a fire he had no claim to, which was already receding within him, despite how urgently he tried to tug it back. *Not yet at full strength, then.*

Oh, what he wouldn't give to experience it again with this woman. It was a power unlike any he'd ever known. One that offered not only immense protection and offensive might but privacy as well.

Privacy that allowed him to kiss Neela and not hate himself for the betrayal of his body. To, dare he say, *enjoy* the touch of another. Of *her* touch.

"Uh-huh," he remarked, enraptured by the final flame as it flickered out, taking all it represented with it. But beyond the arc of her hair, a strange shadow on the snow in the distance caught his eye.

An odd figure draped in suited finery stood at the edge of the tree line. The cut of the individual's sharp jacket mimicked the crease in the front of its slacks, which was visible even at that distance. The being wore no overcoat, nor were there any footprints marking its trail through the snow.

No, it only wore a single smile that flashed colder than any New England winter. Sharp teeth a hair shy of animalistic broadcasted the warning message, but Rhode didn't need to examine it. Oh, he knew exactly what had been watching him.

Who had been watching him.

And it should have been fucking impossible in broad daylight.

Rhode's celestial senses sharpened, twisting the knife in his gut further as the picture before him came into focus. A male who was a good head and shoulders taller than the rest of the charmers leered back at him, his flattened nose and eyes upturned at the corners marking exactly who had witnessed Rhode's little fire show.

Cyro. The demon ruler.

Rhode leaped to his feet and let his rhodium skin ripple over every inch of him. Before the last of the armor could snap into place, however, Cyro offered up a smug little wave from across the way and vanished into the wind.

"Rhode? What's happening?" Neela lifted herself up on her elbows. Her voice brought him back to the present, to what they had just done. To who he had just done it with, and who had seen it all.

"Did you call him here?" he snarled, his hand itching for the weapons at his back.

"What? Call who? There's no one here."

"Don't ask me who. You fucking know who."

"Rhode, there's no one here. No one."

He blinked again, then cast his senses far and wide throughout the arboretum. At the gate, two sets of people had just entered. Mortals. One couple were retirees, the other two arboretum workers returning from lunch. In front of him, he frantically pushed his powers out, scanning the grounds.

No hint of charmers. Aside from Neela, there was not a single marker of the shadow realm anywhere for miles. Had he really imagined it?

Rhode gripped his head. "Fuck!"

"Rhode? Talk to me. What's going on?" Neela offered her hand, but he refused to look at her, refused to examine too closely how his first taste of intimacy since his capture had somehow been caressed by the demon ruler's talons.

Mages, he was going to be sick. Or savage.

His head spun violently until he could no longer delineate his metal from Neela's white coat or the snow around him. It was all, and always had been, one giant cage. So he did the only thing his panicked mind could do to escape.

He left her there.

With wings spread wide, he leaped into the air and took to the skies.

CHAPTER 13

The sun had just begun to sink below the horizon when Neela finally dusted off the burner phone Brass had given her, pried her nearly frozen ass off the bench outside the arboretum, and made the call.

It had only taken the better part of several hours to realize with an alarming amount of certainty that Rhode wasn't coming back for her. Honestly, did she expect him to, though?

Did I know what to expect at all?

There was out-of-her-depth and then there was whatever the hell had happened earlier. He had asked her to kiss him, hadn't he?

Of course he had, because in what world would she voluntarily lock lips with a man who shirked away from her touch as though she had ten kinds of plague crawling all over her?

She'd done what he asked of her. There wasn't one second of that encounter that hadn't involved some kind of fight-or-flight thinking on both sides, she was sure of it. It was a literal game of survival, with no power-ups left and no health bar to regenerate.

So she'd kissed him. And he'd promptly left her ass in the

snow like a forgotten bag of vegetative waste that would have to endure another freezing winter before the town came and picked her up, moldy and sodden.

Neela's knee bobbed out an anxious rhythm. She *should* be furious. Should be gleefully counting off the ticking minutes that took him farther away from her. Or at the very least, basking in the amazing experience of not only having a hand in their rescue operation but calling forth a crucial power that only *she* could pull off. Her, of all beings!

But instead, all she could think about was the kiss.

More.

The way he'd spoken that word against her lips hadn't been a simple plea. She'd heard plenty of those in her lifetime and uttered a fair amount of them herself. No, with Rhode, there was a passion to it, painted with some sort of urgent arrogance that belied the devastating look of disgust he gave her before the snow from his boots plopped onto her face as he got gone.

Unfortunately, it was his disgust that made the most sense. Disgust she knew, after all. The concept had practically been her babysitter, let alone the chief motivating factor in making sure that she maintained as low a profile as possible around her sire.

She was used to the stuff, knew its shoe size, and could even make friendship bracelets that featured all of its favorite colored beads.

Seeing it carved onto Rhode's features, though, after being cradled beneath him, feeling the insistent hardness of his body responding to hers, and scorching against him as the fire *she* called forth did the same to the branch above them, well . . .

Just because she was used to degradation didn't mean it sucked any less.

Neela zipped up her coat, not even caring that another one of her curls got snagged in the zipper. It seemed like a small price to pay for the secrets Rhode knew she was holding. Secrets she hadn't had a chance to reveal.

Maybe that was why he'd bolted when he popped those fiery peepers open and those dawning shreds of realization finally wound their way into his psyche. Regret was no one's favorite flavor, and he'd looked like he'd just swallowed two scoops of the stuff.

If he ever allowed her to explain, would he even understand, though? Or would it just send him to the skies again?

Had she even earned the right to care about him one way or the other?

A black SUV parted the misting snow, which had only begun to ramp up from flecks to flakes, and parked in front of her. But when the window rolled down, a woman's long blond braid—which was clearly revolting against the icy precipitation—nearly leaped out of the winter coat collar it was tucked into. The smile that greeted Neela was both soul-shatteringly sweet and just a hair too knowing.

"Please tell me Rhode didn't abandon you on the side of the, um, road," the woman said, already grimacing at the unintended rhyme before the words finished coming out of her mouth.

"Please tell me Brass sent you and the heat's cranking in there."

"You bet your sweet tits it is." She patted the outside of the door with her gloved hand, bestowing a curious amount of affection on the inanimate object. "I'm Drea, and you're cold, so let's continue this chat inside."

Neela already had one cheek on the fine leather before Drea finished her sentence, and though Neela's lips were still feeling the tingle from earlier, that didn't stop her from orchestrating the best low whistle of her life over her new surroundings.

"If I had a vehicle like this, I'd not only give it a waxed pet down daily but would solely drive it while wearing a pair of those cotton white gloves museum curators have on when handling precious artifacts."

Drea pulled onto the street and winked a violet eye at her. "I know, right? This was a gift from my soul bond, Chrome."

Ah. Figured. "What was the occasion?"

"That, by some miracle, I hadn't fallen through the rusted-out floorboards of my old car or died from carbon monoxide poisoning caused by the thing's longer-than-street-legal failed emissions test."

"Oh, wow. Well, I can say with complete certainty that this is the nicest car I've ever been in." She didn't need to elaborate that it was also only the *second* car she'd ever been in and discreetly crossed all fingers and toes the news wouldn't get back to Molly in some way.

"Really?" Her bright eyes creased at the corners. "I'm going to hold you to that, if you don't mind. I love Molly like a sister, and we used to live together in what is now her apartment, but she said she gives me one month tops before the back seat is riddled with Twizzler wrappers and I have to explain to Chrome why the leather's sticky and the vents smell like caramel macchiato."

"I suppose there are worse things to smell like."

"My thoughts exactly! Yeesh. If the man thinks he's keeping me from my iced coffees while he gets to leave his peppermint gum wrappers lying around, he can take his spare set of keys and shove them so far up his—"

"Hey, you know, I never said thanks for the ride. I really appreciate it."

Not wanting to step into any more family angel drama than she'd already waded through, and also not wanting Drea to accidentally blow through a second definitely-no-longer-yellow traffic light, Neela thought it best to steer the conversation in a different direction.

Drea seemed to ease up on the gas at the same rate the heat left her voice. Soon, they were strolling the speed limit with the rest of the lethargic traffic. Because, you know, small towns and whatnot.

"No problem at all. Brass and some of the others are out on patrol tonight. Chrome and Bronze are watching over Molly's apartment, so don't be surprised if the next-door neighbor Mrs. Carmine hollers something out her window about too much foul language. Which is *so* ironic because I've heard that eighty-year-old cuss out the UPS delivery guy with more linguistic flair than an auctioneer." They pulled up to a stopped traffic light, and Drea leaned closer. "I think she secretly loves the guys since they keep seedy people away from the parking lots, but she just maybe resents that she hasn't been able to keep up with a lot of the younger lingo, you know? The woman's a doll, but she still has a cable subscription. There's only so much pop culture and modern vernacular you can glean from that."

"Seeing as this is the longest I've been aboveground in my entire existence and the only man I thought I recognized from before abandoned me in the snow a few hours before nightfall, I can kind of relate to feeling a bit lost." Neela chewed the inside of her cheek as the car slowly accelerated through the light. *Silently* and slowly, mind you.

God, it hadn't even been five minutes, and Neela had already managed to steer the second conversation she'd ever had with a woman straight into shit's creek.

"Chrome and I found him, you know. Rhode. It's been— Look, it's not my story to tell, and I can't say I love the situation I'm in."

"What situation?"

The sigh Drea let out was so deep, Neela nearly felt it echo around the hollow in her own chest. "The one where the man who I'd literally do anything for wants nothing to do with the man who, for some reason, let me, of all people, care for him when he had every reason in the world to give up on life."

Neela tried to absorb that idea but couldn't reconcile the

heat she'd just experienced beneath Rhode's touch with the ice he'd practically cut her with as he flew off.

"The man gives me whiplash," Neela admitted. "I can only imagine what it must have been like for you when you were caring for him."

"Here's the thing, though—and believe me, it took me for-fucking-ever to realize this—but his circumstances don't really have anything to do with me. Rhode and I share a connection, sure, and Chrome and Rhode absolutely have a Mt. Everest-sized reckoning barreling toward them at some point, but it's not my place to try and worm my way inside his past, except to give the hard parts of it a soft place to land when the pieces start breaking free. Look, beyond what the others have already shared, we don't know more about Rhode's prior situation. He's claimed memory loss since day one, and even though Chrome *loves* to call bullshit on that, I don't care if that's the party line Rhode feels he needs to tote to keep himself safe. None of us can imagine what he's been through and what he's had to over-come mentally to even fly or fight again."

I can imagine. Far too well, I can imagine.

When Neela didn't say anything, Drea flicked on her blinker and pulled them into a strip mall parking lot.

"Why are we here?"

"Because retail therapy does a far better job of topping off the dopamine than bedroom sulking." Then she jammed the gear shift into park. "Besides, friends don't let friends wear the same outfit for more than a day in a row, unless it's, like, the *good* pair of jeans."

Shopping. As in, walk through a store, browse the racks, and —Neela's lower lip curled under her teeth—*try on* clothes in a fitting room. It was the most mundane of mortal tasks but something she'd always longed to do.

Neela's throat quivered. "I didn't know—"

"Save the questions. We've only got another hour until these places close, and if you want to feel like a new woman before *gently* handing Rhode his ass for the way he treated you, I suggest we walk and talk."

"Wait." Neela had already swung her car door open, but her hand froze on the handle. "What are you talking about?"

Drea was out of the vehicle and sauntering up to the first shop, her long braid swaying with canine-like enthusiasm. "I know where Rhode likes to go when he needs space away from the others, and I'll tell you where that is, if you promise to try on that hunter-green sweater dress in the window. Ooh and the brown calf-length boots!"

Neela barely made it through the boutique's door before her arms were piled high with garments and gratitude.

CHAPTER 14

I t was close to ten thirty in the evening when Rhode pushed himself off the cinderblock wall of the Happy Hands, Happy Paws animal shelter. After finally having enough of the sole parking lot light's sad interrogation technique, he used his power to disable the rhodium-coated electrodes in the facility's alarm system and ducked inside.

Not gonna lie, *that* had been a neat trick once he'd learned how to do it.

The shelter was one of the few animal rescues in Aurora that had a physical building to house dogs available for adoption. Most of the other rescue operations in the area lacked such funding, so the proprietors usually relied on volunteers to foster the dogs until the animals got swept up into (hopefully) loving homes.

The concept made about as much sense as non-dairy cheese. Apparently, having keepers with *more* money and resources meant you got to spend your days and nights in a cage, save for the few mandated potty breaks and some cuddle time that was more for the shelter volunteers' enjoyment and community service hours than the dogs' satisfaction. But if your caregivers had *no* money? Well, that got you a nice, warm home with free-roaming privileges, a few toys, canine friends to commiserate with, a couch to lounge on if you were lucky, and a kitchen full of scraps to snuffle off the floor.

That was the thing about gilded cages. The exact makeup of the bars was entirely irrelevant.

Because the best, most efficient jailors always knew that even if those doors were flung wide open, no inmate would budge. The true prison was always a mental one, and that facility was unfailingly locked up good and tight.

Rhode pushed through the back hallway, being careful to stay far away from the dim sepia-toned emergency lights that did far more to remind the poor animals of what they couldn't see than what they could. Even the temperature controls in the place managed to hitch another car to the nightmare train of canine psychological warfare. The thermostat for the main floor was just a hair shy of health-department healthy and tended to unexpectedly dip below sixty degrees Fahrenheit when the thing was operating on the programmable schedule.

Which, conveniently for the mortals, only ever happened at night when the animals were in the building alone.

But they had fur, right? And as long as the building's pipes never froze and they never failed an inspection, the nonprofiters could just keep on nonprofiting in the name of altruism. Because they were saving lives— No, what did the mortals call it again?

Ah, yes. They were finding the dogs their *furever* homes.

The chorus of soft snores and canine whimpers swelled against the rattling heating system that was doing its level best to show up for a job twenty years too late. Among the symphony of slumbering dogs, one kennel in particular always stood silent, as if its occupant insisted that, even during sleep, best behavior was still rewarded.

And he'd be right.

Rhode stalked past an assortment of terrier types and doodle mixes until he came to the single cell he always sought out whenever his mind got too full of his problems, not the least of which was his most recent Cyro hallucination.

Or the golden-haired demon who simultaneously gifted him power and robbed him of it.

Equally, the bulge of his arousal was also the gift that kept on fucking giving. It had taken the better part of an hour before it had finally subsided and he was able to sink into the desperate distraction of his beloved ritual visitations.

The black mask and nose greeted him before Rhode's bulk had even come into full view of the cage's door. It hardly mattered to the creature, as the fluffy tawny tail wagged with an excitement that belied the stern, pensive posture of the giant animal.

Owing to the beast's size, it was given the largest accommodations available, but even that wasn't saying much with how many kennels were built into the space. Adequate headroom was only really adequate for those animals who were adequately average.

"Hello, old friend."

The male dog relaxed its mouth and tongue and offered licks through the holes in the gate, but its deep tan chest never gave up the bark Rhode suspected it longed to release.

"I know. Silence is safety." Rhode did his best to ensure all the hard-to-reach spots on the animal got their love, especially since those were the areas that likely never got the attention they needed on account of his size and stature. After all, what high school volunteer, who was only there for two hours a week for college resume padding, wanted to get up close and personal with an intimidating and reserved guardian breed when the happy lab mixes were already rolling over for pets? Laughably few.

Above the dog's kennel door sat a piece of white paper that

was stuffed into a plastic sheet protector, condensing the animal's entire life into its age, weight, and likelihood of adoption.

Name: Lucky

Age: 3

Weight: 125lbs.

Breed: Anatolian Shepherd Mix

Then there was the ever-condescending four-sentences-max paragraph distilling the animal's entire worth into bite-sized selling points.

And why this particular dog was, in the mortals' minds, *special needs.*

Furry Facts: Lucky came to us from Oklahoma, where he was found wandering the streets after his owners were incarcerated for drugs. We don't know how he lost his leg, but he has a wonderful temperament and is fiercely loyal and protective. However, he does have travel anxiety but gives the absolute best kisses once he gets to know you! He'd be perfect for a homebody family who loves giant teddy bears and has a fenced-in yard.

Balancing on its one back leg, the dog gently pawed at the cage door when Rhode paused his petting for too long. The enthusiasm stretched across the dog's fangy and in-no-way-ferocious smile made Rhode's frown tip up just a bit.

"Why they chose to call you Lucky, I'll never know. It doesn't suit you in the least." The dog seemed to snort his agreement, turned around, and, with no small amount of ceremony, presented his sizable butt as the next part of him hoping to receive affectionate scratches. The copious undercarriage was offered up with a mix of eagerness and reservation as his boxy head swung around. With assessing brown eyes, he waited to see whether the request would be honored or denied.

A low rumble vibrated through Rhode's chest that might have been construed as a laugh on anyone else. "Always, sir. Let's have it."

Lucky scooted his hindquarters as far back as the kennel would allow, and Rhode obliged the pup in the small routine they'd come to share over the past few months when Rhode had found himself seeking out another sort of sanctuary.

As he worked his fingers over the dog's muscular form, he stared at the creased paper above the cage door and scoffed at the ridiculous name the mortals had given the beast, along with the equally ridiculous notion of what circumstances warranted the emotion.

Like Rhode, the dog had long been overlooked for his usefulness and had come to be defined by the limb he lacked instead of what the rest of him still had left to give. At three years old, and going on the sliding scale of mortal equivalent years, Lucky's age might as well have seen him, if he were a human, failing to launch out of his mother's basement while simultaneously aging out of dependent health insurance status a good five years prior. He was too old to be adorable, too independent to be easily trained, and far too disabled to be socially acceptable.

Rhode could so fucking relate.

What he couldn't patch into was how the mortals thought luck had anything to do with the dog's worth. Was Lucky truly lucky? The open mockery of the animal's condition that the moniker implied was so vapid, so simperingly asinine, that it bordered on depressing. As if, by virtue of being picked up off the street and being nursed back to whatever semblance of health passed for adequate once one's limb had been amputated, the dog should be grateful. Grateful to live out an untold number of days with stale, though somehow reliable processed food as his only source of nutrition, while having a designated patch of grass to pee on during mortal-approved windows of time.

Grateful for the cell, because to the well-intentioned caretakers, the converse could only ever be unfathomable, of course.

Rhode leaned in close and whispered, "Luck has nothing to do with it, and you and I both know that. If you were my companion, I'd give you a proper name, one that suited both of us better."

"What would that be?"

The icy tendrils that froze Rhode's limbs quickly eased as the honeyed floral notes of Neela's voice kissed them away. And while his hackles nearly grazed the ceiling with the realization of his sanctuary being invaded, Lucky's stayed infuriatingly still. Not only that but the damn animal had the gall to turn around and offer the newcomer his belly, of all things.

Traitor.

"How did you find me?"

Her sharp steps, no longer the dull patter of her thickly treaded boots, clacked gently on the concrete floor as she moved closer. "Drea."

"Ah."

"So, what would you name him? The dog?"

As if some blatant understanding passed between him and Lucky that they were no longer blessedly alone and some more decorum was in order, the animal righted itself to where it sat upright. The dog assumed the calm, affable stance and expression that he'd no doubt always hoped would win him favor among potential adoptive families.

"Cerberus," Rhode said before he could think better of it.

"Cerberus?" She moved closer, but he couldn't bring himself to look at her. "The three-headed dog who guarded the Underworld in Greek mythology? Funny, I don't see any snakes coming out of him."

"You'd be surprised what true ferocity looks like and what lengths creatures will go through to conceal it." He rose from his petting position, folded his arms, and leaned back against the wall, never taking his eyes from the dog. For some reason, it seemed far safer to keep his focus there.

"I gather it's easier to talk to him than anyone back home. From what I hear, dogs have an amazing ability to listen without being judgmental assholes." The words were as much of a proclamation as her presence there was to begin with. Touché.

"I would name him Cerberus because if he bore the name of one of the mortals' famed mythological beasts, perhaps he wouldn't be overlooked for his defect. Perhaps he'd command the attention and respect he's so deserving of long enough for any interested parties to see that he's not only worthy of being adopted but capable of being an invaluable part of any family."

Neela moved about in his periphery, only to settle next to him with her back against the wall, arms folded in a posture that mimicked his mood. "Names are important."

He snorted. "Yes, they are." But when she didn't pry more out of him, he took a deep breath and, lulled by the sonorous canine snores echoing off the cinder blocks, let free bits of a burden he somehow knew would be kept safe within those walls. "You called me Axtar when you first saw me in the mechanic's parking lot."

"I did."

"You claim to have known me from . . . before."

An ominous silence was all that answered him, and the invitation to fill it was as inescapable as it was inevitable.

Despite the red carpet he'd laid out for her to speak, she took no bait. Only offered him a sharper hook to ensnare himself on: a single raised eyebrow.

Dammit. Very well.

Rhode took a deep breath and kept his eyes trained on Lucky. "After my time in Cyro's camp, I could not bring myself to identify with the name I had once been called. As Axtar, I was a spy commander in the Empyrean's forces. A celestial weapon that served a higher purpose. But when Cyro—" He swallowed thickly. "After, I took on a name that was as much a part of what I'd become as what I'd hoped to be. If I could become the thing itself, the thing he made me, not only in physical prowess and power but with an entirely new identity, if I could embrace it instead of hate it, then I'd somehow manage to cut the nightmares' tethers over me."

Neela shifted at his side but didn't move to touch him. "Did it work?"

He scoffed. "What do you think?"

When she didn't respond to the sneering jab he'd intended to rile her with, his anger and indignation had nowhere to go. By saying nothing, she assuredly cut his fuming off at the knees, as if she somehow knew, somehow reminded him, even, that those emotions were not welcome in a place such as this. The animals didn't deserve his pity or anguish. They only deserved whatever peace they could find in the few hours of unbothered slumber.

Unbothered, at least, until he had shown up with his foul mood and heavy burdens.

Neela let her arms fall to her sides, and the soft brush of the cashmere cuffing her wrist grazed his arm. It was a shock both lovely and lilting, and his fingers couldn't help but sway closer to enjoy the contact. Still, they both looked onward, keeping a watchful eye on Lucky as he curled into an obscenely large fur ball and started to doze off.

Mages, how he wished he could sleep so soundly.

Neela inhaled a soft breath. "I think I should have found a way to reach you long before I overheard Cyro mention your name." Then it was her turn to shudder as the temperature, and their circumstances, plummeted to chillier levels. "After it was proven that I was officially no use to Cyro and also couldn't be killed, I eventually earned enough default trust that allowed me to move freely around the compound and help in what way I could, provided I wasn't in anyone's way and wouldn't interfere in any of Cyro's affairs. Well, one such affair that I volunteered for was to oversee the basic needs of his prisoners."

Rhode's heart skipped a beat.

"I-I remembered you. Your name, your original name, at any rate, was all I ever knew of who you were. I didn't know your history. My only job was cleaning your cell and making sure you were fed and watered. Beyond that, I had no context for anything about you, except the fear I felt when you had been rescued and I no longer knew what happened to you."

Neela took in another bracing breath and stepped farther away from him, taking her faint heat and softness with her. "That's a fear I can't live with, and it's why you made me realize that I can't bring myself to let anything so terrible happen to another soul if it's within my power to prevent it. So, yes, Rhode, as I said before, I'll help you take down Cyro, but don't think for one second I'm so easily discarded that I'm not worth including in this fight."

She turned away from him and walked toward the back door he now saw was still propped open. In the parking lot outside sat a familiar black SUV with its taillights on, still running. Still watching him.

Still expecting him to fuck up.

As the door slammed shut and the push bar clicked into place, sealing him in with the asylum's other inmates, a foreboding hollow clanged around his mind, resounding in his back teeth.

Neela had never meant to stay, only to stand her ground.

CHAPTER 15

"I don't know whether anyone's ever told you this before, but you guys need a better war room." Neela picked at a dried red spot of something on the scratched-up farmhouse table in the middle of the angels' great room and wondered, not for the first time, whether what she'd discreetly gathered under her fingernail was ketchup or blood. With the nearby sectional sofa arranged around a condensation-ring-laden coffee table positioned only a smattering of feet from a breakfront weapons arsenal that small countries would kill to have, she wondered at the strange sort of balance the angels had managed to find in their underground utopia.

Breakfast omelets and military artifice. Freshly baked cinnamon buns and celestial armament. To be among the press of shoulders and literal boulders as they all cupped their French press coffees and, in Iron's case—and she could not believe she was about to say this—an espresso demitasse cup, while she sat hunched over a table that could have easily been thrifted from any decent estate sale, she was slapped with no small amount of irony.

As odd as it might appear, this was a family. It was in the

subtle ways condiments were passed while the angels pored over no fewer than half a dozen tablets or how Tungsten never even so much as dropped a single breath in his conversation as he scooted back from the table just enough to allow his mate, Tammy, to join him on his lap. The kitchen was, likewise, a thriving hub of activity but was anchored with more purpose and enjoyment than the servitude Neela was used to.

Eggs puddled with goat cheese and sprinkled with neat flecks of chives had just as much of a place at this table as the news she'd recently shared regarding Cyro's latest hideaway location. She might as well have told them that Cyro had figured out how to have Mount Vesuvius release its Pompeii sequel all over Italy, and they'd probably just start triangulating flight trajectories and weapons schematics while still criticizing the rise time on that morning's batch of sourdough bread.

The whole thing made her heart squeeze to previously unclenched levels.

This was a home, in all its unabashedly peculiar and admittedly dysfunctional glory. Silence was only awkward because of what it *did* say, rather than what it omitted. It was never expected or, even worse, endured. There was no tolerating another's presence simply because they couldn't be removed from the equation.

No, judging by the tepid tension in the air and the empty seat she'd been told was usually occupied by Chrome, there was always the expectation that shit would be worked out and they could get back to their sausage and strategy sessions like it was any other Tuesday.

Except the subtle glances toward the noticeably absent party's usual place setting and the rows of several stony jaws begrudgingly chewing around that fact made the crater-sized hole she'd caused bloom to galaxy-sized proportions.

The unit these angels and their mates formed was a precious commodity, and there was no escaping the awful truth that she'd had a hand in the events that brought them to where they were: fractured, untrusting, and on the brink of whatever looming terror her sire had planned.

That ended right the fuck now.

Bronze heaped another pile of scrambled eggs onto his plate and nodded appreciatively at whatever was on Iron's screen while still addressing Neela. "Nah, there's no need for any fancy meeting place. We've got the best lighting right here. I mean, have you *seen* those mortal interrogation rooms, with their harsh fluorescent bulbs?" His shoulders shuddered in mock offense. "No thanks. I don't need that crap stealing my highlights and making all this au naturel auburn look like it came from a box. Besides, it's a bitch to move the espresso bar, and I am *not* settling for fucking drip coffee."

"Is it that much of a pain to move it? Aren't those just countertop things?" Neela asked, genuinely curious, and then instantly regretted it when every pair of eyes in the room looked at her as if she'd just announced she liked to kick puppies or shave kittens for fun. Even Rhode, who'd eaten nothing all morning and seemed to prefer propping up the cavern's most sizable granite wall, regarded her with an eyebrow arch of derision.

Steel shucked off his apron and plopped down a fresh tray of hashbrowns. "Our kitchen uses water from the hot springs deep below the mountain. Moving the espresso bar would mean we'd have to change the water source for the coffee."

"So, no, it's not moving." Iron lifted the petite cup to his lips, where his russet beard almost swallowing the porcelain seemed like a warning in and of itself.

Neela swallowed. "Point taken."

Titan leaned forward and swiped a finger across his tablet. "I can't believe Cyro's new hideaway has been below that Wonders of the Wilds theme park this whole time."

Bronze shoveled some eggs into his mouth before saying, "I

also can't believe how big of a hard-on the creators of that place had for Disney. Did they really build an entire faux utilidor below the park? How the hell did Disney let them get away with that?"

"They didn't," Iron clarified. "One of the original investors of this place knew the facility managers over at the Orlando park back when the Mouse's House was first built and offered up their knowledge of the underground tunnel system for an entirely unkosher cut of the new park's profits. It'll come as a surprise to no one that nondisclosure agreements were deeply violated, the other investors found out, and the tunnel system below Wonders of the Wilds was promptly shut down shortly after the foundations were put in. Now the workers have to schlep garbage and take their breaks next to ugly HVAC sheds like at the rest of the theme parks in this country."

Neela shifted in her seat, growing increasingly uncomfortable at the way they unknowingly described her previously lived reality—as some abandoned lair that only existed in the first place due to another male's scheming. They weren't wrong, per se, but the analysis and obvious analogy hit a little too close to home on many fronts. "Yeah, well, one person's trash—"

"Is the relic there?" Rhode cut in, expressing about as much interest in the hows and whys of her home's origins as he'd expressed about anything since she'd seen him that morning.

"Yeah, it's there," she confirmed, for some reason both grateful and irked by his abrupt change in topic. "The tunnels run the entire span of the park below ground, but the entrances have long been sealed off to mortals. They're still magically warded but far less so in the wintertime when the park's not operational. If you all are to go in, I'd recommend entering from the portion of the park that sits above my greenhouse. From there, that leads to, first, my private suite of rooms and then the rest of the complex beyond that. If we go in that way, it's less guarded. Because magic doesn't work on me, my quarters always had to be physically patrolled, instead of spelled, and well, let's just say monitoring my whereabouts wasn't always the choicest task when security assignments were handed out."

"They're not going. Only I am."

Neela had never heard the collective slamming of an entire service-for-twelve set of serving ware, ceramic mugs included, hit a table all at once, but she was nothing if not primed for a constant barrage of firsts in her life these days. One by one, every gruff voice in that cavernous hall rose up in an auditory wave to crash upon the sole sound of objection from the man who had yet to move from the wall he'd claimed since he'd first arrived.

"Out of the question—"

"We're a *team*, or have you forgotten—"

"If Chrome was here, he'd sure as shit have something to—"

The thunderous clapback of Rhode's rage was the only answer he provided, and it was enough to glue Neela's butt firmly back to the bench she'd commandeered.

Irises of deep umber morphed into the silvery-white flames she'd last witnessed when she'd been crushed beneath Rhode's powerful chest—a chest that was seemingly growing in size to match the tension in the room.

"You doubt me? You all doubt me still? I am a *spy*. Have I not bestowed enough? Bled enough? Fought hard enough? If I've given you no other reason to trust me, at least trust in that. No one, my *brothers*, has a record of service to match the length and breadth of mine, I assure you." Then that opulent metal armor snapped over his skin in a display of not only strength but offensive will. Weapons were drawn—more of those sickle blade things—and tendrils of blue flames swirled around his arms.

Shit. Not good. So very not good.

Neela didn't have to visit an animal shelter again to have the picture drawn of a panicked, desperate animal only to have it dragged out for those who loved it the most to gawk at. Especially after she left said animal licking a new set of wounds. She needed to do something before someone else got hurt at her expense.

"Excuse me! Rhode and I need a minute." Neela leaped off the bench, grabbed Rhode by the flaming arm, and dragged him down the first corridor she saw.

To her great surprise, no one asked her why she was so calm seeing his fire or how she knew it was safe to touch.

And to her even greater surprise, Rhode didn't fight her as she pulled him away.

CHAPTER 16

Rhode's rage was a practiced undertaking, and that was about the only thing in recent memory he could honestly say he was proud of. When examining all the good he'd accomplished in his existence, his ability to only fly off the handle when called to do so had turned into a calling card of sorts. An expertise. A skill set so rare and valuable that, in a different time, full-blooded Empyrean warriors had learned to tread with care where his temper was concerned, ensuring it was only called upon in pursuit of the enemy rather than misdirected elsewhere.

Well, all of that careful toe-stepping had flown right out the fucking window, apparently, and maybe that was for everyone's benefit.

Loose cannons were liabilities. Any sentinel in that room would be the first to say so, and they had, in no uncertain terms. And he sought to, what? Convince them that suffering somehow equaled service? That his time trapped in the proverbial trenches negated the eons that the others spent in *actual* service, with *actual* skills strengthened through familial bonds he had been severed from long ago?

Dammit, he was better than that, but hell if any part of him could see that beyond the temptation of what vengeance offered or the—

"God*dammit!*" His shoulder slammed into the wall's granite corner before Neela, who never looked backward and was seemingly annoyed at his sudden lack of propulsion, grabbed him and yanked his arm harder, until he had no choice but to follow.

"Door . . . Door . . . There must be a door around here . . . *Ah! Door! In here.*"

No sooner had the sting in his muscles subsided when the door latch clicked behind him and the motion sensor lights fired up. Once he finally got his fire and fury under control, he slowly tried to center himself among the great mountain's soothing minerals and . . . sacks of chickpea flour? "Why are we in the food pantry?"

"Because this was the first place I could find with an unlocked door that could afford us some privacy."

"And why would we need privacy?" he gritted out.

Neela whirled on him and pointed a finger at his chest. "Do you even really need to ask me that? Because if you had any ounce of awareness, you'd be able to tell that you were about to go all Silver Surfer meets Human Torch in there, and I don't think either of us would have appreciated the ramifications of *that* temper tantrum."

Cold clarity returned to him. "Temper. Tantrum? Never, in all my years, has a female spoken to me as if the very fury of the Empyrean was being wielded by none other than a toddler."

"Yeah, well, what would *you* call it when the person pitching a fit is too stuck in his own emotions to be able to hear that his family's complaints about him are one hundred percent—"

"If you think for one *fucking* second that I'll let you—"

"—unequivocally—"

"—insert yourself where you don't—"

"*—wrong!*"

"—belong . . . Wait, what?"

"What?"

Neela staggered backward and threw out a hand to support herself against a shelf containing commercially sized cans of San Marzano tomatoes. Likewise, Rhode felt a similar ricochet, but her barbs didn't slay so much as stun him.

Had she just said . . .?

And then he saw it. The deepening pink creeping high into her cheeks, the upturned creases in the corners of her eyes threatening to dip southward. The way her expression didn't just soften but somehow melted and reformed into an icy awareness that always came when one tried to mask their wounds.

"Shit. Neela, I didn't mean—"

But she cut her gaze away and examined a basket of baby purple potatoes while she cleared a gather of emotion from her throat. "What I was trying to say is that your family is wrong, Rhode, and trust me, I'm not just saying that to try and make you feel better. I have zero interest where that's concerned." A near-silent sniffle pricked his celestial senses before quickly dissipating beneath her words. "I'm saying all this because when something's worth fighting for, sometimes the desire to correct the misconception can be lost behind the desire to be correct. And believe me when I tell you that I don't say this because I'm smart. It's just that I have firsthand experience with sticking to problems a whole lot longer than most others. It kind of comes with the territory when, as you pointed out, one has a habit of not belonging." Glistening honeyed eyes found him, and he cursed himself for having put the sheen there to begin with.

Then cursed himself anew for admiring the unique shimmer, as well as the way his fingers itched to cradle her red cheeks and call his thumbs into service to swipe away the first tear that might fall because of his callousness.

"Why do you think neither you nor my sire have managed to chase me away yet? I promise you, it's not for lack of trying but because I am as persistent as you are important to what Cyro has in store. And if you would stop fighting me for more than one damn second, I'd be more than happy to explain my theory on the subject."

Rhode's ire had finally begun to ebb, but he wasn't entirely sure he was grateful for the relief. While his rage fled him, other emotions and observations filed in. Neela's tattered tunic had been replaced with a hunter-green sweaterdress that seemed to cradle every abundant curve of softness with a whispered invitation written for him alone. Expertly brushed brown leather boots hugged each generous calf, enrobing her legs in a confection that left only a slice of ivory skin at her knees to tempt him, which was another test of will he hardly needed.

Just when in the hell had she gotten all of that?

And then he remembered the black SUV that had sat parked outside the animal shelter. Drea's vehicle.

Did you expect her to stay in the same tattered clothes you found her in forever? It's not like you offered to help her in that regard.

No, he hadn't, on either front. Though he'd have been remiss to admit, even to himself, that he wouldn't have experienced at least some small joy in ripping those tattered clothes off her.

Shit. No.

This wasn't him. Whatever madness had him fighting with family and screaming at the only being who could help him was a new type of mental warfare. One he would make damn sure he demolished before another bout of rage got the better of him.

Rhode stepped forward and guided Neela's hands away from the innocent produce. When she let him, thank the mages, he took it as the good omen he needed but most certainly didn't deserve. Riding that wave of fortune, he slid his palms up her arms, appreciating the way her limbs felt when kissed by cashmere, and cupped her shoulders. Instantly, that now-familiar burn began to swirl within his core, filling his muscles with a tender recognition his body seemed to search out at every opportunity.

"I am sorry. It was shameful of me to behave the way I did."

Neela sniffed, then tried to back away, but his fingers tightened on her shoulders. "No, hear me. I cannot find the words to honestly apologize unless you're near enough to feel the truth of them. I was . . . not myself."

She reared back and lifted a brow, taking his measure as well as testing the veracity of his words. Her searching gaze pricked at parts of him that were still far too tender to suffer such scrutiny. Was she seeking out her own truth or searching for the bits of his that were so buried beneath the rubble that there was no hope of any such golden rays ever reaching them?

The truth—the *real* truth—wasn't solely that he hadn't acted as himself just then but that . . .

"I'm not entirely sure I know who my true self is any longer," he confessed in a harsh whisper.

Those knowing eyes softened a tad. "Good."

"Good?" He reared back slightly, equal parts confused at her remark and relieved she was still talking to him.

A tremor of fortification stilled her shoulders. "I think I can help with that, at least."

He quirked a brow at her. "Oh?"

"Now that I know who you are, *what* you are, I believe I know more about what Cyro plans to do with the other half of the relic." She stepped out of his hold, and that time, he let her, though she took a part of him with her as she chewed a fingernail and paced a small circle in front of the mountain of cereal boxes. "I think he might be using the relic's magic to fuse remnants of your celestial DNA with parts of himself to create beings that can survive in the light and, therefore, breach the walls of the Empyrean."

A chilling stillness choked off all movement to his limbs while words died on his tongue.

No...

"And this time, there's no reason it won't work," she continued before ticking off her fingers. "He's got his dark magic, a powerful relic of the Empyrean's gates, and your celestial DNA. The relic was the piece he hadn't quite managed to figure out before you were freed. But now, I'm sure it's only a matter of time before he finds the right combination of all that and mashes it together to create some super charmer capable of doing what I failed to." A remnant of pain tightened her vocal cords, but she managed to push her words through regardless. "So *that's* why you're more integral than your brothers realize. *That's* why they're wrong about you."

Then a concerning pallor chased away what remained of the bitter emotion he'd put on her face. Neela dug her fingers into her hair, pulling so tautly at the hairline that even her brows seemed alarmed. When she lifted her face to his again, any glimmers of confidence that had originally emboldened her enough to drag a raging seraph from a room full of Empyrean warriors had receded. All that remained was the uncertain tight lines pulling her features into an expression of fear he'd last seen when she was trapped beneath the charmers' net.

He liked it not at all, and his fire agreed, churning violently within him.

Neela's lip quivered before she stilled it and lifted her chin. "And I'm about to take you back to the one place I finally managed to free myself from."

CHAPTER 17

Rhode followed Neela beneath the amusement park's entrance archway, which proudly declared that they should all *Have a Wondrous Day*, and marveled at yet another element of mortal society that had evaded him: recreation.

The early afternoon sun was as deceptive and ineffective as any other ray of sunshine would be when tasked with warming frozen metal. The amusements all bore animal themes of one species or another, but no amount of fearsome mechanical menageries painted to look like serpents or sharks seemed either ferocious or, frankly, enjoyable when crusted with frost or tucked beneath weather-beaten tarps.

He tried to imagine what such a place would look like with children scurrying throughout the grounds and their parents, precariously balancing cell phones and melting ice cream cones in each hand, chasing after them.

There was a natural immersion practice he often did when he was alone and deeply entrenched in meditation. During those sessions, he would sometimes manage to make the outside world slip away fully. Walls would fade to open fields. The cold floor would fall away, until he was embraced by nothing but clouded cushioning that supported even the heaviest parts of him. In those deeply mesmerizing times, which were becoming harder and harder to visit, he'd sometimes imagine what it would feel like to live without the burden of what came before. To truly exist in an airy state of fulfillment, where it wasn't hard to play the part the other sentinels enjoyed so much.

Devastated things weren't free to stroll grounds such as these, but in those quiet and hard-to-attain moments, when he could truly bask in minutes-long periods where personal peace ran just as freely as gleeful children, well . . . he supposed an amusement park was as good a place as any to fuel the happy thoughts.

Too bad guilt had taken up permanent residence in the esteemed role of the monkey on his back ever since Neela had quietly tugged him along toward the very hell she'd fought her way out of. The hell they were both returning to.

Spying on, he mentally corrected. Not returning to. Not yet. In the game of espionage, details and distinctions mattered.

The crisp chill in the air was nothing compared to the frigid ten-foot gap Neela maintained ahead of him as she led them farther into a section of the park called Tundra Takedowns, which seemed to offer far fewer high-thrill roller coasters and far more zoological-based attractions and theming. Rides such as the Caribou Bumper Benders and Muskox Mayhem were housed either beneath a canopy or indoors entirely, creating an even more desolate awareness of what she was leading them toward and what was stretching out between them.

Any moment, he was waiting for the familiar comfort of his weapons' cold metal kissing his body to remind him why he was trailing after a woman who wanted as much to do with him as she wanted to be there in the first place. But when he closed his eyes and tried to feel the hum of the metals singing back to him, all he got was a whole lot of silence. No reverberation. No purring thrill of anticipation at soon being called into action to finally end the one being who had tainted him with the very power in the first place.

Instead, all he got was a soothed ego that, while newly calm and satisfied over the assurances of the other sentinels' thoughts about his place in their household, still turned the rest of his mood sour with every jilted step Neela took away from him.

If he had to pass one more happy polar bear with its tongue lolling over its incisors while Neela was hell-bent on being anywhere else but there, he was liable to torch every wooden caricature cutout just to give them both something to look at that was a more eye-catching distraction than whatever was happening between them.

Chaos he could handle. Silence he could not.

"Neela, a moment." Rhode jogged a few paces to catch up with her, and while her steps slowed slightly, that pert nose of hers still angled straight toward the ground. Mages, he would have had better luck catching her attention if he were a patch of ice painting the asphalt, but even then, he suspected nothing would thrill her more than to leap over him in supreme avoidance. When she didn't look up and only hiked her collar higher against whatever nonexistent breeze had yet to offend her, he took her meaning loud and clear: *he* was the offense.

"Hold." Rhode gently gripped her by the shoulder and angled himself in front of her.

Given the choice between dealing with her advancing problems or dealing with him, she reluctantly chose the latter and finally stopped. "It's not that much farther. If we keep going, we could be there before—"

"You've used up all your anger by aiming it at me instead?" A thoughtful display of confusion played across her face, and he used the opportunity to try and wedge into whatever good graces she still might have held for him. "I don't think that's wise, do you? Not if we're about to encounter more demons."

She folded her arms across her chest, and that lovely indignation flamed the apples of her cheeks. "Glad you're finally getting around to the elephant in the room."

"I see no elephants." Rhode extended his arms and made a show of sweeping them around. "Unless you count that Mastodon Mountain attraction we passed before we turned into this area of the park. I'm still not sure what a rock wall has to do with an extinct elephantid, but if the other amusements are anything to go by, the mortals who did the theming most likely couldn't refuse the potential for the alliteration." Yeah, he was being a sarcastic asshole, but it was a length he was willing to go to assuage his guilt and clear some air between them.

Neela's top lip quivered, and though she shut the movement down almost as fast as it appeared, it didn't stop Rhode's celestial senses from snagging on it and taking the win for what it was: the makings of a smile.

"I'd rather have your annoyance than your anger."

"Since when?"

He opened his mouth to speak but was stunned when no answer came. Surprisingly, the lack of that awareness, or perhaps the change in its perception, was a deterrent to the hardened balm that had so long cloaked his frame against the harshness of her kind.

She was a demon. A charmer. Cyro's get and potential heir to whatever hell the bastard was further cooking up.

Yet, when Rhode looked at Neela, very little of the hatred-colored lenses he saw her kind through seemed to cloud his vision. Not anymore, at least. Instead, his eyes delighted in focusing on other parts of her. Lush curves, golden spun-sugar hair, and a sensuous smile he had trouble recalling due to him giving her a lack of occasion to use it. There were far too many constant assaults on his senses, and dammit, he wanted *more*, but his desire was disturbing somehow. Physical attributes aside, there was a hollowness slightly dulling her aura that not only called to his wretched internal aches but seemed to seek out something from him as well.

Acceptance? Admiration?

Forgiveness?

"What?" he asked, hoping she'd dismiss his forgetfulness at what she'd asked him, while still very much wanting to hear her voice again.

"Since when would you rather have me annoyed at you instead of angry? I was under the impression you'd take as little of either option as possible and were only tolerating as much of me as you could stomach. You've made it perfectly clear where you think I belong, and that place is about as far from your side as possible."

Ouch. Her words were a firebrand across his chest and stood their own against some of the harshest inflictions ever leveled against him. Perhaps because her words were so well deserved. Perhaps because he had been seeking his vengeance from the wrong charmer and, instead, should have been offering his own amends.

"You are mistaken."

"Am I?"

"Yes."

"If you expect me to believe that, you're going to have to say it without looking like you're being actively disemboweled."

Rhode winced. Damn, this woman had more barbs on her tongue than Iron's mace. And still, he found himself deserving of every single one of them.

Before he could summon whatever sort of facial expression Neela would find the least amount of fault in, a growing warmth spread throughout his core, infusing his muscles and spirit with the lightness he'd only ever experienced through deep meditation. A sense of peace, calm, and understanding, fueled by his fire instead of the need to quell his ever-present fury.

It was usually a fleeting sensation, but it lingered within him and gave him the wherewithal to offer up some of that soothing energy by way of voicing gratitude.

And because he couldn't resist, a not-so-small bit of showmanship.

"Words are failing me," he said, shaking his head. "It has been quite some time since I've had to answer for my own emotions, and I fear I have yet to improve the skill set."

"Yeah, well, welcome to the club of sentient beings. It's a common affliction among its members and has no known cure."

Apparently.

He chuckled softly, more to hide his discomfort with his spoken truth than the reality of her rejoinder. "No, I don't suspect there is one, but perhaps small strides toward rectifying my behavior aren't entirely out of the question. At least, not yet."

Then Rhode turned to face the building behind them and pulsed his power into the mechanical latches and electrodes that had long been shut down for the fall and winter seasons. Slowly, gears cranked, doors lifted, and starved light bulbs connected with newly completed circuits. Maneuvering his power had become more natural, more centered and grounded in the lightness that came from his enlisted fire. The act was easy and, dare he say, almost pleasant, the way his muscles responded innately to wield the metallic magic that he'd hated for so long.

But for some reason, standing next to Neela, with flecks of gold in her eyes that mimicked the twinkling lights adorning the building's sign and internal sundries, his metallic manipulation didn't feel alien or abhorrent. Something was different. Something felt . . .

"Grateful," he rushed out, then cleared his throat and looked out across the myriad of games and machines that had come to life because of his power. Because of her connection to it. "I am grateful, Neela. Grateful for you."

That was all he could say. Somewhere, buried below the rubble of his past and the atrocious dig site of his present sat the proper words he needed to use. Phrases that spoke of true emotion, of familial ties and vengeance earned and private memories that chose to make themselves known while others merely grazed his consciousness. Entire tomes articulating every confusing need and desperate desire sat concealed beneath what he was not yet strong enough to clear away.

But for now, he could do this. He could meet her where he was and where he knew she would happily wander.

"Cyro will remain where he is. A supreme spy never rushes and cannot excel at reconnaissance without mastering patience over performance." Then he extended his hand toward the arcade and waited for her to take the first step. "I think it's time to learn a bit about your world. Not Cyro's, but yours."

Neela's eyes widened as they flitted among the games' glowing lights. "You opened the Arctic Arcade for me?"

Rhode nodded but still couldn't read her tense expression. And to his profound relief, he soon realized he didn't need to.

Because that time, when she grabbed him by the arm, he happily followed.

CHAPTER 18

It felt like a trick. The cruelest, most cunning machination designed not only to lure prey into a web but stuff it full of so many enticing emotions that it had no choice but to lie down, belly up, and sigh in rapturous defeat. But after many long moments passed and nothing swept in to steal Neela's joy, she thought that maybe, *maybe* Rhode had truly meant this to be a peace offering, one that filled her little gamer heart to bursting.

Bursting, ironically, with her own form of gratitude, though he had no way of knowing it.

Neela stepped into the center of the arcade and couldn't decide which dancing display of lights should command her attention first. "Do you know how often I dreamed of coming here?" she asked, hovering her fingers over the jets of an air hockey table that was just begging for a puck. Neela reached around toward the goal, gingerly plucked the hard disc from its cradle, and plopped it onto the cool blue surface, laughing as it skated away from her finger each time she poked it.

"I do not." Rhode joined her at the hockey table but kept his hands braced behind his back like a reserved home inspector scrutinizing the latest construction. "But I should like to hear of it."

"Really?" She swallowed hard and watched a display of mixed emotions war on his face.

"Really."

Not feeling entirely up for the acrobatics required to interpret his statement, she gleefully glossed over it to clarify hers. Seemed safer, at any rate.

Neela abandoned the hockey table for a wall of Skee-Ball machines whose backsplashes glowed with eager red numbers that promised high scores in the thousands for those brave enough to compete. Before she even looked to see whether any balls were free, the metal catch holding the row of balls back was released, and nine polished orbs scuttled down the ramp, ready and waiting for her to play.

She smiled at Rhode. "Your handiwork, I take it?"

Instead of the stoic nod and monosyllabic response she was expecting, however, he walked over to her side, retrieved a ball, and rolled it down the ramp. To her infuriating surprise, the ball bounced off the rim of the fifty-point slot and settled comfortably and conveniently in the hundred-point cylinder. The red lights above went all sorts of ballistic, flashing and strobing in anticipation of more points. The tinkering carnival music pinged its metallic notes, and even the angel at her side couldn't help but crack a smile as he leaned down for another ball.

"Uh-uh. Not so fast." Neela swiped the ball from the holster and sent it flying before it fell into the way-too-freaking-large ten-point catch basin of shame.

The dark chuckle next to her seemed so ominously off in a place of joy such as this that she honestly wasn't sure Rhode had ever had an excuse to laugh before. Like, an honest-to-goodness, belly-busting, tears-leaking-from-your-eyes, can't-breathe kind of laugh.

The realization was as shamefully heartbreaking as it was

savage in its ruthlessness to steer the conversation toward greener pastures.

"I tell you what. Open the lane up next to this one and we'll have a good old-fashioned Skee-Ball battle. Winner gets to hear the loser's dreams."

Rhode eyed her thoughtfully. "And what if the loser's dreams are not worth sharing?"

A somber warning crackled beneath the inflection of his words.

"That's for the winner to decide."

They stood there so long that the heft of the Skee-Ball in her hand seemed not to only weigh down her arm but the joy of the wonders around her—wonders she'd only ever seen in videos and vivid clips of social media friends gathering together in carefree pleasure. No worries, no evils, no agenda. Just . . . joy.

Was it some sort of fool's errand she was teetering toward? She knew, more than most, how wide the chasm between them was. But was she crazy for still wanting to at least *try* to cross it? For the sake of what they could prevent?

For the sake of what they could protect?

She was about to drop her ball back in the slot and wedge her disappointment good and deep beneath it when the familiar thunderous roll down the ramp next to hers answered her worries.

Rhode's ball missed the hundred-point ring by a wide margin, settling home into the broad ten-point bucket. A throw-away toss, perhaps, but she was happy to take it for the response it was.

The knot in her chest lightened as she declared, "Game on."

AFTER NINE GRUELING rounds of Skee-Ball, which *had* to end on an odd number of plays because, as it turned out, both she and

Rhode had a bit of a competitive streak in them and a de facto winner *had* to be declared, Neela was finally ready to admit defeat . . . but not before the three cycles of pinball, five NASCAR driving races, and way too many embarrassing attempts at every crane game in the joint.

Embarrassing because, as Rhode pointed out when he handed her the third identical hot pink glow-in-the-dark cat pillow, the claws were mechanized with rhodium.

So, yeah, not her finest win, but still, the pillows were cute.

Rhode leaned back against one of those crane games holding an inordinate amount of plushies against a chest that had no business cradling things so soft and flashed more of his achingly beautiful smile than she'd ever seen him show before. Was he even aware he was doing it?

"Happy looks good on you. Has anyone ever told you that?"

His smile fell abruptly, as if caught with its pants down. "No," he answered a bit breathlessly while his mesmerizing chest expanded with each easy inhale. "But Skee-Ball is a rather fun game."

"Games usually are," Neela said, collapsing sideways onto the faux motorcycle seat from the BMX racing game across from the Skee-Ball wall. "That's why I love them so much. Especially when you win. Congratulations, by the way."

Rhode bowed slightly, and she couldn't help but smile at how out of place his starchy regalness felt among the giant Charizard dangling over his head.

"Thank you for allowing me to master a new skill."

"I wouldn't say you *mastered* Skee-Ball, just got in a few lucky—"

"I meant humility."

Her heart bottomed out from the shock of his words. "What?"

But Rhode didn't turn away. Instead, his troubled beauty

softened, and she had to remember who he was and *wasn't* to her but also why they were there.

"It is a humbling thing to not only admit when you have wronged another but to experience such determination, such an integral investment in the rectification of that wrong, that the correction often repairs afflictions within yourself you had long forgotten needed mending."

Neela shook her head. "You're talking in circles, and after the light show I've been spinning under for however long we've been here, I'm going to need you to speak in plain sentences."

"A dream, then." She quirked her head in curiosity, but he merely nodded his encouragement. "I am the victor, and as such, you owe me a dream. Wasn't that the agreed-upon spoil of this war?"

And just like that, their present situation came back to shake up her insides. Crap. They'd made a deal, hadn't they? Neela blew out a shaky breath, stood, and tried to center herself. *Here goes nothing.* "My greenhouse is belowground but not far from the arcade here. During the summer and into the fall weekends, I could sometimes hear the music through my cinder block ceiling. The melodies always changed based on which games were being played, who was winning, losing, etc., and also what was being blasted through the speakers. Sometimes, perhaps on rainy days, I gathered attendance at the park was slow enough that the employees working the arcade had enough freedom to go off script and blast whatever music they wanted."

Neela wandered toward a nearby photo booth and rested a hip against the stall, eager to have something sturdier for support than just the racing vehicle beneath her. "It always seemed so extravagant in some way. That no matter how many people were above me, there was always an ebb and flow to the life force of the music, both from the speakers and the games themselves. I would sit in my greenhouse, and I swear I could tell exactly who was playing what based on the sounds that vibrated through the tunnels. Young families, teenagers, rowdy cousins, grandparents with canes and motorized scooters, I could hear it all, and I would dream what it would be like to be a part of that. To have someone stand behind you, rooting you on as you worked the crane joystick, tongue out, eyes squinting, examining the angles of the claw's trajectory from every possible side. Or to have a doting partner spend far too much money on the basketball knockout game to win the exact number of tickets needed to gift their sweetheart with the one thing that would light them up from the inside."

Neela shifted absentmindedly and nearly fell back into the photo booth's curtain before she caught herself just as Rhode sprang to his feet.

"It was a family you dreamed of?"

"Maybe. I don't know."

Oh, she knew. As sure as her hair frizzed the moment the humidity level hit seventy percent, she knew exactly what she dreamed of. However, ever since her fear had chased her into the chaos that was the mortal lands, a whole new set of wants and desires had begun to take shape and morph around her formerly once-constant goal.

Rhode took a step closer, and the blue and red lights from the adjacent police chase video game painted him in perplexing contrast to the metal she knew him to command. The metal he'd used to open the arcade for her.

Then that small smile, so seldom in its appearances, returned for a repeat performance, lifting the angles of his face into an interesting piece of art, one she wouldn't mind staring at for as long as he'd allow. Her fingers were anxious to trace it, to map each contour of his happiness lest it disappear again and never return.

His haunting tenor voice broke the spell, stealing her focus back to his words. "Was it a memento that you dreamed of, then? Some special keepsake of joyful times shared?"

Neela thought on it a moment, of what having a keepsake or token would have represented for her while she was stuck lounging beneath the earth, longing for the sun and cursing herself all the same for what her desire to embrace the sunlight meant.

Then she thought of the angel before her, who she was somehow bonded to in ways neither of them had truly begun to explore.

Did she want to remember all of that in her prior life, or would she have preferred to forget the past for just one moment and take a piece of her present into the future with her?

As if she even had the luxury of such a choice—

"Take a picture with me," Rhode said. Then he was at her side, holding open the burgundy curtain to the photo booth, an expectant gaze lifting his features as he waited for an answer.

"I-I've never had my picture taken before. Not really. All my gaming profile images are just avatars or animations."

"I have never had my picture taken either."

The symbiotic truth hung somewhere in between the similar statements.

We've both had time and experiences stolen from us.

"What if you don't like it?" Neela asked.

He shrugged. "What if I do?"

"What if *I* don't like it?"

His gaze darkened. "Then I'll know something about you that no one else does."

A secret. A treasure. A token. Something shared voluntarily, beyond whatever supernatural bond and haunted past that had claimed them both.

A new start. Small but still sacred.

"I think I'd like that," Neela agreed and ducked her head beneath the photo booth's curtain.

CHAPTER 19

Rhode had fought in countless battles, uncovered secrets from enemies who'd sworn against their souls to never reveal, and there he stood, arm shaking beneath the slight weight of the photo booth's curtain as he held it open for Neela and wondered what the hell had possessed him to offer such an invitation.

He and Neela, alone in a box with barely enough head clearance for him, never mind the enormity of what she'd shared . . . and what he'd offered.

A photo. Together. Next to each other. Possibly even—

"Are you going to come in?" Neela asked, poking her head out and eyeing him curiously through the gap in the curtain he still held open. The bulk of her flaxen curls dangled over one shoulder and swayed enticingly in the empty space between them, as if offering a bridge toward some great beyond he'd yet to cross but which Neela had already conquered.

Conquered. Now *that* was a word far too keen for the circumstances. He hadn't meant to conquer anything beyond the guilt that had gnawed at him for his behavior—behavior he alone would have disemboweled any angel in his legion for displaying. Yet somehow, guilt had turned to pity, which had then morphed into some harsher grip of anguish.

What Neela described was far too close to a predicament he'd previously seen no way out of.

Loneliness.

Owing one last look around the arcade to ensure they were still by themselves and marking their coats and various game prizes exactly where they left them on top of the air hockey table, he swallowed past his apprehension and slipped inside.

"Why do I feel like I'm in a coffin?" he asked as he took a seat on the hard bench next to her.

"Because this is where party fun goes to die?"

He barked out a sardonic laugh. "Then why do the mortals even have such a thing?"

Neela craned her head back and started reading the instructions on the screen in front of them. "I think so introverted people can have an excuse to get away from the crowd they were societally forced to be a part of while still documenting the fact that they actually attended the event."

"Again, why attend at all if it only causes them discomfort and shame? Seems like a ridiculous price to pay for misery."

Neela pushed some buttons and smiled at him. "Misery loves company. Now smile! It takes three frames, and then it should give us a printout."

Rhode snorted, then shifted against the seat, hoping to keep certain parts of him far and away from certain parts of her. Perhaps it was an excuse to avoid the camera lens, but as the flash went off in quick succession, something about her words struck him. When the slip of photo paper shot out from below the screen, he understood what it was.

Neela's smile was all wrong. His ornery face aside, each of the three photos revealed a stiff, artificial sort of forced happiness in her that he instinctively knew had no place in an arcade photo booth meant to capture delight and laughter. Though the corners of her lips lifted on command and neat rows of teeth stood at photogenic attention, there was no true joy in it. Her golden eyes didn't sparkle, despite the camera flash's best intentions to capture it. Even her shoulders sat just below her ears, wrinkling the fine cashmere of her sweaterdress's top to awkwardly mash her figure into an unappealing shell that was far from accurate.

Where was the petal-pink flush to her cheeks that had last lit her features when she'd scurried to name all those damn trees at the arboretum? Where was the sunglow's radiance in her eyes that flashed her excitement when she'd first seen the arcade's lights fire up?

This artificial bland visage wasn't the memento he'd promised her, nor was it the explanation he felt he owed her.

No, that was, as she'd so keenly pointed out, misery, pure and simple.

Misery in the form of a required yearbook photograph taken of the student who had no means to pay for the keepsake.

And it pissed him the fuck off.

"Something's wrong with you."

Neela's eyes widened. "Excuse me?"

"You're not happy."

"I'm not *not* happy," she hedged, gesturing toward the photo booth's screen. "It's fine. It's great. I've got my photo, and it's something I never thought I would have. Not really, at any rate."

"But you're not *happy*." Then he snatched her hand from the air, and she gasped when the groan that came out of him surprised them both. Rhode's eyes fell closed as he remembered the last time his hands were on her.

And his mouth.

One by one, he kneaded the pads of her fingers, relishing the way her pupils pulsed as she watched him and how the blood beneath her skin ebbed and flowed back to his touch in eager increments.

Mages, even her fingertips were warm, where his body had only ever known icy savagery.

It wasn't fair to have all that heat wrapped up in such a delicate grasp, not when the fire within his core punched against the cage of his body as she began to curl her fingers around his.

Fuck. They were only hands, for god's sake, but blood was blood, and he couldn't help but track the pale blue of her veins as they tunneled down her palm and beneath her sweater's soft cuff.

The booth was too hot, too stifling. Oxygen had become a rare commodity as he sucked in precious little of the stuff. Clarity, whatever had remained, quickly turned to necessity. Fire roared beneath his veins, and an urgent part of him wondered—no, *needed* to know whether Neela was just as hot as he was.

His lips, eager explorers as they were, descended onto the soft skin of her wrist. One kiss, then another, then a curious swipe of his tongue charted her vital lifelines and told him everything he needed to know.

"You are hot," he rasped out, straining to speak for fear that if he parted his lips from her for too long, he'd never remember the way back.

"It's hot in here," she said, though she surprisingly didn't pull away from him. "The booth is, uh, stuffy."

"Too hot?" Another press of his mouth against her skin and his cock punched at the zipper of his slacks.

Soft puffs of her encouragement tickled the hair on the top of his head.

And then he felt it. The insistent yank on his silk collar. When he followed the tug, he was met with those golden eyes, blazing with wonder and unspoken questions—questions that would mirror his in another time, in another circumstance.

But there was no other time, and in the hushed privacy of

the photo booth, nothing would have stopped him from devouring her mouth as she lightly, tenuously set her lips upon his.

There were reasons they were there, he was sure of it. Sound, logical reasons why he'd unlocked an arcade for the sole purpose of seeing her smile. Because if she was smiling, she wasn't miserable. If she wasn't miserable, she could work more adeptly at their reconnaissance mission, so he might finally access the information he needed to bring down Cyro.

All of that had gone right out the fucking window as he possessively groaned into her mouth, his fire beating an insistent rhythm to the pulse of blood thickening his cock. One of his knees dropped to the floor, then the second. He was a beast ruled solely by hunger after humanity had abandoned him long ago.

And then, like any beast, a ferocity took hold, one that a part of him roared to surrender to while the last remaining shred of his decorum shut the door on the scene and turned its back.

Good.

Approving murmurs vibrated through Neela's mouth and shot straight down his spine, curling his hips against the hard frame of the bench. His hands dropped hers and slid to her hips, eager to grab onto something, to mold his grip to curves that contoured perfectly with his palms.

He dragged his mouth away from hers, tracing a trail of cashmere that ended inches from his lips, which tingled with the anticipation of another heat source entirely.

Neela's thighs fell apart, and the sly woman gripped *his* hand, led it beneath her dress, and welcomed the backs of his knuckles to the damp cove hiding behind her underwear.

"Is this what you want, little demon?" he asked as he stroked her desire through the thin fabric. With each caress, his fire answered. An erotic call and response to a passion he never thought he'd experience.

"I want to be happy. Your touch, this . . . this . . . *bond*, whatever it is, I think it can do that. Do you want this, too? Would it make you . . . happy, as well? Is that what we're doing here?"

Happiness. What a concept, and not one that had ever applied to him. Before he'd met her, he'd been imprisoned. Before he'd been imprisoned, he'd been at war. There had only ever been orders, schematics, actions, and actualities. Emotions were left for the celestial mages to manage, for the souls who'd entered the Empyrean under the sentinels' supreme guard, for the mortals to indulge in for the few years they had available to them.

But it was never for him. Happiness had always been a private indifference. Something for others with more frivolous concerns.

Wasn't *that* what they were doing, though? Wasn't happiness the driving force behind this . . . carnal act, this tempting tryst?

Would it alter his course in any way if he indulged in the molten heat emanating from her slick desire that was doing a bang-up job of thickening his own?

His hands answered for him, followed by his mouth. Suppressing the harsher edges of a roar Rhode only ever reserved for battlefields, he pulled the drenched fabric aside and slid one finger, then a second into her glistening arousal.

Neela's hands shot out to the walls at her sides. "Holy shit!"

But those were the last words he was interested in hearing. From there on out, he wanted only moans.

He sank his fingers farther into her, curving them sharply in the direction her soft pants and quivering muscles urged him to go. Mages, she was glorious. Peering over the soft mound of her curves, he smiled at her head thrown back, eyes pinched shut, and breasts heaving against their cashmere prison in time to his ministrations.

But it wasn't enough. Nowhere near enough. Greedily, he hooked the backs of her knees over his shoulders, spread her even wider, and set his tongue upon her tight nub with a veneration he hadn't known himself capable of. Neela bucked against him, desperately trying to squeeze her thighs closer together. Such a feat would impede his vision of her coming apart under his mouth, so he used the strength of his shoulders to stretch her legs farther and settled his hand against the delicate softness below her ribcage.

Her panting turned to prayers as he played the secret parts of her like the finest celestial instrument. Every slow crescendo and riveting note wrought by his tongue was mirrored by the desperate grips of her hands anchoring in his hair. The gentler his kisses, the softer her fingers' caresses.

But he didn't want gentle. He wanted fierce. He wanted fire.

Rhode added a third finger and sucked her clit until her magnificent hips roiled against his face in great undulating waves. Her cries were a symphonic flood of pleasure that preceded the burst of arousal exploding on his tongue.

Then, to his great surprise, his name came next. It was just one shout, one ecstatic declaration of the lover's name who happened to negotiate her undoing, but it was *his* name and damn if he didn't love how it reverberated through the arcade's high ceiling, slamming around the building's cluttered walls until the refrain hit his ears anew.

Neela's legs gave a final shudder, and he gently lowered them to the floor but not before bestowing several kisses in secret places along the soft flesh of her inner thighs.

Once he'd righted her dress, the sight before him made him want to hike it up all over again. She was just as he thought she should be. High color in her cheeks. Genuine smile lines bracketing her mouth. A hungry fire in her eyes.

All of which *he* had put there.

"Are you happy now?" he asked, clearing the gravel from his throat but having little interest in removing his hands from her hips. "Or do I have more work to do?"

Neela laughed, the sound carefree and jubilant. "Oh, I'm happy." Then she eyed his tented slacks and made to reach for him. "But I'd be a lot happier if—"

An explosion shook the meager frame of the photo booth before thick gray smoke funneled into the arcade.

CHAPTER 20

Too many things happened at once for Neela's mind to make sense of. Whatever heat that had still been swirling around her skin was quickly shown the door by a cloud of acrid black fumes.

There was no time to interpret anything about her situation other than to make sure her lungs were still pumping in the good stuff, which was quickly dwindling in supply.

Before she could even sit up, a heavy cloth was draped over her and Rhode's arms were beneath her knees and upper back, lifting her lax limbs from the precarious position they'd yet to rise from. Her world became impossibly darker and ten times more confusing as her body fought for air.

"Where . . . What . . . I can't—"

Labored breaths and deep grunts were the only answers to the questions she struggled to force out. The smoke was thick but not so engulfing that it had a perpetual source. Though Neela couldn't see much beyond the small fragments of light peeking through the bottom of whatever Rhode had draped her in—the curtain from the photo booth, she realized—she knew enough of the arcade's layout to know they were going in the opposite direction of the main entrance.

Seconds later, Rhode shifted her weight and barreled through a separate door. When asphalt finally kissed her knees, she whipped the curtain off her head and sank back against the side of the building. A lone smoking canister was rolling around on the ground outside of where they'd originally entered, sputtering its last clouds of black-to-gray-to-finally-fading-to-white smoke like a windup toy on its concluding rotation.

"A smoke bomb. Not fire," she coughed out. Her mental gears clicked into place before she even had time to explain. She'd watched enough myth testing to know exactly how long a smoke bomb lasted and why it was used.

It was the decoy before detainment and lasted two minutes max.

Rhode was already on his feet, blue flames bursting brighter and higher along every inch of him. Startlingly white metal swirled behind eyes she almost failed to recognize. His power was stronger, hotter, and infinitely more menacing than what she'd seen of it before.

The flames licked around his body like silent sentinels shifting into attack formation. Except no flames were firing back at them, which meant—

"It's not magic," she cried. "It's just a smoke grenade. Nothing's burning!"

"Not yet."

The growled warning was all she heard before a line of angel fire punched out from his taut arms and slingshotted off his fists toward two bodies draped in black tactical gear who had leaped out of a stowed ride vehicle.

She hadn't even noticed them. Shit, where had they come from?

Then the blood in her veins froze as she took in their appearances. Black skull caps protected pale bald heads. Facial tattoos that, from that distance, could easily be mistaken for eye black. But the gold irises flashing high and hard in her direction? Those gazes were as familiar as her own.

Charmers.

What *wasn't* familiar, though, was what the men carried. Mortal artillery weapons. Not magical ones.

Charcoal-gray clouds drifted overhead, smudging the darkening sky and casting final swathes of shadows over the concrete walkways and alabaster signage.

The sun had just about gone down enough for the demons to risk an appearance in the last wisps of daylight. Neela mentally tried to tabulate just how much time she and Rhode had lost by indulging in fanciful fun and racing hearts in the arcade. Too much. The demons had found them.

Found *her*, judging by their choice of weapons.

"Rhode!"

Her cries were lost to screams as one charmer took Rhode's flames right in his shoulder, while the second one threw himself behind a metal garbage can, leveraged a gun she'd never seen before over the lid, and fired.

Neela was barely to her feet when Rhode shifted his stance and reared back so his chin was facing the sky. In the most amazing deadly dance, the flames coating his massive chest rose even higher and snatched the fired red and white circular pellet out of the air, incinerating it instantly like the world's most efficient bug zapper.

The resulting cloud singed her nose for a brief moment but didn't affect Rhode in the slightest as his fire protected him from the residue.

When the tickling in her nose finally subsided, she realized why Rhode wasn't affected by whatever they'd fired at him. The bullet didn't contain dark magic. It was a nonlethal projectile filled with pepper spray and meant entirely for her.

Shit, she needed a weapon. Something. *Anything.* They were

in literal demon territory, throwing a dance party on Cyro's roof, and it was only a matter of time before backup was called in the form of corrosion bombs, acid attacks, and chemical warfare specifically designed to destroy the angels in their metallic forms.

Rhode had blades, but they were back in the arcade with their coats. Should she risk running back in? The charmers obviously weren't prepared for him, only her.

"Hide," Rhode barked. "I have them."

"The hell you do! They're not after you. They're after me!"

"They're not after anything except their own ends. Now, run!"

"They can't kill me, remember?"

But his battle cry ate up her words in a trail of fire as his wings spread wide and he bolted for the charmer still firing pepper bullets. Neela risked a glance at the other demon and immediately went queasy when nothing remained of him except a pile of steaming ash.

Then a low ominous hum drowned out the jovial music pumping out through the arcade, creating the singular soundtrack of her nightmares.

A portal.

Neela threw herself behind a bench and watched in horror as three more charmers poured out of the blazing circle of magic. Their gaits were slow, smooth, prowling, as if they were late to a party that had been on their calendars for weeks. Two had gold bands hugging their necks, while the third one, the largest, had three.

Two elite charmers. One apex.

"Shit," she whispered through gritted teeth. Rhode had sensed the same party guests joining them, apparently. When he turned from the other charmer, who was still screaming with his lips stretched wide and eyelids peeled back as blue angel fire licked up half his body, no more fire adorned the angel's frame.

But there were wings—wings and metal. Rhodium armor coated every inch of his body.

The apex was the first to charge forward, followed by the two elite.

No!

Decision made, Neela waited for the distracting sounds of their boots hitting the pavement before she scurried through the back door into the arcade. Thankfully, most of the smoke had cleared out, and after a few stumbling strides, she located the air hockey table where their coats hung limply over the edge. She tossed her white puffer aside and rooted around Rhode's wool trench for any bladed and bulleted thing, all of which were infused with his angel fire. When she came away with a haul of things she'd never heard of but never wanted to know intimately, she filled her arms and ran back to the door.

The sight that awaited her was one she'd never forget.

Rhode's chest, still gleaming the silvery-white of his metal, was a horrific cross-hatching of brutal slashes. His fine silk shirt had been shredded from his body. Blood oozed from intersecting angles as his muscles strained with each press and release of strength. As before in the mechanic's parking lot, his wings whipped violently in circling arcs, slashing at the two elite charmers who continued to get their blades into Rhode's sides, despite taking hits of their own.

The apex, for all his eager arrogance, stood by and watched, arms folded across his barrel chest, golden eyes tracking all three players.

It was almost as if he was . . . No, that couldn't be right. Was he . . . *bored?* Like the dude was waiting for the table before him to finish their meal so he could enjoy the seats they'd kept warm?

Or so he could pick off the parts that only the butcher knew were the best cuts of meat.

"Fuck. That." Neela dropped the weapons at her feet, picked

the closest one, a small pistol of some kind, and started firing off shots.

Not at the charmers Rhode was actively battling—she wasn't that skilled or stupid—but at the apex. For all the bastard's magic, he was just as susceptible to angel fire as the rest of them. Fatally so.

The flaming bullet sank into his thigh. The apex grunted with the impact, then started to growl and drew the attention of the other two.

Her distraction worked. Good thing, too, because that was about all the excitement she had in her.

Neela crouched beneath the failing strength of her adrenaline, and her palms hit the blacktop. "Rhode! Now!"

Flaming opal eyes whipped to hers, and a shadow of recognition passed between the two of them. His metal was brittle, but his waning fire wasn't.

Rhode's chest heaved with a great roar. Blood trickled down the sides of his armored face where new slashes had penetrated his metal. Then a surging blast of blue flames skated over the tips of his wings, and he whirled. With a swift spin, his wings sliced through the necks of each elite, leaving his angel fire to incinerate the rest of the trembling bodies as they fell to the ground in spasming heaps.

Hot tears pricked her eyes as they connected with Rhode's. Through the smoke stiffening her cheeks and the ash permeating the cooler air, she smiled stupidly wide. So wide it hurt.

Rhode didn't reciprocate, but neither did he look away. His flames had sputtered out, and his rhodium armor faded to flesh, but God, he was a mess, streaked with blood and sweat and charred stuff she didn't want to think about too closely. Great heavy breaths filled his full chest and inflated his lower abdominals, forcing the muscles into sharper angles to contrast the deep grooves at his hips and weeping gashes at his sides.

But he was still breathing and staring at her as if, at any

moment, she would peter out like the very flames that had just saved them. Like, if he didn't get to her, there would be no hope of resuscitation.

A final slice of sunlight caught Neela in the eye before taking the rest of the rays with it as the star sank below the horizon. She slowly sat back on her heels, shifting a bit when her knee hit something sharp, and held her arms out to Rhode in invitation. "We did it."

Just as the corner of his lips started to lift in a relieved smile, they fell back into their familiar grim line. Then a frown. Then opened with a roar. Opal flames seemed to light his eyes, but that couldn't be. He'd just spent all his angel fire. Why would—

A creeping pain crawled up her knee, scraping a trail of gnawing agony along the only part of her leg uncovered by her dress or boots.

"Neela!" Rhode ate up the ground separating them. When he reached her, he gripped her shoulders and settled her onto his lap while he grabbed the pistol she'd dropped and aimed it in the direction of the apex. One shot went off, then another. A grunt, followed by the familiar crackle of combusting flames.

But that couldn't be. She'd already shot the guy with an angel fire bullet. He should be dead, if not close to it.

"Hold still, Neela. Hold still— Fuck!"

"Wh-what? What's happening?" The pain answered her question, though, causing her leg to shake and spasm.

"The apex," Rhode growled out.

Then those gears from earlier, the ones that she thought had already clicked so solidly into place, stalled out and shut down her whole mind machine. Apex didn't use mortal weapons, only ones of dark magic. Wasn't he dead, though?

I thought . . . I thought . . .

The demon had been alive enough to strike her with his magic.

And for the first time in her life, it had wounded her.

CHAPTER 21

Neela dropped into Rhode's arms like a stone, her eyelids fluttering with a spasm that mimicked his erratic heartbeat. Fire roared through his veins as he briefly looked behind him to confirm that, yes, the portal had disappeared and the three charmers were nothing but steaming ashes painting the asphalt.

The charmer in his arms, however . . .

"Neela—" he said thinly, trying to keep the worry and confusion out of his voice.

"Mmm . . . Hurts . . ." She moaned behind lips that had already begun to pale along the creases.

"There could be more coming. I have to move you. It-It might be uncomfortable."

Neela closed her eyes and nodded sharply. "Do it."

Ignoring the gouges along his ribs and the sharp cry she let out when he cradled her to his chest, he stretched his battered wings and got airborne. Not wanting to soar too high lest their presence call undue attention to themselves, he skirted the arcs of the nearby roller coasters, riding their descents until he saw the only place even remotely defensible: behind a dumpster at the back of a neighboring lumber yard. Plenty of construction vehicles and metal to work with and even more wood to ignite should he need it.

That was, if his fire hadn't been entirely spent already.

Rhode touched down in the fading shadow cast by the dumpster and settled Neela across his lap.

"I've never—" She swallowed around a cough. "I don't . . ."

"Quiet." The word came out harsher than he meant it, and he cursed himself before gentling his words. "Easy. Let me see."

" . . . you're . . . angry . . . not my . . . fault . . ."

"Shhh, save your strength."

Rhode settled her gently onto the pavement and pulled the hem of her sweaterdress up her thigh, then hissed. On her right knee, just above where the boot's leather kissed her calf, her pale skin had begun to crackle and peel. Dark char outlined her kneecap, the edges of which began curling outward from the corroded pockmarks in the center, attacking any clean flesh it could find.

The apex's magic hadn't been designed for *her* but for the sentinels. It was a dark perversion crafted over years to fight back against the angels in their metallic forms. Cyro had long ago tasked his demons with cultivating magic that could rust, corrode, eat away, or molecularly destroy the sentinels' metals.

And it seemed that the bastard had perfected the formula, improving it so it worked on their flesh forms as well.

Rhode sat there and watched in horror as the sickly spell crept higher over her knee, until the very swell of the lower thigh he'd had his hand on moments ago began to pucker and shrivel. The more intently he watched the taint, the faster it seemed to crawl. It was already a challenge to keep her hands from clawing at it. If she did manage to touch it . . .

He, more than anyone, knew a fucking contagion when he saw one.

Neela's moans turned to whimpers, then panting hisses as

his soul bond tried to fight off a magical enemy she couldn't understand, knew nothing of, and had no hope of defeating.

But he did. He knew all of those things. And it terrified him.

Rhode cleared his throat. "Neela."

Agony raged in her eyes but did little to fight off the poison quickly consuming her.

He tried again. "Neela, I have to—"

Then the screams erupted out of her, deafening ear-shattering wails that were the telltale mark of any dying animal. And the siren's song to any predator within a ten-mile radius.

Shit.

Rhode held her down in the manner of all battlefield wounded, knowing full well comfort was not part of the operation and wishing with his entire being that he could offer it to her.

On instinct, he held her limbs still, straining to contain her writhing body so she wouldn't . . . Wouldn't what? Hurt herself further? So he might prevent her from inadvertently biting her tongue lest she choke on the blood and leave the dark magic with less active prey to devour? Fuck!

His mind whirled, cursing every ounce of angel fire he no longer had because he'd used it in service of his own worthless protection earlier in hand-to-hand combat. But hadn't she healed him once before? Something about their supposed bond, something—

While Rhode focused on the charred skin flaking off her inner thigh, a notion he'd just glossed over clung to his paranoid list of solutions. Prevent her from biting . . .

Biting.

Tongue. Mouth.

A kiss.

He didn't know what propelled him to consider the idea fully, but out of options, time, and security, he lowered his mouth to the ruined skin of her thigh just above her kneecap and sealed his lips to her. Instinct had him sweeping his tongue over the shriveled skin. Once, twice, then a third time, kissing the site with a sad, yet urgent reverence.

Then she stilled. The screaming stopped. The femoral artery beneath his tongue slowed its frightful pace by a degree, then another. A sudden flush of warmth infused his chest and cheeks but not the kind his angel fire recognized.

This was a new power. One he'd never asked for and had violently tried to reject but was commanding with a general's call.

Between one kiss and the next, the skin beneath Rhode's lips warmed and smoothed out, until his mouth met a healed strip of new pink skin. He dragged his tongue higher, kissing the next patch and the next. Soon, the anticorrosive properties of the metal he governed had taken shape, enrobing Neela's skin in a protective layer that absorbed every ounce of vile tarnishing magic that had been heaved at her.

Magic, he realized, that very much *did* affect her when she was in the mortal world during the day.

A fact she'd swore to him was not possible.

Rhode sat up a bit, pulled the tattered remains of her dress back down, and cupped the side of her neck. She was breathing normally again, those full lips of hers flushing a deeper shade of berry as color returned to her cheeks. Her eyes tracked him as he methodically examined every part of her, checking for any corrosive magic he might have missed.

But his gaze returned to those lips and then to the questions floating behind her shaken eyes.

"You kissed me," she said, no doubt addressing the first of many unusual occurrences of the evening.

"I did." He nodded solemnly, struggling to keep his warring thoughts in check. When he couldn't do it any longer, he leaned forward and claimed her mouth. It was a hard brush of lips and a quick, solid reassurance that health had returned to both of them.

Trust, however . . .

He broke the kiss. "And you lied." Rhode pulled away, setting her as far apart from him as he could without hurting her, and stood. "I shouldn't be surprised that treachery tastes so sweet. I've never had much of a sweet tooth, however."

At that, Neela vaulted upright. "What are you talking about?"

Rhode found his phone in his back pocket, hit a button, and brought it to his ear. While he waited for the call to connect, he glared at her. "I won't abandon you again, but nor will I let you live without explaining why."

When the call was answered, he stepped away to make the arrangements that needed to be made. When he returned, Neela was on her feet, with her hands stretched out before her, palms open and pleading, but he turned away before he could see more.

"Why? Why what? I don't understand, Rhode."

"Why you told us you couldn't be wounded or killed when I just witnessed how you very much fucking can be. Why those charmers expected you to be here but came prepared to dispatch both of us." He stalked toward her, a desperate fury overcoming him as he gripped her throat and angled her mouth to his but held her a breath away. "Why you begged for my touch, for supposed *happiness*, just long enough to ensure that an adequate amount of the day had fled so your fellow demons could attack me."

It was the silence that finally did him in, both from her stammering lips and his vengeful soul caving in after being denied the answers it was starving for. Hurt flashed hot and heavy across her features, but it was no match for the fury that punched through his ragged chest when it replayed the betrayal perpetuated by his own soul bond.

Rhode dropped his hand and softly pushed her away from

him. Despite nearly losing her leg, she didn't stumble. She merely stood there with a gaunt expression that was almost as hollow as he felt.

"Titan and Iron will be here soon. They'll escort you."

"Escort me where?" she asked, her voice quivering.

He gave her his back and looked to the sky, measuring the distance the dark clouds traveled and how long it would take before he would be able to leap into them.

"Your cell."

CHAPTER 22

Drea and Molly quick-stepped in front of Neela but were barely able to make any headway due to Iron's and Titan's broad backs walling them into a pocket as they led the way toward wherever the hell they were going to stash her. Behind Neela, Brass's soft but insistent footsteps rounded out the shittastic symphony of her circumstances.

Somehow, due to a feat of flexibility beyond Neela's comprehension, Drea's six-foot-plus frame ducked low and had managed to wedge itself in between the two sentinels before turning around in front of them to finally get their attention. "This is bullshit," she asserted, throwing her hands wide as she shuffled backward to keep pace.

Titan gingerly moved her out of the way and kept walking. "This is protocol."

"It's *bullshit* protocol," Molly fired back, though Brass was able to grab her hand and hold her before she tried to get around Iron. Now, *that* was a back Neela didn't want to go up against, no matter how much she'd love to heel-kick the bastard between the shoulder blades for going along with this.

Ten feet ahead of their adventuring party was Rhode. Even

from this distance, Neela could tell that the annoying scalp wrinkle at the back of his head hadn't lost its tension in the slightest, nor had the hard set of his shoulders as he stormed a trail in front of them. She didn't know what was more ominous: Rhode's stark avoidance of her or the dark granite tunnel she was being led down. Or was it *up*? At one point, the ground beneath her had seemed like there was a slight elevation to it, which her right knee did *not* appreciate whatsoever, but then, after a few turns, things had seemed to level out. The walls became smoother, and beneath the evenly spaced lanterns, the crags and shards she'd expected to see had faded away until there was no longer a discernible way to tell which hallway they'd come down.

It was so very different from the underground life she'd lived before popping up to the surface. Cyro's homestead had always been one of bare necessities and temporary measures because of the desire, or perhaps the need, to move so often. There were no stationary electric lanterns to light her way back to her room, only floating orbs of green magic that her eyes barely tolerated. Since humanity's existence, they'd mostly set up shop in vacated mortal dwellings or abandoned sites. Whatever was left behind was what the charmers had to work with, and that meant only the most minimal of structures ever saw any sort of renovations.

Absolutely nothing was carved smooth.

Smooth meant care. Smooth meant an artistic touch and a desire for comfort and beauty.

All things that were the exact opposite of what she'd known. That was, except for in her suite of rooms and her greenhouse, where, with her sun lamps and electric lights and multimonitor gaming setup, she could manifest her desires without fear of her sire's interference because his magic couldn't harm her there any more than it could harm her anywhere.

Or so she'd thought.

But as Rhode stopped in front of a metallic door up ahead and her steps slowed to mimic the halting caravan, her mind reeled over every truth she thought she'd known and came up more shaken than sure.

"You are *not* putting her in there," Molly barked. "No fucking way."

"Rhode," Drea pleaded, placing her hand on his forearm as he unlocked the door. "I'm sure there's a reasonable explanation for all this. There has to be. Neela did *not* lie to you. She's your soul bond! That's like saying the sun has secretly been plotting to poison all life on Earth while simultaneously *growing* all life on Earth. It doesn't make any sense!"

"Don't talk to me about sunlight," he snarled under his breath.

The door creaked open and swayed on its hinges while everyone stood in the hall waiting. It was a strange halt to the proceedings, one that reminded Neela of opening a bottle of red wine, only to have to wait on that first sip because the contents needed to breathe. Whatever the hell that meant.

Neela peeked around Iron's shoulder into the room, and her jaw dropped. If this was what Rhode considered a cell, then their barrier to understanding each other was even wider than the chasm of their silence.

The room was a carved cavern of modest comfort and unstated luxury. If she thought the hallway's granite walls were smooth before, this room's foundation put that all to shame, boasting a fine polished shine she'd only seen on the finest opal or pearl gemstones. No adornments covered the walls, and if she'd lived in such a rich mineral palace, she wasn't sure she could bear to cover them either. There was beauty in simplicity, and the room's structure had surpassed beauty some time ago, screeching into solid opulent territory.

And that was only the tip of the iceberg in terms of surprises. Simple yet functional furniture stood like monoliths in the silent space. A solid dark oak dresser sat along one wall, catty-corner not to one but three matching armoires so large they could easily have held an entire family's worth of seasonal clothes, bulky winter wear, and still had room for formal attire.

A large bed with simple gray cotton sheets fitted to military precision anchored the stone room, and at the foot of the bed was a massive chest long enough to house pool cues or, if the angels managed to figure out how to get one down there, perhaps a compact vehicle.

There were no mirrors, not even in the small bathroom connected to the space, from what she could see of it at any rate. The suite was entirely barren of adornment but was more than adequate in size and amenities. It was quietly comfortable, if incredibly lonely.

Hardly what she'd consider a cell, though how often did the angels need to take prisoners? The chilly thought sobered her. Was that what she was? A prisoner?

"In." Rhode's harsh order pulled goose bumps from her skin, and her feet were already marching before she could question what she was walking into or why.

Her heels barely click-clacked over the threshold, amid Drea and Molly's very vocal protestations, when movement down the hall to her left caught her eye.

There in the meager lantern light stood Chrome. His arms were folded across his massive chest as he leaned a shoulder against the wall, boots crossed at the ankle, and face so fixed in its consternation she couldn't imagine there was any hope of warming it toward even a placid grin of indifference.

And she was right. Rhode spared the other angel a glance as the rest of their party fell silent.

"Chrome . . ." Drea whispered, obviously somewhat relieved to see him, but her eyes shared the same wariness that crossed the other angels' expressions.

Chrome didn't nod, didn't acknowledge her in any way, didn't take his focus from anyone other than Rhode.

The air in the tunnel thickened so much, Neela tried to swallow back the tension just so she could breathe freely again. This wasn't right. Whatever had happened between these two, whatever rift her presence had caused, it was tantamount to two planets converging toward a cataclysmic explosion. If the course wasn't corrected soon, the ripple effect would have untold devastating consequences.

She should say something. Plead, beg, scream, just *something*. This was her fault, and it wasn't right that this family should suffer so harshly as a result of saving her—of *knowing* her.

Neela retreated from the room slightly and directed what little voice she could find toward Chrome. "If there's anything I did, know that—"

"*In.*" Rhode pressed a palm between her shoulder blades, the first touch he'd given her since he'd revived her, and guided her forward with surprising force. Not gentle but not unyielding either. She stumbled but quickly caught herself and straightened.

Drea glared at him. "Don't be a dick, Rhode." Then she gentled her expression and smiled sadly at Neela. "We'll get this sorted out as soon as possible."

"Precautions," Titan elaborated, if one could call that an elaboration.

Neela suspected that what the second-in-command *wanted* to say was, "Precautions against a charmer invasion. Precautions against a demon insider and would-be traitor. Precautions against an infiltrated spy who has access to our soul bonds and the underground home we all share."

"I understand," she offered quietly, even though she understood about as little of what the hell was going on as how she was even still breathing, let alone standing upright to argue over semantics. But making waves was not worth it, not when her supposed soul bond refused to even look at her. The way the fingers he'd touched her with instantly recoiled into his palm was enough of an indication to prove that the few people she'd started the day off with in her corner were quickly jumping ship.

Neela smiled back her understanding to Drea, clasped her hands in front of her, and waited for the door to slam.

There were shoddier places she could be. Hell, she imagined a hard floor, leaking stone walls, rodents, maybe a dilapidated pallet, and a bucket of dubious liquids. A girl could do far worse than a clean mattress and sheets when trying to clear her mind and figure out just how the hell the male who had begun to consume more than just her thoughts suddenly—

Rhode stepped into the room with her and, without touching the solid metallic door, willed it to slam closed.

CHAPTER 23

Neela waited for the fear to hit her, for the uncertainty of her situation to send her screaming into a corner as far away as possible from the man blocking the doorway.

Except that fear never came, nor would she categorize what Rhode was doing as *blocking*. Once the door closed, he just sort of stood there facing it. Sure, tension radiated off his back in gusts strong enough to register on the mortals' hurricane wind scale, but it wasn't like he was making strides to ease their circumstances. If anything, he seemed to think *she* was in the wrong somehow. If that was true—which it emphatically *wasn't*, but she'd yet to get to that—wouldn't he be more . . . smug about it? After all, she'd binged more than her fair share of murder shows in her time, and not a single one came without an arrogant detective or seen-it-all beat cop.

Accusations were one thing. Interrogations were another. And she sure as hell had questions of her own, not the least of which was how he could go from worshipping her with his mouth the way he had earlier to somehow kissing away whatever was killing her. And then, in the very next breath, using that same mouth to call her a liar.

But they were no closer to getting the information they'd come for; he'd dumped her there in the most comfort-meets-value-stay prison cell she'd ever seen and didn't even have the good sense to at least open up the conversation.

Well, if he thought her weak or complacent, he had another thing coming.

There were only so many personal attempted murders a woman could deal with in her life before she eventually started snapping back.

"Where are we?" Neela asked, no longer giving a rip how much venom found its way into her voice.

Ooh, and Rhode had figured that out, too, judging by the way his back muscles twitched when her question found its mark.

Uh-huh. That's right. Mama ain't playing anymore.

But the voice that answered her was filled with so much gravel, she almost missed the words entirely. "My room."

Neela took in the bare granite surrounding them again. "You-you live here? I thought you said you were taking me to a cell."

His chin touched his shoulder, but he never lifted his eyes to her. "That is what I did."

She not only saw it but felt it. The overwhelming sadness of the circumstances that had brought them both to where they were. Truths that were clouded in more questions than either of them had answers to. Pasts that were far too cold to ever truly have a chance at thawing out on their own.

The loneliness. The isolation. Time stolen when you never even realized it was a limited commodity to begin with.

Neela hugged herself at the enormity of the realization. "It makes sense why you would think this place is a cell."

He scoffed and gave her the full breadth of his body. "What would you possibly know of my thoughts?"

"I know you think I'm a liar." One of his brows lifted, but she ignored the unspoken accusation. "I know you think I have ulterior motives or that I'm in cahoots with the other charmers." Then she dropped her arms and stared at him with more gumption than she'd ever needed to muster. "And since you're so content to draw conclusions without so much as asking me for mine, I'll grab the floor for myself and say my piece." She waved a hand in his direction. "Listen or not, I don't care, but I will *not* be intimidated by you." Neela swallowed past a wave of emotion brought on by memories she hadn't shared with another living soul. So it was fitting, perhaps, that the very soul in question she was about to unload on was also somehow inextricably linked to hers.

Freaking lovely.

As far as deep breaths went, Neela's next one was pitifully shallow, but there was only so much available real estate in her chest at the moment. So what choice did she have but to finally offload some burdens?

"I won't be intimidated by you," she repeated, "because, for more years than I can count, I cared for you." The truth lifted free from her throat and widened the opening of her heart to let long-buried memories come pouring out like water from a firehouse. "I didn't know I could die because all my earliest memories following my inception were filled with so much confusion and agony that, even though I was told death wasn't a possibility for me, I *so* wished it was."

Rhode didn't say anything, just held his stance by the door like some stone gargoyle poised for danger but unable to move. At least she had his attention, though. The way his eyes tracked her as she gained momentum pacing around the room was enough encouragement to continue.

"I won't insult you by asking whether you have any idea of

what it's like to wish for such a thing. I can imagine you do, but that won't stop me from enlightening you on my experience regardless."

His jaw twitched. She'd struck a nerve. Good.

"When Cyro called for me after my inception and we discovered that I couldn't portal like the others, I had no inkling of what that would mean for me. I only knew him as Cyro, my sire, our leader. Among the charmers, he wasn't exactly paternal, but he wasn't *not*, if that makes sense. When you're responsible for another life, no matter how that life came about, there's still an element of care inherent in the relationship. Sometimes that care comes naturally and is nurtured. Other times, that care is acknowledged and then willfully abandoned, but that's the thing, isn't it? For a bond to be abandoned at all, it must first exist." Those words hung there for a moment, heavy and expectant in the confines of the cavernous room.

"The look on Cyro's face was so different after he realized the flaw in my design. I had always come to know his smooth mask of aloofness as his default setting. He never smiled, nor did he scream and rage. He just always . . . was. Controlled, intentional, even-keeled. Until me."

Neela paced along the wall farthest from where Rhode stood and imagined, as she sometimes did back home, that there was a large picture window illuminating her efforts. "I had no inkling of what his next step was going to be. No warning signs, no room set up. Nothing. I remember standing before him, unsure whether he was pleased with my performance or not. There had never been any discussion of what the desired outcome should be by me trying to portal. No hypothesis to test. He simply told me to do a task, and I tried to obey."

Her throat began to tighten, but she pushed through, quickening her steps in response. "His hand came up first, and I remember being mesmerized by how long his fingers were. I didn't have fingers like that and always wondered how he crafted my smaller hands, or my hair, for that matter. But I stopped thinking that the moment he snapped those long fingers and a hail of green magic leaped for me. My hair, my most identifiable feature aside from my sex, was the first thing to be engulfed in the flames, followed by my more delicate skin —earlobes, eyelids, and such. I don't know how long I stood there screaming before I finally collapsed and lost consciousness. But when I woke with freshly healed skin and hair still brushing my shoulders, that was when we all knew I was different." Neela stopped and glared at him. "The wrong kind of different. And it seems I'm still paying the price for that, even from my soul bond."

Rhode closed his eyes and held the blink for two full inhales before his umber gaze found hers again. The balled fists were new, though, as was the skim-coating of shame that seemed to tighten his features.

"It went on like that. For days and weeks and years and *eternities*, until, through the power of sheer perseverance and having no fucking choice, Cyro just gave up on trying to kill me. For the first time ever, the demon ruler had to acknowledge true defeat." Then her voice softened, and she looked around the room, wishing like hell there was something to hold while feeling so exposed—a curtain, a chair, anything. Because with her next breath, she scooped out what remained of those heartbreaking days. "And as a result of his defeat, I found you."

Rhode's eyes flashed. "What?"

"I asked you once whether you knew what it was like to care so deeply for something where you were the sole creature in existence truly capable of helping the other."

"I . . . Yes, you did. I remember." His voice had lost some of the rasp but none of the enigma.

Neela nodded back her tears. "Well, you want to know what I remember? I remember feeling so alienated, so lost in a universe whose language I didn't speak and among others who refused to teach it or really talk to me unless they had to, that the only way for me to exist was to find purpose elsewhere. I found that purpose in caring for you, Rhode. I remember you lying on that stone slab as I scraped off and cleansed from you whatever I could of the day's ordeal. I didn't know who you were, but given my experiences with my sire and the research notes I'd find each night near your cell, it didn't matter. I could read between the lines and guess what was happening, what they were doing to you." Her breath hitched. "What they were trying to make you become."

"Don't," he growled, stepping toward her.

"No, *you* don't. It's my time to talk, my time to stomp my feet and tell you the things you don't want to hear. Because I *remember you*! I didn't lie to you *because* I remember! I remember everything of what you used to be, limp and lifeless most of the time, desperate and disoriented the rest. I never touched you then because of what I knew they'd done to you, or how, in your lucid moments when I was in your cell, you would reach for me but never spoke or saw me. Imagine, the one being whose life depended on *me* for survival, never being able to truly know me or even so much as open his eyes to see that I was right in his cell with him the whole time, that he wasn't alone the way I had been for so long."

There was no hope of putting the lava back into the volcano. Neela's whole soul erupted with pent-up ferocity, and she was powerless to do anything other than rail at him.

"So imagine how fucking elated and devastated I was when you were rescued because I knew you were finally free," she screamed, "but you were also finally free of *me*!"

A thundering energy rattled through the stone around them as Rhode lunged for her with furious sparks lighting his eyes. "You want me to be free of you?" he roared, gripping her shoulders.

A pang of hurt struck her at the implication of his words.

"That's what you truly want, isn't it?" Neela whispered. She didn't know how to answer him but was pissed as hell that her earlier uncertainty hadn't left town once her desperation had decided to unveil its narrative. "Deep down, *you* want to be free of *me*."

Then his hand gripped the back of her neck, and the heat of his skin branded her. "I fear I will never be free of you."

Rhode's fiery lips crashed against hers, finally claiming what her heart could never truly deny him.

CHAPTER 24

No amount of water could have extinguished the inferno boiling Rhode's blood as Neela spilled every torturous detail of her existence. Rage would have been an easier thing to rein in. Rage had boundaries, clearly delineated borders that one knew what they were getting into once they'd crossed them. A short burst of fury, a roaring tidal wave of temper, and then it was expended as soon as it came on. Calm shores returned. Trees stood upright again. Life went on.

But not for him. Never for him.

He'd have ashes before he'd have her doubt or her fear.

Every word she said was another nail ripped up from a coffin he'd fabricated with sheer force of will. How she managed to unearth it, let alone find a way to bury him anew with her brazen truths, was a miracle of the mages.

No, he realized. *A miracle herself.*

One he feared he could no sooner extract from his soul than the Eternal Flame's spark within him.

Abandonment had been his bedfellow for as long as he could remember, but in actuality, it had been nothing more than an excuse. An excuse to find Neela, only to risk losing her again to a force neither of them was capable of understanding.

What he did understand with absolute fucking certainty was that he needed to have his mouth on her.

The kiss was a thunderclap, an auditory outrage harmonizing with the angel fire singing in his veins whenever his hands were on this woman. He leaned in farther, anchoring his arm at the small of her back and dipping her so far backward that there was no possible way he couldn't taste all of her. He greedily stole every hyssop-scented sigh and tickling caress that her flaxen tendrils would grace him with. When his lips no longer brought enough of her to him, his tongue took over. Neela's breath hitched at the sly intrusion, then advanced in another way, with her searching fingers pressing into the sides of his hips.

"Mages, how are you this divine? You're . . . you're . . ."

Rhode couldn't think, couldn't call forth enough words to string anything together that wasn't rooted in urgent, primal needs. The need to claim, to capture, to caress, to protect from whatever dared threaten to take her away from him.

"Fuck!" he growled into her mouth before grabbing her ass and spinning her around the room. The edge of the mattress soon bumped his calves and buoyed him with the certainty that there could be no other conclusion for what the fates had planned for them.

But only if she consented to tumble over that precipice with him. And if she didn't, could he blame her?

The thought was a sobering shock of ice to the fire that threatened to erupt out of him. What if it was too late? What if her presence in his life was some other trick crafted by Cyro to further control and manipulate him? What if the luscious lady who filled his hands and had slowly begun to root out and fill other hollow parts of him could only ever be a carnal fling? A desire exorcized?

The sobering chill snaked down his spine but fell short of invading the rest of his nervous system when Neela bucked her hips forward and knocked them both onto the mattress. When she settled above him, her soft body molding to his and her breasts pressing against the strength of his chest, her might answered what his could not.

Neela lifted off him slightly, then sat up entirely while her thighs cradled his hips. A single palm braced insistently against his sternum, impressing upon him more words than he'd ever thought to say. "I'm so done with being afraid, Rhode. And despite what you may think, the one person I'm *not* afraid of is also the same person who hasn't left my thoughts for a second, not even on the day I thought I lost you." Neela slowly shook her head and smiled sweetly. "Whatever you want this to be, I'm game, because somehow you and I are both still alive to experience it together." Then she blinked a few times, and something regretful and solemn passed over her expression. "It doesn't have to be more than that."

Rhode's fingers curled along her torso, claiming the negative spaces between her ribs for the handholds he needed, and he had to work *really* fucking hard not to leave bruises.

Did she just say . . . ? Did she not want . . . ?

He never let himself think of the sheer volume of years lost. If he did, he wasn't sure he'd ever truly be free. Even if his body was whole and hale, finally fit enough to command the new power that he was just coming to appreciate as a gift instead of the curse it had been for so long, there was something far different about being a prisoner of the mind.

If he knew the exact number of lifetimes he'd never see again, well, madness would be a kindness.

But to realize that he hadn't been entirely abandoned? That Neela had been in his corner, in his fucking *cell*, all that time, quietly repairing and cleaning away whatever filth the charmers had forced to leak out of him?

He hadn't been alone. In his darkest moments, she'd been there, and he wasn't equipped to deal with the kind of humbling awe that truth draped over him.

But the truth of her draped over his body? Of that connection not needing to be something more?

She was wrong, and he would take no small delight in correcting her.

Rhode reared up and cradled her face inches from his. "The fuck it does."

He captured her mouth in a kiss so hard, so raw, that it spoke every word of emotion he'd never been able to reach when it came to her. He was a seraphim commander, a master of espionage and coercion, and if he couldn't figure out how to impress upon her just how vitally his soul craved hers . . . then he didn't deserve the relief that had somehow only ever found him through her hands.

"Do you know how long," he murmured into her mouth, "I've been waiting to tear this dress from you?"

Neela smiled against his lips. "You know, under normal circumstances, I would never advocate for this, but…"

"But?"

"Do it."

The finely spun threads gave no resistance as he grabbed the front of her collar and pulled. Her breath hitched but was quickly followed by a sigh that Rhode would happily die listening to.

But he had no plans of dying quite yet.

His knuckles brushed against black lace that expertly curved around breasts his mouth watered to taste. Another package. Another present. Another secret promise.

When she arched her back, he took her offering with relish. The lace's design was like an intricate puzzle box that hid the very treasure he couldn't go another moment without kissing. Neela's hands slipped along his scalp as she moved his mouth where she wanted him. When his lips bumped against the little mound of her nipple through the fabric, he nurtured his treasure with undue attention.

"Shit, Rhode. Oh my God."

Neela's head fell back as he plumped her breast, coaxing more of her into his mouth, while he plied the other with his fingers.

There was more of her than he could contain with his mouth or hands alone, and his cock fucking knew it. Each mounding caress of her breasts drew an answering throb that beat insistently against his thigh.

"Mages, you're perfect. You're everything. I need to see more. I need to see all of you, little demon. Please."

"Always."

Always.

The word smoothed over raw wounds with its promise of the future. He sighed an unknown relief against her sternum before placing a kiss there.

The rest of their clothes fell away on that one promise, until he lay bare before her, and she resumed her perch above him, straddling him like Lady Godiva atop her gelding. Her luscious hair fell to the tips of her full breasts, with select tendrils curling around her nipples like golden ribbon adorning a precious package. She smiled at him as she steadied herself below his abdominals, eyes alight with mischief and something that seemed to form a tether inside his chest.

Had he really thrown her into the same lot as the other charmers? In what world could he possibly mistake the golden beauty situated above him as anything other than fate's excellence?

Rhode reached for her, but instead of lifting her breasts to his mouth again as he longed to do now that they were freed of their bindings, he stopped and instead skated his fingers along the smooth undercurve of each globe.

Damn, he loved her body. Loved how full and heavy her breasts were, how they settled over the top of her rounded abdomen, adding more allure to the curvature of her waist where his hands itched to settle.

There was nothing harsh about her. He could see that now. No evil magic or vile intentions. Only pure, shining perfection. The finest threads could never do her skin justice.

He sat up and pressed a kiss to her stomach, holding it there for several heartbeats. "You are far softer than any garment."

Her lilting chuckle pushed her farther against him, and his abs curled in response. "Not too soft, I hope."

A wicked gleam lit her eyes, and then, mages damn him, she took his cock in hand.

"Fuck, Neela." Rhode's head hit the mattress as she squeezed the base with a devilish insistence that belied the tenderness she gazed down at him with.

Then that hand slowly drew down to the base of him, taking special care to ensure her thumb's knuckle pressed against the bulging vein beneath his shaft. The move expertly elicited the groan from him she was no doubt searching for, along with a pearly drop of arousal that was only the beginning of what he hoped she'd claim from him.

He wanted to give her everything—his secrets, his sorrows, his fucking sanity. All of it was hers if he could continue to lose himself in the embrace of this woman.

But her stroking was relentless and pulled sounds from him that would threaten to tear down the mountain if he didn't get inside her soon.

Rhode lifted his head and looked down the plane of his torso at his cock's glistening tip, at the woman who had, mages almighty, bent forward to place a gentle kiss on the weeping head before she lifted up and angled him toward her slick entrance.

His answering thrust was rough and unexpected but

controlled enough to ensure she felt only pleasure. Her powerful thighs became the anchors beneath his hands as he pistoned his greedy hips into her over and over again, rocking in time to her swaying breasts. Every so often, he curled forward, capturing a taunting nipple in his mouth and tugging just to hear the hiss through her smiling teeth.

Her core was a tight sanctuary that welcomed him home with each plunge, a salvation that, little by little, chipped away at the tight coil of tension that had been permanently placed on his body. Always on alert. Always ready to strike, to kill. A fire never to be released.

Until now.

Her soft moans coaxed him higher, hotter. Fuck, he'd chase those sounds anywhere they'd take him, if only for the privilege to combust beneath her once he'd found them.

"Neela . . . Oh, God . . ."

She answered his benediction with a prayer pose of her own, arching her back and slamming her hands down on his thighs. Her breasts quivered in time with the tightening fist of her body as it dragged his orgasm from him while riding out her own. Rhode shot up and clutched her to his chest, holding on as he cradled the very life he held impossibly dear. Her heart shuddered against his, pulsing in time to the waves of passion that had begun to lick up his spine.

Whatever barriers he'd carefully constructed around Neela had exploded into tiny shards as his angel fire flared to life, burning off the fumes of his ecstasy.

Rhode cried out when the power of his soul finally burst through its cage, instantly dissolving the shards of its previous confinement. His full angel fire, unrestrained with the complete strength of the soul bond, roared into existence, set free like a phoenix—

A phoenix that was about to light the damn sheets on fire.

"Shit!"

He grabbed Neela quickly before any bedding could be singed and settled on the floor with his back to the stone wall, her panting body still clinging to him as she laughed into his neck. That glorious hair, slick with sweat, stuck to his forearms and biceps as his fire finally started to die down, claiming her as his own just as her soul had claimed him.

Gingerly, with more care than he'd ever been taught to wield, he lifted her hair from her neck to kiss her pulse point and froze.

"Rhode?" Neela asked, still trying to get her breathing under control. But when she tried to push away from him to see what he was looking at, he kept her close.

"Stay still."

"Why? What's happening?"

Rhode stared at the small iridescent symbol tattooed behind her earlobe, which, if it weren't for his angel fire illuminating it briefly before the flames extinguished fully, he would have never seen.

Did Neela even know it was there?

And more importantly, if she *did* know it was there, did she understand whose name she bore on her body?

CHAPTER 25

Neela's body was still weathering the aftershocks of her orgasm when she sat up in Rhode's bed and accepted a bottle of water from a mini-fridge she hadn't noticed was tucked next to the nightstand.

It was the one concession he seemed to allow to any sort of comfort, and it was freaking spring water. Not even the mineral stuff.

Her heart flapped around like a fish on land while she twisted the cap off and took small sips. That was all she could manage when Rhode offered her one of his T-shirts and said they needed to talk before he headed to the bathroom, gloriously naked and heading in the wrong damn direction.

Absolutely no one, be they charmer or mortal, wanted to talk after sex. The few dalliances she'd had with other demons had been fast and fleeting but had scratched an itch that would flare up from time to time. And if what the mortals led her to believe was true, in their world, postcoital conversation had a shelf life directly tied to whichever partner had the lowest melatonin stores.

Neela fiddled with the cap and lifted the sheets higher

against her chest, worrying about what would come at her from the other side of that door.

No, she *refused* to believe that what she'd just shared with Rhode was anything other than cell-altering. Or, in her case, soul-altering. So, yes, talking about it would be a good thing.

When his fire erupted around them again, it had felt different somehow. Mutely warmer and just . . . *essential*, almost like the stuff was as much a part of her as the hand she'd had in bringing it to life.

And if what Molly and Drea had told her about the soul bond was true, that fire would last for eternity, protecting Rhode through whatever might come his way. It didn't matter that the metal he commanded and armored himself with was painfully brittle and essentially useless in hand-to-hand combat. If he had his full fire, he could live. He could *thrive*. No more time stamping his strength or requiring that he recharge beneath the mountain each night.

It was the greatest gift she could think to give him, one that would have saved him from untold torment had she known it was possible before.

Neela cut that train of logic off real quick because dredging up the past was hardly ever useful.

But he was finally well, healed physically, and fully powerful. If Cyro came for him again, her sire would be met with a far different being than the one he'd chained to a slab of rock.

Soft tears of thanks pricked her eyelids, but she blinked them away lest they fall and dampen Rhode's sheets. Looking down to ensure no tears had already managed to escape her notice, she observed how the charcoal-gray bedclothes formed around her naked body. The hem of the flat sheet was cool as it draped over her breasts, the undersides of which rested on top of her ribs.

She had to laugh at that. She'd never seen one of her ribs in her life, let alone any of the muscles that showed up to work each day to pad her skeleton. They were there, of course, providing the structure for her frame and foundation.

But they weren't what Rhode admired.

Mages, you're perfect.

She could live an untold number of days and never get enough of replaying Rhode's declaration about her while he feathered gentle kisses along her round stomach.

She wasn't so naïve to think he meant more than what that word *perfect* could actually entail. Perfect was *perfect*. Indisputably ideal, without flaws or faults. Lord knew she didn't come close to that. But by the tender way he caressed her body, whispering little moans of approval and breathing in parts of her no one had ever bothered to linger near, let alone love on, he was speaking about a different kind of perfection.

Her angel had a preference for what her body alone offered him, and no amount of bathroom brooding was going to rob her of the perma-smile he'd put on her face because of it.

The door creaked open, and Rhode walked out wearing a pair of khaki-colored linen yoga pants, which swayed, loose and forgiving, throughout his hips and thighs, but cinched tightly around his ankles. The rest of him was blessedly bare and highlighted every rung of muscle that she'd yet to explore.

Better start making a to-do list . . .

Before her mind wandered too far from the earlier subject at hand, she asked, "Are we going to have The Talk now?" But when the mirth she was hoping to ignite in his eyes never appeared, a sinking feeling slammed into her gut.

He eyed the bed like a serpent in the grass. "May I lie next to you?"

Neela lifted the sheet. "If you have to ask, then I didn't do my job right."

Again, her joke didn't land, but at least he climbed in. Progress, not perfection.

And that was when she noticed the compact mirror in his hand. "Are you going to do my makeup? Because if so, based on your complexion, I'm not sure I trust you to get the contouring right."

Neela waited . . . and waited . . . *Please laugh. Smile. Freaking blink. Something to tell me you're in there and you're okay.*

When his strong chest lifted, she held her breath, anticipating something that would set the happiest moment of her life up in flames.

"I saw your tattoo," he remarked as casually as one would comment on afternoon storm clouds rolling in.

Oookay . . . *Not* what she was expecting to hear. "Tattoo?"

"Behind your right ear."

It was her turn to stare blankly. "Huh?"

Rhode gently turned her head to the left and positioned the mirror so she could see her ear. The soft glow from the night-stand lamp was enough to highlight the strange shimmering symbol that only seemed to appear when he moved the mirror at the right angle toward the light.

"What the hell is that?" Neela swatted at the back of her ear as though a family of mosquitoes had just taken up residence there, but she felt nothing. No raised bumps or indentations. Just smooth, warm skin.

"You've never seen it before?"

"How the hell is that even a question? No, I've never seen it before. I didn't even know I had it."

Rhode closed his eyes, inhaled slowly, and nodded before opening them again. "It's a symbol of the Empyrean that only manifests in the light and can only be read by beings of the Empyrean, as it's written in our celestial language."

Using reflexes she'd never understand, Rhode snatched the uncapped water bottle from her hand seconds before it tumbled from her grip and soaked the sheets.

"Okay, back up several seconds. I need a shit ton more information, because what you said does not compute. Where did this come from, and why can't I get it off?"

"Stop scratching at it or you'll rub your skin raw and start to bleed. You can't get it off because it's a part of you." Then he lifted her right wrist and turned it over beneath the light. "Just like this is a part of you now."

As if calling down the secrets of the universe to explain himself, he rubbed a thumb over her wrist, which bore another shimmering symbol written in a language she didn't recognize.

But that time, she wasn't afraid. That time, she knew exactly what he was asking her to comprehend.

The soul bond.

"This says Axtar, doesn't it?" Then she lifted a very insinuating, very condescending brow. "The name you yelled at me to never call you again."

That got a reaction out of him. Rhode lifted her wrist to his lips, enclosed her palm within his, and rested their combined fists against his warm chest. "I was not in my right mind, perhaps."

"But you are now?"

He squeezed her hand, impressing what felt like earnest yearning into their embrace. "Without a doubt. I can no longer deny the soul bond any more than I can deny my own name."

Whatever hope that had fluttered in her chest in anticipation of what he was about to reveal suddenly had holes blown into both wings.

For Rhode, it wasn't a choice, just an eventuality that finally came to fruition. One that, yes, he'd been far from enthusiastic about in the beginning but had finally accepted.

Accepted but not desired, no matter how perfect he found her body or how well the two of them fit together. To him, their relationship—situationship?—was the mortal equivalent of paying taxes.

Neela nodded, suddenly feeling far too naked to have any

further conversation that required her to string more than one or two words together. So she did what she'd done her whole existence: deflected as best she could and tried to sink into the background while he said whatever he needed to.

"The tattoos?" she reminded him, eager to get it over and done with, despite however gnawing her curiosity might have been over the new marks on her skin.

"Because of you, I can now access all of my power."

Read: Because of our fate-mandated teamwork, I now have the power to level up.

"With my full angel fire, Cyro has no hope of touching me. With your help, it'll be a cakewalk getting the relic back before he can use it to cause further harm."

Read: You've got the cheat codes, and I've got the invincibility. Together, we can beat the game.

She didn't want to hear any more, but she also couldn't deny him the happiness he deserved after all he'd endured.

She could be happy for him. She really could. She *should* be. And there was no reason they couldn't still enjoy each other's company. They were soul bonds. That constituted more than friends with benefits, right?

But as she tried to rationalize what her life ahead would look like and inadvertently began tuning Rhode out in the process, she shivered when he cupped the side of her face and ran his thumb over the mark behind her ear.

A mark she'd never known existed.

"I know this symbol, Neela, and I think I know why you're not like any other charmer."

She nodded her encouragement, still too raw to speak. "Hmm?"

"It's also the reason why you're like no other female I've ever met."

Oh, boy, he could *not* say that stuff to her, not when her world had yet again just been upended. She was plucking up the courage to say as much when another woman's name fell from his lips.

"Ciara. This was the name of another seraph in my legion long ago. One of my best trackers." A sadness ghosted through his eyes as he caressed Neela's jaw. "We lost her on a patrol mission. Her body was never recovered. But seeing this now, and the way you've carried it on your skin this entire time, I'm willing to bet that the item Cyro recovered from that battlefield and used during your inception process was one of Ciara's flight feathers. This symbol likely formed on you as a manifestation of Ciara's spark."

Neela pushed aside her sorrow to make sense of what he was saying. "Really?"

"Yes. To Cyro, it would have been just another seraph's feather that he found, one that could be connected to the Empyrean but with no known origins beyond that. He had no way of knowing it was a female's feather he stole, which is what, I suspect, contributed to your gender." Then he lifted a brow at her. "Unless he used female seraphim feathers in other experiments?"

"No, he didn't," she confirmed. "But why did magic harm me earlier, when it never had before?" Then a horror struck her, and her cheeks heated. "I never got an opportunity to thank you, by the way, for saving my life. Again."

His hand moved to her bare shoulder and rubbed soothing circles into it. "Consider us even."

God, did he have to keep doing that? Touching her, consoling her as if they were anything other than essentially ballroom dance partners with more comfortable clothing—or *no* clothing?

Or maybe that was how he viewed the two of them. Partners who were free to touch, to taste, to make love, but never more.

Then she looked into his hard face and was struck with a memory of how he'd looked when she first saw him. Skin so pale that every artery and vein track told a different tale of where he'd been abused and misused. Thickly matted hair down to his mid-back, which was originally blond but had been bleached to a ghostly white, devoid of every protein and mineral due to the experiments. A scraggly beard that was his only form of modesty, covering whatever body parts its unkempt length could reach.

Back then, he had been Axtar. He'd whispered that word to her once, in a fever dream of delusion, she suspected. But she knew. She knew it had been his name.

And now, he was Rhode. A fallen seraphim commander who was part of a team of warrior angels. A cohesive unit. A family. The thing she'd always yearned for.

The truth lay cloyingly thick in her heart as the path to certainty began to solidify in her mind.

How on earth could she deny him this? What he'd found, what she'd somehow managed to give him, was lightyears beyond a symbiotic connection to another. She'd given him health. A family. A home.

It was exactly what she'd dreamed of for herself, so why the hell would she begrudge him the ability to finally enjoy his life?

She wouldn't. She couldn't. That had become abundantly clear.

And if there was room for her in his life, in whatever small way the soul bond allowed, she would latch onto it with open arms and hang on for as long as her grip held out.

"To answer your question," he said before dropping a kiss on her shoulder—*damn him*. "I believe you can be harmed in the mortal lands because all of Cyro's attempts on your life were done in the shadow realm."

Neela stilled, mentally retracing every horrid experience ever done to her. It was a practice she never did, for obvious reasons, but his conclusion, if correct, was too much of a bombshell to go unchecked.

"Oh my God, you're right."

Rhode nodded, opening his arm wide for her to sidle up to him, as if they both knew such a revelation couldn't come without some measure of physical comfort. The call of his smooth chest was too irresistible, and she huddled closer, puddling her cheek to his hard pec and smiling to herself when his heartbeat kicked up. Was that reaction for her or a byproduct of the soul bond connection?

Does it really matter?

"So I can die," she murmured.

Rhode tightened his arm around her. "Yes."

"Magic can harm me in the mortal lands."

"Yes. But it can also save you. That's why the soul bond magic works on you, Neela, because you carry part of Ciara's Empyrean legacy within you, despite your charmer parentage. Empyreans live and thrive in all forms of light. We're made of it."

Neela took his words to heart and tried to concentrate to see whether she felt any warmer, any lighter, lying next to him.

She did.

"Cyro never understood that," Rhode added.

"He didn't?"

"No. If he did, he would have known that the true worth and power of any life can only be measured once it has ended." Rhode painted idle circles onto her arm, and his voice seemed to drift further and further away. "You were wrong, you know."

"Surprise, surprise."

"I did know you were there," he whispered.

Neela lifted up and rested her chin against his chest, but he was already staring down at her.

"A part of me did know, I think. When I was in that cell."

Her heart slingshotted around her ribs. "You told me your name, but it was only during one visit. Right after they had brought you back from . . . Anyway, I wasn't entirely sure how lucid you were. You kept chanting that word as part of a phrase but never opened your eyes or anything, even after I tried to wake you up, so I just assumed it was your name. It went something like 'I . . . Axtar, not Tyrus.' Or maybe it was something similar. I don't know. It was a long time ago. I never figured out who Tyrus was, and you never mentioned either name again."

The play of his fingers stilled, but he didn't remove his hand. "Tyrus is Chrome's celestial name."

She sat up then and noticed the tattoo on his forearm, the one that was a mark of his office as a seraphim commander. Neela extended her hand toward it, but Rhode ducked his arm beneath the sheet. "What do those symbols mean?"

His eyes assessed her. "You can see them?"

"Yes . . ."

"Chrome branded me with the symbol himself, used his angel fire to etch it onto my skin when he appointed me to the post. The celestial eye affixed atop a flaming scepter. It's only visible to the sentinels, the celestial mages, and my soul bond, apparently."

She tried not to feel joy at the sense of belonging that thrummed within her, especially at the obvious sorrow it brought him. "Does Chrome know about what really happened?"

"No." He shifted his gaze toward the wall. "No one does."

"Why not? Why not explain and help them understand?"

Then Rhode swiped a hand through the air and lifted her off him. "Don't do this," he barked, then walked over to the trunk at the foot of the bed.

Neela wrapped the sheet around her more tightly. "But why, Rhode? They can help. We can *all* help."

"Because I volunteered for Cyro's treatments!" he snarled. "I injected myself."

CHAPTER 26

Rhode yanked a sweatshirt from his trunk and punched his arms into it. No fucking way was he going to have this conversation while so much of him was exposed. Hell, a damn hazmat suit wouldn't have offered him enough coverage. For some wounds, no amount of protection could ever be enough to prevent the gashes from splitting wide open again.

Rhode ran his fingers through his short hair and tried not to think of what it once looked like. And the worst part was that Neela knew. She *knew* how infested with lice and fleas it had been. How the vermin had gnawed at his scalp so terribly that the only relief he could expect to find was scraping his head against the stone and hoping the salt of his blood was enough to starve the pests to death.

It had never worked. Nothing ever had.

Rhode finally settled on the edge of the trunk, making damn sure no part of that bed was touching him. Neela was too much of a distraction, and he knew himself, knew that if he felt even her pinky toe through the covers, he'd lunge for the opportunity to sink into her again and avoid the responsibility of telling his soul bond the truth in favor of the responsibility of giving her pleasure.

"Before my capture, Chrome and I were responsible for overseeing a defensive mission against Cyro and his advancing armies. They were getting too close to the Empyrean's gates, and every spy legion I sent out for information came back in pieces. Wings and limbs would be dropped from magic portals that Cyro and his charmers opened up in our territories. The bastard was stretching us too thin, splitting our armies into directions we couldn't sustain with our numbers. Now I know why."

"Why?"

"We never knew how he made more of your kind, only that for every one we took out, half a dozen would sprout in its place. If he was creating armies from his own person, with his dark magic, and then regenerating, well, it makes sense now why we were never able to keep up with him."

"Hindsight's twenty-twenty," she said.

"So it is. At any rate, I soon learned that an intelligence breach was the reason my entire legion of seraphim scouts had been slaughtered and their mutilated bodies returned to us outside our gates. They were *my* angels. I sent them there. And Chrome trusted my judgment." Rhode shook his head, hoping to fling the memory a thousand miles away from his also-too-trusting soul bond.

But he couldn't. He owed her and promised her as much.

"The night before the Sealing—"

"Sealing?"

"The sentinels' final act of salvation. An all-or-nothing op. Using magic bestowed on them by the celestial mages, all the sentinels stood outside the gates of the Empyrean and drained their power to seal off the gates so no one—neither Cyro, souls, nor the sentinels themselves—could ever enter Heaven again. Not until Cyro and the entire threat to the Empyrean had been eradicated. Unbeknownst to the sentinels, however, enacting the Sealing blasted them out of Heaven and sent them plummeting to the mortal realm with little hope of returning."

Understanding stilled Neela's movements.

"Anyway, the night before, I insisted Chrome send me on a final mission to hunt down the source of the breach. He refused, of course, most colorfully, I'll add, but I didn't give him a choice, and he knew it. Our numbers were dwindling, and if we couldn't stop the bleeding, we might as well have opened the fucking doors for the charmers regardless. So I left with a promise not to fail him."

Rhode swallowed down the bitter memory and the lie it had turned into. "Before I reached the shadow realm, a portal opened above me, and I was shot down. But because I was by myself and not among a legion of seraphim, the charmers that apprehended me surmised what I was there to do and brought me to Cyro, who recognized me instantly."

Mages, his head was heavy. His neck, his temples, everything throbbed with a renewed ache that had only ever truly ebbed when Neela had begun to run her fingers through his hair.

But, no. He had to get through this.

"Like any good commander, Cyro was after information."

"What sort of information? Battle plans and such?"

"No, not battle plans. The battle planner."

A curious crease formed between her brows. "But wouldn't that be—"

"Chrome."

Neela sucked in a breath, and no matter how hard Rhode tried, he couldn't *not* turn to her, nor could he stomach keeping things to himself any longer.Mages, he was so damn tired.

"Cyro wanted Chrome, our intelligence master, and since I

had zero interest in giving him up, we struck a bargain," he gritted out.

"A bargain? Why would he offer one if he already had you captive?"

"Because if he had my cooperation on a particular matter, he assured me that he'd have no more need for Chrome or the desire to locate his whereabouts."

"I see. And you agreed to this right away?" It was clear Neela was trying to parse out the timeline of events, a glimmer of hope sparking in her eyes that perhaps the worst of his suffering had been condensed to just the time she'd known him.

How it hurt to break her heart again.

"You know I did not, little demon," he said gently. When she closed her eyes, he wished he could close his as well. "It was eons before such an offer was presented to me. Prior to that, well, I won't give you the details, but suffice it to say, when the time had come to consider giving up the torture I had known in exchange for a new sort of torment, one that Cyro himself admitted was experimental in nature, there wasn't much left in me that could refuse."

"To protect Chrome?"

Rhode nodded. "He was—had been—my brother. When I tell you that I would have died a hundred thousand deaths if it meant keeping him safe, know that I speak from experience. So Cyro's bargain wasn't really much of one, if you ask me. As long as I've known of Cyro, I knew that he'd always been on the hunt for a way to breach the Empyrean's gates, and as you know, aside from you, charmers cannot exist in the light. He'd been ravenous for a workaround, and then one day, he came to my cell and told me that after many failed attempts, he might have found one that would work."

Before Neela could latch onto the words *failed attempts* and let them drag her down into darker places, however, Rhode intervened and smiled. "Just so you know, you are by far the best failed attempt that the world could ever hope to know, and I'm quite glad I was able to experience several of your failures firsthand. Perhaps we can even engage in more of them."

The eye roll was what he had hoped for, but Neela's delicious nose wrinkle was the cherry on top. "Ass."

"On occasion."

Talking to Neela had become so effortless, despite the friction he'd had to overcome to get to that point. The give-and-take between them was something he could get used to and made his chest lighter for it.

"Cyro was looking for a weapon against the sentinels, as well as a warrior who could breach the Empyrean. He hadn't yet acquired the relic at the time, so he was testing the assumption that, because I was a being of the Empyrean, I would be able to still enter the gates *after* whatever testing had been done to me. He was searching for something that would command metal as the sentinels did but would be resistant to so many of the weapons that the charmers crafted to combat the angels. Corrosion, rust, acid—those tactics were what made up the base of their magical warfare, and that worked quite well against the sentinels' metals, steel, titanium, bronze, etc. They were all highly susceptible to it. But he wanted a warrior who commanded metal *and* who was resistant to all of that but who could also walk among the Empyreans. He sought out to create a metallic angel army of his own but one immune to the magical warfare that crippled the sentinels. And I was his test subject. That was, if I agreed."

"Oh, Rhode . . ."

He placed a hand over her ankle, finding he needed her strength more than he thought. "No sympathies, little demon. We cannot change the past. And what choice did I have, really? Return to the torment I knew, knowing my weakness would ultimately lead to a target being placed on Chrome's back? Or forge ahead and consent to be turned into whatever Cyro would make of me, while my brother remained safe? It was, as the mortals say, a no-brainer.

"So, I consented, provided that the administration of the materials was on *my* terms. I refused to be forced, and Cyro saw no reason to object. Shortly after, I was handed a syringe of silvery-white liquid, spelled so that my body would accept it. They had chosen to test rhodium for its anticorrosive properties and being inert when it came to most aggressive chemicals. The metal isn't known to tarnish, tolerates high heat superbly, and is also very rare. All qualities that would prove useful if the sentinels ever met someone like me in combat.

"With nothing left to lose, I took the injection, and that was when my hell truly began."

"The spells . . ."

"Yes," he acknowledged. "I wasn't prepared for the amount of trial and error that went into spell casting or the effects the dark magic, when mixed with the rhodium, would have on my makeup. I lost . . . everything," he cried out, dropping his head in his hands. "The rhodium, combined with the magic, corroded my body at first. The burns were . . ." He took a deep breath. "I can't even begin to describe what it was like to have your skin flayed off from the inside out, only to have it grow back again and again, to take new concoctions again and again, hoping for a different result but never going so far as to truly wish for death because if I died, nothing would stop Cyro from going after Chrome.

"So I continued with the treatments and experiments. Some turned me to solid metal but didn't allow for movement, so I was no better than a patient on an operating table, fully alert but frozen to the slab and able to feel everything they did to me. And try everything they did. At one point, they drained as much of my blood as they dared to, only to replace it with equivalent doses of whatever latest poison they were testing. This went on and on and on, until one day, after a particularly brutal session, I faked unconsciousness just for a few hours of a reprieve, for a few cowardly moments without pain. It worked. They weren't able to get any new test results until I was awake anyway, so they left me alone, but by the time they were set to return, Chrome and Drea had already found me, freed me, and brought me here. Only in the months after, during my private recovery, did I discover that Cyro's experiment had finally been a success."

Rhode inhaled deeply for the first time in ages. Good thing, too, because Neela chose that moment to throw off the covers and fling her arms around his neck. He welcomed the warmth of her bare body and lifted her, along with the rumpled discarded sheet, into his lap.

"Shhh, it's okay," he soothed, stroking her hair, wrapping her against him, and comforting her as she comforted him. "Every fucking night, I wish I could say that my time with the charmers is behind me, but I can't. During my time there, I grew comfortable with the loneliness, the isolation. It's why I keep my quarters so sparse, why I insisted on rooms so far away from the others. For some reason, a room full of decorations and wall adornments felt like it should be meant for other people, not me. When you go so long without even the barest of necessities, even a bar of soap is a luxury. Imagining my life with the lavish trappings that the sentinels regularly enjoy, or even what I'd enjoyed as a seraph in the Empyrean, always seemed like too large of a hurdle for my mind to consider crossing." Then he pulled back slightly and cupped the back of her head. "Until you."

Something shifted in her demeanor, though. Eyes that had been misted with unshed tears darted around the room, taking in bare wall after bare wall. Her teeth claimed her bottom lip, refusing to set it free, even as her skin beneath his fingers began to pebble with goose bumps.

"Neela? What is it?"

"Rhode, there's something—"

Three loud consecutive bangs resounded against the metal door to his suite. "We've reached a consensus," Iron hollered. "Meet us upstairs when you're ready."

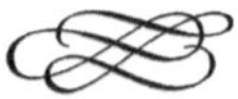

CHAPTER 27

Neela was halfway up the stairs to the den's great room when Drea nearly bowled her over on the staircase.

"Oh my God, he let you out! Thank goodness!" The bubbly blond threw her arms around Neela's neck, and Rhode had to steady both of them from behind lest they each kiss the granite.

Though, like the angel would let anyone break their neck on his watch?

"Your legs are too long. Seriously." Neela squeezed back.

"A blessing and a curse. That's why Chrome had to triple-check the leg-room specs on my car before I got it."

"Smart man." Neela pulled away but couldn't miss the grunt that Rhode tried to disguise with a throat clear.

The angel was as silent as a cemetery most of the time, so whenever he made accidental noises, there was usually very little *accident* behind them. Once they sorted out the mess with her sire, she'd turn her attention to Rhode and Chrome's mess of a relationship.

The tension between the two of them was killing her, not to mention the guilt.

Drea leaned over Neela's shoulder and narrowed her death stare at Rhode. "Did you sort your shit out? Because if I need to grab the other girls so we can start voting on everyone's actions and formally turn this den into a democracy, so help me God, Rhode, I'll do it. I don't care how long you've been alive. You *cannot* treat people like that without talking first. Like *adults*. You know, grown-ass organisms with smartphones and fully developed cerebral cortexes who are more than capable of intelligent discourse. You cannot just take a woman, who is clearly a victim in her own right, *not believe her*, and throw her into some padded cell while other grown-ass organisms decide her fate all because they happen to have wings and penises!"

"Drea," Rhode warned.

"No, don't *Drea* me on this." She turned and, thankfully, unclogged the stairwell bottleneck so they could all move. "I've never pulled the patient-caregiver card before, but I thought you and I had a connection. Or at least some sort of understanding."

Her arms were waving over her head, and Neela thought it best to join Molly when the brunette rolled her eyes and patted the vacant spot next to her on one of the farmhouse table benches. It wasn't a hard decision. The girl was offering solidarity, snacks, and a front-row seat, so, yeah . . .

"Drea," Rhode said a bit more forcefully.

"I can't believe you scared her like that, scared *anyone* like that, to be honest. I mean, it's not like this den isn't full of people with their own bags full of problems. I challenge you to find one person in here who *hasn't* made at least one questionable decision in their life. But you know what? We *talk* about our shit—we talk, therapy up, atone if needed, forgive where we can, and move the fuck on with our day because life's too short to treat people like garbage."

"Drea!"

"What?" she yelled, then spun around to the room full of

people with eyebrows scraping the ceiling. But those violet eyes didn't truly widen until they finally got a good look at Neela's appearance. Drea squinted, then lolled her head to the side. "Why are you wearing Rhode's sweats?"

Neela was holding a sour cream and onion chip poised above her tongue when everyone's focus shifted to her. Rhode walked over and, intent on answering the question for her, pushed down the cuff of the sweatshirt she'd borrowed—*his* sweatshirt—lifted her wrist to the room, and let his name on her skin speak for itself.

Silence wasn't a foreign concept to Neela. If there had been a soundtrack to her life thus far, it would have featured one giant staccato stretch of her lone footsteps, punctuated here and there with video game scores and YouTube song parodies. But the silence that stole the breath of every single pair of lungs in that room was some truly blackhole-worthy shit.

Iron's eyes flashed topaz before he blinked it away. "Excuse me." Without another word, the massive angel chucked his beer can in the recycling bin—because, yes, apparently even immortal angels still recycled—and stormed off down the hall.

She barely had time to ask what was going on before the room erupted. Titan and Tungsten stood, exchanged some unspoken words of understanding, and, after seeing Rhode smile and kiss Neela's tattoo, flew into a riot of back-slapping congratulations. Rose and Tammy, twin sisters and soul bonds to Titan and Tungsten, hugged each other, while Steel ran to the kitchen, grabbed a verdant-green bottle from a separate fridge, and started pulling down champagne flutes. Bronze and Brass went to the pantry.

Chrome was nowhere to be found.

Molly gave Neela the good old side hug and offered her the bag of chips. "You'd be surprised at how well these puppies pair with champagne. There's something about the combo of high acidity and salt that just hits."

"I hadn't realized this was such a cause for celebration." Neela grabbed some chips and quickly threw them into her mouth so she didn't have to answer questions she didn't know how to navigate.

Drea stalked up to Rhode, never once breaking stride as the prime sentinel and second-in-command parted for her like she was royalty.

Which, in a lot of ways, she was. Neela hadn't realized it at first, but after knowing what Rhode had been through, *who* he'd suffered through it for, and what Drea had to do to reach him and pull at least small parts of him back from whatever brink of despair they'd been teetering on was truly awe-inspiring.

It was a feat Neela had yet to accomplish, despite wearing the trappings of the soul bond title.

A hollowness bloomed beneath her breastbone, and she wished she could crawl into the chip bag for the surface-level comfort that would greet her there. Jeez, could she be any more of an imposter? A dupe adorned with proverbial diamonds who had been lifted onto some pedestal because of how she'd magically reformed the angels' scarred seraph while—oh, hey, look— also turning out to be one of the *nice* demons.

Meanwhile, Drea had been the true queen in all of this, and as Rhode gripped Drea's elbow and whispered into her ear what Neela sincerely hoped was a whole lot of sentences that started with *I'm sorry*, she had to remind herself that this was right. This was good. She *wanted* him to have loving, meaningful relationships with his family. He deserved no less.

Then why did it hurt so much?

"Thank you, everyone," Rhode said quietly, bowing his appreciation. "It has been . . ."

Neela's hand froze, suspended in the air between her mouth and the chip bag. It had been, what? Exhausting? Raw? Enjoyable and convenient? What *was* she to him? Did he even know?

Did she?

Ugh, all the questions were about to make her eyes twitch, and for the first time since these people had welcomed her into their lives, she wondered whether she wasn't better off in her old life where all she had to do to combat her discomfort was sign off and close out a game.

Meanwhile, Rhode grabbed the back of his neck and seemed to root around to find the right words to finish whatever proclamation was obviously expected of him.

When he finally did find the words, Neela was reminded why she wished he hadn't.

"It has been a journey, to say the least. One I am much further along on than hours ago, thanks to Neela." Rhode grabbed her hand, and for a moment, she thought he was going to hold her fist high like she'd just won a knockout round in boxing. Instead, he slid close to her, rested a hip on the edge of the table, and threaded his fingers with hers.

Neela's cheeks heated, and she tried her best to fade away behind Rhode.

Thankfully, Titan, ever the elder statesman of the group, wasn't one to let festivities linger for too long without getting down to business. Neela didn't know the angel that well, but she suspected he took great delight in wrangling the group back in. That and probably reminding everyone when last call was if they ever went out to get drinks among the mortals. Maybe even organized the bar tabs for the group. She wanted to kiss the angel for the much-appreciated change in focus.

"Unfortunately, we've lost the element of surprise when it comes to the charmers. Cyro knows that not only are we now aware of his location but also that Neela is with us."

"He doesn't know that I can command angel fire, nor does he know the extent of my metallic capabilities."

Tungsten folded his arms across his chest. "I'm not entirely sure the rest of us know either, my friend. Will you share with us?"

The soft encouragement on the prime sentinel's face was the most trusting comfort Neela had ever seen called into action. Dear Lord, he was like a golden retriever but one trained for service duties. If she ever had someone look at her with the sort of neutral hope Tungsten looked at Rhode with, she wouldn't hesitate to spill her entire life to them, as well as come up with some bonus stories just to make sure the deal was fair.

God, this family loved Rhode. They really did.

Neela's heart skipped a beat and then nearly exploded when Rhode squeezed her hand. It wasn't a pulse of persuasion or a press of reassurance. It was something else. Something . . . hesitant?

Curious, Neela looked up, but the stiff set of Rhode's shoulders and the bob of his Adam's apple answered her question. He was nervous. Did he . . . did he *need* her?

But when her soul bond's flare fluttered to life inside her, she had the answer in spades.

Yes.

And she didn't delay in delivering her answer.

I'm right here. Neela leaned her shoulder against him, hid their joined hands between their bodies, squeezed back, and held it. Held it for as long as needed, which wasn't nearly as long as she'd feared.

"It is . . . a long story." Rhode sighed.

Then several things happened at once. Glasses stopped clinking, chips stopped crunching, and butts found seats as Rhode recounted, in only as much detail as absolutely necessary, the intention of Cyro's experimentation plan on him. The mechanics of his metallic power. The anticorrosive elements. How, despite the harm he'd suffered mentally, that physically Rhode couldn't be harmed by the same dark magic the demon leader had used on the rest of the sentinels. Neela's heart bled as, for the second time that day, he had to rip open wounds that had only just begun to even flirt with the healing process, let alone get on a first-name basis with the idea.

When it was over and Rhode had squeezed out every last drop of willpower so that he might finally face his brothers again, he lifted his head. What greeted him was a room full of family, standing shoulder to shoulder, with mates hugging mates, and either tears or swirls of angel fire lighting the eyes of those staring back at him.

It was a family who loved him. A family who mourned with him and for him, a family who fought for him.

A family who would die for him.

The sharp *tsss* of a beer can tab popping open broke the spell over the assembled party. Iron stood behind Rhode and held the beer out to him. Rhode accepted it but not before the giant angel's smile lifted the corners of his russet beard.

The grin was equal parts mirth and menace, relief over a bridge finally crossed and a new leg of the race to head into.

Iron clapped Rhode on the shoulder. "Let's do this, brother."

CHAPTER 28

The next week was a furor of logistics, location scouting, way too much time underground, and nowhere near enough time under Neela's soul bond.

It turned out that busting the seal on Rhode's pain *and* his full power made for a rather ravenous angel.

But like a girl was about to complain? It was, not so ironically, absolute heaven.

Everyone's safety concerns over Cyro's next move had hit Mach 3 levels of unease since Neela was known to be with the angels. One of the armories, because of course there were several, had quickly been turned into more of what she would deem a proper war room, save for the espresso machine, which was, in the end, regrettably relocated. But as Rhode explained, close proximity to their weapons cache allowed for proper examination of next steps. Thanks to what Rhode was finally able to share with everyone, amendments to the angels' tactical and mechanical approaches had become more important than ever.

Cyro was ready to deploy magic that could not only destroy the sentinels' metals on contact during any combat mission but, if the charmers ever managed to examine Rhode's DNA for the right markers, may have found ways to create their own magic-resistant metal and use it against the angels.

There was no shortage of possibilities scrutinized when it came to what Cyro might do, and every night when Rhode dragged his exhausted body back to bed, he'd regale Neela with another weapon the angels hadn't considered Cyro capable of, as well as which weapons of theirs would serve best in which scenarios. Closely wielded blades, long-range firearms, angel fire, shields, flight attacks—not a single option was left unexplored. He, along with every other angel in the den, had taken to walking around like the celestial equivalent of caffeinated zombies. There wasn't a single hard-set jaw among them that hadn't displayed signs of twitching, whether from stress, lack of sleep, or Iron pulling unhealthy amounts of doppio espresso shots and passing them out like Halloween candy.

Amid all the chaos of trying to plot out Cyro's next move and after the consensus seemed to favor Neela staying in the den since she was being actively hunted, she'd made some discoveries of her own.

The first: she missed the sunlight desperately.

The second: she was in deeper trouble than she realized when it came to Rhode.

All those self-proclamations and pep talks about keeping her emotional distance from the angel went right out the proverbial window when he joined her in bed each night. It was like every ounce of mental energy had been so completely sucked dry from the man that by the time he left the others, his physical needs had been so far neglected to the point of starvation.

They exchanged very few words when he came to her. Didn't need to, really. There were so many ways to care for someone, yet so few of them that required connection without speaking, fulfillment without asking, satisfaction without regret or concern.

After the first night she stayed in his room, he'd petitioned Iron to equip his space with comforts for her. Computers, gaming consoles, headphones, microphones, whatever she described when he asked after what her former quarters had looked like, what she had missed most. Soon, the barren space had taken on a new life with the simple additions of color-changing string lights, an Internet connection she almost—*almost*—got down on her knees to worship, and the largest pink-leafed aglaonema she'd ever seen.

But it was the unknown comfort of hearing that door close each night and having his hands seek her out before anything else that settled a soothing calmness into spaces she didn't know could be reached. The angel had a knack for hunting down her tension and obliterating it into pieces too small to ever find their way back together.

Most nights, he'd find her at the desk he had set up. The workspace was one of those electric numbers, with programmable buttons that could adjust the height of the desk should she need to stand and stretch during one of her games. Always, he started with her headphones, peeling them over the back of her head and gently lifting the weight of her hair off her shoulders before dropping a kiss on the tattoo behind her ear that only he could see. Then he'd flip off the camera, which she had taken to having on for certain games, but never the microphone.

It was a dangerous game the spy in him loved to play, and just like everything he did when they were alone, it thrilled her to no end.

"No noises, little demon, or they'll hear you." The whispered reminder was only ever said once, but it was enough to last the hours that would follow.

Rhode would conquer her like a spy invading enemy territory knowing they might get caught at any moment. He'd strip her bare and chart every inch of her with his mouth. In certain areas, he'd take his time, using his tongue to map out the exact curvature of her calf or flare of her hip before it dipped into where his hands gripped her waist. When he'd finally slide into her, though, he always made sure that his mouth was on hers as he pulled her passion into him. The result was a balm to both their souls. Every time his hips curled and he'd thrust deeper into her, he chased away the darkened tendrils of a past that she never fathomed she could truly break free of.

It was a raw, primal gift and one she'd never tire of opening, even if it did come draped in the trappings of their situation rather than true sentiments.

Regardless, they had been the happiest days of her life, until Rhode declared the angels were planning another ambush on the entrance to Cyro's hideaway. As in, the very one she and Rhode had just been ambushed *at*.

"The guy's probably not even there anymore. Seriously," Neela said over breakfast one morning. She was just working up a good schmear of scallion cream cheese on her everything bagel when the most asinine strategy to have ever been uttered nearly soured her already-tart fresh-squeezed orange juice.

Iron sighed and ran a heavy hand through his beard, looking for all the world like no amount of coffee or breakfast pastries could make his day better. "It's called offense. We go in Kool-Aid Man style, take out anything that moves, grab the relic, douse the place in angel fire, and get back in time for dinner."

"Yeah, except Cyro's not an idiot, nor is he predictable. I'm willing to bet both slices of your turkey bacon that he's no longer even there. One important thing to know about the charmers is that we move *constantly*. I don't have to tell you how expendable we are. Trust me, if Cyro's figured out that he's on your immediate radar again *and* that I'm with you, you can bet your ass he knows why and that he's taken precautions to control the game." Neela grabbed her fork and scooped up some capers out of the jar, while Rhode sat next to her silently sipping his coffee. "If I know him at all, not only is he not there anymore but the relic is with him. So you can Kool-Aid Man that place all you want, it won't make a difference."

A startled hush fell around the table. Neela had taken two whole bites before she realized that just maybe she was still a *teensy bit* annoyed over how Iron had unquestioningly sided with Rhode during her little prison march earlier.

Great, Neela. Way to win friends and influence people.

"What I meant to say was—"

Rhode settled his arm around her shoulders and began to knead away the knot of tension at the base of her skull that always flared up whenever lots of eyes were on her. She sank into his touch and was more than content to let him shut her up for a few moments. They had all been discussing things for a good hour, after all. But then a niggling idea floated to the surface, and damn if her mouth didn't latch onto that thing and send it sailing throughout the room.

"Why not use me as bait?"

Rhode's hand froze, and the chilly rumble of his voice hit her ear. "No."

"No, wait, hear me out!" Holy shit, was she about to say this? Neela did a quick mental gut check. *Yup, we're doing this. All systems go.* And then she turned to Rhode but addressed the rest of the table. "I know you've been fighting Cyro for ages, but I've lived with him nearly just as long. I know his habits, his preferences, even his motivations. I know what sets him off, and I also know how his mind works. Whatever offensive action you're planning will be for a battle that, in his mind, he's already fought, won, and has moved on from. He's a futuristic thinker. It motivates every action he's ever taken."

Tungsten nodded thoughtfully. "It does make sense. All these years, he's always been a step or two ahead."

"Exactly!" Neela pointed out. "So why not do something he has no possible way to plan for? Draw him out. He knows I'm dangerous, not for what I can or can't do but for what I represent. He's looking for me in the same way he's been looking for an answer on how to access the Empyrean. I'm a liability he can't afford to have out in the world."

"No." Rhode's audible snap to the word would have stiffened anyone else's spine but not hers.

This could work. This is good. This is . . .

"It's not happening," he said.

"Like hell it isn't!" Neela threw her napkin on the table.

"I won't deny the danger involved," Tungsten added, "but I can see the merit to the plan. It's not ideal, but we now have precautions Cyro doesn't know about."

Rhode stood from the table and flashed his teeth at the prime sentinel. "How can you possibly be entertaining this?"

Tungsten didn't stand, opting for quiet composure instead of chaos. "Because it makes sense. Pure and simple. Neela's right. We've done the ambush routine. I'm not saying it isn't effective," he said, holding his hand out to Iron in consolation, "but perhaps it's no longer the right application for this circumstance. Think, brother. Think of all we have on our side. Not only can you command a celestial power Cyro doesn't know you have, but you can do so to its fullest strength, along with metallic magic none of us can wield. Also, he doesn't know what we know about Neela's true origins or her abilities. The charmers at the amusement park didn't live long enough to report back. We *do* have surprise on our side. Why not take advantage?" Tung's eyes gentled. "Besides, do you really think I would even consider the idea at all if I didn't think you could keep Neela safe better than anyone?"

"Rhode, please," Neela said, grabbing his hand and holding it between hers. "Let me do this for you. For us. For your family. I promise you it will work."

It was a long time before anyone broke the silence that had settled over the room. It was as if everyone was in some sort of mental standoff with each other, with imaginary guns held from both arms and aimed at whoever voiced the biggest threat.

It wasn't so much a pregnant pause but a perennial one. But just when Neela couldn't take it anymore, Iron stood from the table, swiped his breakfast sandwich to go, and said, "If we're doing this, I better get as much done during the day as I can. Some of us still need to recharge at night, and if I've got to keep one eye out for Cyro and the other one making sure Rhode doesn't go fucking postal because his soul bond has a death wish, then I'm going to need to have a goddamn geriatric bedtime." Iron gestured at Rhode. "You know what to do." Then he pushed his plate toward Neela before he grabbed his coffee and left.

It was a long time before Rhode finally broke the silence.

"I can't tell you how much I hate that you're right," he said as he pulled Neela against him and settled her head beneath his chin. "I hate it so damn much, little demon." The defeat in his voice was palpable. Then his tone quickly turned predatory. "But not more than I want to fight for you. I trust you, but I know better than to ever expect you to trust me back."

The raw truth of his words felt like venom on her skin, a symptom of the barrier that he always erected between them. She snuggled farther into his chest regardless. "Is it so hard to trust each other?"

"I am a spy," he said by way of explanation.

"And I am a demon."

"Yes. But you are *my* demon, and I'll always protect what's mine. Always."

Always . . .

Achingly private memories of her harboring that similar sentiment misted her eyes. She'd once thought such a thing might be possible between them, when he was no more than a tortured prisoner and she a pathetic charmer who'd foolishly hoped that she alone could save them from the hell they'd been confined to.

It was a different time, though. She knew that now. And this, whatever *this* was between them, had turned out to give her far more *always* than the frazzled fabrications a desperate caregiver could ever hope to offer.

Some parts of the past served no purpose traveling into the future. So no, she didn't need to dredge up anything, not for him. He'd gone through enough, and for that matter, so had she.

His words should have pleased her, but instead, they only made her sadder. Rhode had once thought the same thing of Chrome, that the intelligence master was his to protect, and in the end, he'd suffered irrevocably for it.

She'd never ask him to suffer again, but she didn't see a way out of stopping Cyro otherwise.

So she said nothing. Neither of them did. And as the plates were cleared around them, Neela finally broke from Rhode's embrace to help with the dishes. But when she'd glanced down at where she'd been sitting, an unexpected gift teased a smile from her.

Two untouched slices of Iron's turkey bacon.

The bowling alley was a surprise. Not the fact that Rhode would find Chrome there but that the facility in question wasn't the one Tammy worked for as a marketing manager. That place was a frequent and familiar haunt for the angels, with the owner even going so far as to provide the guys with a private billiard room and a bartender whenever they attended.

But no, this place was . . . Well, he'd go with *different*.

Rhode ducked his head beneath the rusted bell dangling above him, careful to avoid the chipping paint along the door trim, and immediately understood why the bell was there.

The place wasn't so much a bowling alley as it was a nearly abandoned relic of time. The lights were on, yes, but for the most part, signs of life stopped there. The dark green low-pile carpet blanketing the welcome area had worn down to the mesh in spots from decades of being trampled beneath scuffed soles. A small arcade sat in muted illumination off to the side and was the furthest cry from the joyful theming he'd delighted in showing Neela at the amusement park. The setup was as sad as they came, with crane games filled with stuffed animals that had sat in the same position so long the overhead lights had begun to mute their colors. Of the remaining games, one racing and one shooting, both sported a glowing orange coin slot that still demanded twenty-five cents, even though the change machine next to them sat caked in dust, with a hand-written yellowed *out of order* sign taped to it.

"Can I help you?" A young man with an alpaca's worth of hair hanging over his eyes didn't look up from his phone but sank onto his forearms above a front desk that had seen more chrome than customers. The only indication that the man had addressed Rhode at all came from the deliberate pause after the question. The beige name tag identified the boy as *Trainee*.

"You work here, I take it?"

The boy snorted. "For, like, another three days. Then my winter break's over and I go back to school."

A college student. Lovely. "I'm looking for someone."

A quick eye flick was all Rhode got before the attendant's attention settled back on his phone. "Yeah, I bet you are. Dude's over there." His mop of hair was flung wide and waved Rhode toward the far end of the bowling alley. "Friend or something?"

"Or something."

The boy nodded, as if he was either used to noncommittal answers or didn't care what the answers were in general. "When you go over there, just know that your boy's grumpy as hell because I told him we weren't allowed to serve beer at ten in the morning. Whatever." The kid shook his head and finally looked at Rhode for more than a blink, though it was with the penetrating boredom of a generation forced to go through the motions rather than make waves. "You need shoes?"

"No. Thank you."

"Cool."

Rhode didn't stick around to no doubt see the relief on the kid's face at not having to perform a task he was hired for.

Instead, the seraph made a beeline for the sole lane that was actively having bowling balls thunder down its ramp.

Chrome was by the ball return, staring down the conveyor's chute as if he was expecting it to offer some sort of retribution in the form of polished resin. Rhode waited for Chrome to acknowledge him, for there was no question the angel knew he was there.

Knew he was there and still didn't want anything to do with him.

Chrome's hunter-green ball popped out of the conveyor, but the angel didn't grab it. He just stood there, back to Rhode, with his head bent toward the ball.

Rhode shifted on his feet. "I wouldn't blame you if you wanted to throw that at me."

It was as much of an icebreaker as he could muster, and mages, did it feel utterly ridiculous given the things the two of them had shared and lived through. How in the holy hell had he let it get to this? Theirs was a history that spanned whole existences. Worlds had literally come and gone during the stretch of their friendship, and now they stood there, in a dilapidated bowling alley, like strangers who cringed at sharing a parking lot, let alone lifetimes.

Not to put too fine a point on the rejection, but it fucking *hurt*, and after hurting for so long, Rhode never thought *this* would be the torture that truly unraveled him.

Chrome's hatred was a powerful thing. Rhode saw that now and regretted every moment he'd let the fireball get that big. The sentinel's loathing had turned into a living, breathing thing that raged with a life of its own. Most beings had the capability to be soothed. He had his Neela to help him realize that. This, on the other hand, had unraveled to the point of uncertainty, mistrust, and despair.

And *that* he couldn't allow, even if it meant Chrome chose to sever him from the sentinel's life entirely. Permanently.

He would deserve no less.

"You're not worth marring the resin. Just had this polished." Chrome leaned down, ran a gentle hand over the gleaming bowling ball, and took his next shot. The ball careened down the lane with a force Rhode suspected was more of a challenge for Chrome to temper than triangulate. It hit slightly off-center, knocking the bulk of the middle pins down but left two lone soldiers standing on each side.

Chrome cursed. "If you came here to fuck up my game, you're doing a bang-up job."

"I came here to explain."

"Nah, no need." Chrome waved a dismissive hand at Rhode and looked up at the hanging television—tube, not flat screen—to check his score. The beard painting the angel's square chin was new and wouldn't have looked half bad if Chrome hadn't let it consume half his neck and cheeks. "Damn splits."

"Chrome—"

"Iron and Tung already talked to me. No, correction. Tung talked to me while Iron, I'm pretty sure, was just asked to be there as a blocker in case I lost my damn mind again and decided to break more shit that wasn't mine."

"You had every reason to react the way you did."

"I know." The statement was the period at the end of a lifetime's worth of resentment. "Tell that to Molly, though."

"She'll forgive you."

Chrome shrugged and let the topic die.

"What did Tung tell you?"

Charcoal eyes flashed the molten silver of Chrome's fire but seemed to be fueled by melancholy rather than malice. "What do you think he told me?"

Rhode took a deep breath. "That I wanted to see you."

"Well, you found me. Congratu-fucking-lations." Chrome grabbed his ball from the ball return and sent it sailing toward the pins again. That time, he hit the left pin just right, and the thing careened to the side, taking the other pin with it.

Mages, this would be so much easier if—

In a race to lose as much patience as Chrome had already lost, apparently, Rhode rounded the corner of the ball return and ignored the sticky wood floor as he squared his shoulders in front of the lane, pins to his back and Chrome to his front.

The sentinel narrowed his eyes. "What are you doing?"

"Trying to get your attention."

"Looks to me like you're trying to get your head taken off by a bowling ball."

Rhode leveled his chin but didn't move. "If that's what it takes."

They stood like that for a long moment, letting the tension charge whatever stage Rhode was about to willingly step onto. He wasn't one for pretty speeches or motivational pep talks. He'd not done a single one when commanding Chrome's spy legions, instead preferring to stick to the hard truths of what they would face and the tactics that would see them through the mission.

This was different, though, and uniquely painful, even for someone like him, who'd known endless pain. One never quite got immune to the stuff.

"I didn't tell you what happened to me because I wanted to protect you."

"Oh, bullshit." Chrome waved him off and moved to get his ball. "If you came here to insult me, you wasted your time."

"Wait!"

"Yeah, that's the wrong fucking thing to say to me. Word of advice: don't tell someone whose very existence has been defined by waiting to, you know, keep on trucking."

"Goddammit, Chrome, I didn't tell you about my wings or my power because you're the reason I have them in the first place!"

Chrome's hand stilled above the bowling ball. "What?"

Rhode ran a hand through his hair, tugging at the roots. "When I was shot down, Cyro was going to take my wings, and I was prepared for that. I was prepared for any type of physical torture that bastard could have dreamed up. My soul's spark would have returned to the Eternal Flame, and I would have died happily knowing my purpose as an Empyrean warrior had been fulfilled. But when he laid your well-being across the path of my final salvation and gave me a choice of either giving you up or turning myself into what I have become, believe me, brother, when I tell you it was no choice at all."

Chrome straightened. "What are you saying?"

"I'm saying that there is nothing I would not give up in this world, in the previous one or the next, if it meant losing you for good."

The floodgates didn't just open but were battering-rammed to splinters. Rhode held nothing back. Not how he had been shot down, what manner of torture they'd enacted, or even the bargain he'd struck that he would never bring himself to regret. For the first time since he'd been freed, he told Chrome about what he'd always remembered, which bits he chose to keep to himself, and fears he'd never shared to another soul, dead or alive. The minutes ticked on, and still, Rhode didn't stop. Not when a screensaver covered the game's scoreboard or when that pissant attendant was ordered to go check on the two of them and see whether they planned on finishing the game because maintenance would be arriving soon to service the lane.

As if oiling down a pinsetter was suddenly going to make the establishment's long-lost customers reappear.

Rhode made it a point to keep going, though. He poured every bleeding second of his existence in captivity into Chrome's eardrums, leaving nothing out. His fears, doubts, occasional hopes, and far more frequent disappointments. He spared nothing until every last memory was scooped out and delivered to the sentinel in whatever condition those memories happened to be in.

Perhaps it would have been a more cathartic experience if Rhode wasn't standing in the middle of a bowling alley alongside bench seats that had seen more sweat than sanitizer and below a suspended ceiling with tiles so stained they sagged.

By the end of it, though, that damn bench seat, not his best friend, was the thing that caught Rhode when he finally needed something else to support himself besides determination and resolution.

Then Chrome grabbed a seat next to him and, in a similar show of mental exhaustion, leaned his forearms on his knees. "You can't do that. You can't come in here and say all that to me, telling me I was the reason you were in that fucking hell all that time. You don't think I blame myself enough? I was the one who sent you out there in the first place!"

"No, I volunteered to go, and you know as well as I do that I didn't give you a choice. There were no good choices, Chrome. Deep down, you *know* that." Then Rhode gripped Chrome's shoulder and dug in his emphasis. "And I wouldn't have done a single thing differently. When I took my oath as seraphim commander, I didn't just speak the words as a soldier. I spoke them as a friend." His throat tightened. "As a brother. You were one of the seven sentinels, and there was no way I could have existed in a world where I would have led Cyro straight to you. Trust me when I say that I never blamed you once, never held any judgment or regret toward you. When you found me and I realized all that I had become, I was fucking terrified, not only at the new powers Cyro's magic had manifested within me but at how you would look at me if you knew. And I thought that if *you* knew, I ran the risk of Cyro knowing as well, but I was so wrong. So much has changed since I'd last seen you or the others. I didn't know about the battles you'd all waged with the charmers since my capture, nor did I know the powers the group of you had come to master."

Chrome's shoulder muscle jumped beneath Rhode's hand, but the seraph wouldn't relent. Not now. "I didn't know what sort of place I could have within your family, among the sentinels. The parts of me that made me a seraph have been burned away and replaced with powers similar to yours but also very different. I had not shared your bond with the others, had not even lived life in the same world as you all had. And there you guys were, half of you soul bonded, for god's sake! When you and Drea brought me to the surface, I thought I was as much an imposter as I was an Empyrean warrior. I could no more relate to you than my surroundings. The only thing I *could* rely on, could still understand and hold true to, was my ability to keep Cyro from you and the others. To do that, I had to keep you at arm's length, and it hurt every fucking minute."

Chrome's gaze had turned somber, and Rhode could see the angel reliving those early days after the rescue in a play of mixed emotions that warred across his bold features.

"I never meant what I said, Chrome. I would have *died* without your compassion, without Drea's care. Of course I knew you never expected anything in return." Then the corner of Rhode's lip lifted. "I suspect if I had tried to truly thank you in any real way, you'd have ordered Drea to shove an oxygen mask on my face and run screaming from the room in search of something to punch."

The gruff chuckle lifted the sentinel's shoulders, and Rhode released a breath. "In emergencies, gratitude is implied, you know," Chrome added.

"Even among friends?"

Chrome ran a hand over his jaw. "But not always among brothers."

Rhode sat there, still as stone, while he listened to Chrome.

"I never wanted you out of my life. I was beyond angry and

equally as hurt. Ax, I've only ever wanted you back. It was a miracle of the prime mages that I found you, and when I couldn't reach you up here," he said, tapping his temple, "it fucking ate me up inside that I had somehow failed you again."

"You didn't fail."

"Yeah, I did. Because I didn't do a good enough job of letting you know that, short of *not* lying your ass off and telling Drea that her cooking's the best you've ever had, there's not a damn thing you could do that would ever take you out of this family."

Rhode had to grin at that. "I would *never* say such a thing to her, but something tells me you may have learned that lesson the hard way." He cocked a brow.

Chrome shook his head and smiled the smile of a thousand fools. "Why do you think I got her a new car?"

Rhode barked out a laugh loud enough to shake the already shaky foundations of the bowling alley. And when Chrome's laugh joined his and rounded out the chorus, it wasn't long before tears leaked from both their eyes.

Chrome was the first to wipe his away and regain his breath. "Oh, man, that felt good."

"Yes. Yes it did."

Then Chrome held out his hand, but when Rhode did the same, Chrome didn't grab his palm. Instead, he rolled up Rhode's silk shirt sleeve to reveal the mark of the seraphim commander, then inched up his own sleeve. When their forearms clasped, it was with an embrace that had first been forged in service of the Empyrean but had since been stoked in service of each other.

"Welcome back, asshole."

Rhode rolled his eyes. "Thanks. It's good to be back. Neela will be relieved to hear it. She, uh, was the one who made me realize I finally needed to speak to you."

"Smart woman."

"The smartest. You know," Rhode said, leaning back against

the bench and propping his arm up along the rim, "it's taken me quite the journey to wrap my head around, but I think this partnership she and I have—"

"Hold up." Chrome raised his hand. "Partnership?"

"The bond."

Chrome's face twisted into pretzel proportions, and Rhode wondered whether the sweat smell was truly coming from him or the bench. "That's not how this works."

"She is my partner," Rhode asserted.

"Nah. Oh, man, is that how you're looking at your mate? As a partner?"

It was Rhode's chance to turn on the confusion. "Neela is—"

"Not a fucking lawyer who's trying to get her name on the same bill as yours. She's your *mate*. Your other half." Then he leaned forward and held out his hands as if he were trying to explain trigonometry to a kindergartener. "Look, with Drea and me, when she breathes in, I breathe out. When she wakes up, I'm not letting her feet hit the floor without making sure she's already got a smile on her face. And when she's off with Molly or one of the other girls doing something, my trigger finger doesn't stop twitching until I have her in my arms again, even though, logically, I know she's fine and, though I still can't conceive of it, probably having the time of her life without me."

Chrome paused to let his words sink in, but Rhode couldn't respond right away. All he could think about was every single interaction he and Neela had shared. How there wasn't a single thing he'd done for her that he didn't look on as part and parcel to their arrangement. He'd just assumed that what he'd felt for her hadn't been his own feelings but had somehow been generated by the magic of the soul bond.

But if he took the bond away...

"If you took the bond away, would you still want her?" Chrome finished for him.

Rhode's jaw tightened. "Don't fucking ask me that question.

Of course I would want her! I always want her. She's . . . she's . .
."

The reason he had a brother and a family again.

The reason he had lived through the experiments.

The reason he was more powerful than Cyro could imagine.

And he'd treated her like a coworker instead of the constant source of light and joy she had become.

Chrome leaned back against the bench and folded his arms across his chest. "Oh, man, you are so fucked."

"I have to go."

"Yeah, you do."

Rhode bolted from his seat and was out the door before the pins fell down again. But as he took flight, the crashing sound chased him far into the sky, bolstering him in a way he'd never experienced before.

It was the sound of a perfect strike.

CHAPTER 30

In a turn of events that would surprise no one, Neela's assumption that Molly's restaurant would be nearly abandoned on a Tuesday at eight o'clock in the morning and thus serve as a quiet haven of caffeine consumption was the furthest thing from the truth. It was the weirdest mix of clientele but one that also introduced her to another hobby she'd never thought she'd enjoy: people-watching.

Neela blew the steam off her coffee and decided that, yeah, she could definitely appreciate this life, warts and all. Near the window, a group of two seniors huddled by the baseboard heaters for warmth. One woman, a blond who wore enough costume jewelry to fill a museum exhibit, stirred a cup of woefully oversteeped tea while her friend, a redhead with more fuchsia lipstick on her teeth than her coffee mug, *thunked* a tote bag onto the table, pulled out her body weight's worth of fashion magazines, and began searching the dog-eared pages.

Huh. Good to know someone's still funding those things.

Then a heated conversation ensued involving a lot of acrylic nails pointing out articles where some obscene trend or another clearly offended them. Either that or they were arguing over the price of jewelry they could never afford anyway.

And that was just at one table by the window. The rest of the dining room featured a revolving kaleidoscope of customers: some regulars, judging by the way they knew the menu, and some tourists, judging by the way they didn't. Either way, they were all smiling over the morning's light snowfall and sharing their collective joy around Molly's newest menu items: gingerbread buttermilk waffles and the roasted pumpkin, bacon, and egg breakfast sandwich.

Whatever it was, Neela loved it. It was as mundane as mundane got, and she'd never realized just how vital the simple things had become for her lately. They weren't just a foot in the door to living among the mortals but her entire leg being hurled over a ledge with one foot dangling behind her.

All that remained was the helping hand to guide her safely the rest of the way, to do the big scary living-aboveground thing with her and tell her it would all be all right.

Instead, she was stuck in limbo as if she were waiting on a permit review from a town planning board.

It had been a few days since she'd brought up the whole *use me as a decoy* plan to Rhode and the others, and while she was satisfied in her determination that it was the only way to draw Cyro and the relic out from hiding, she'd also secretly hoped it would draw Rhode out of his shell as well.

Neela sipped down her coffee and tried not to think about how she hadn't seen the man since then, except for late at night, as had become their custom, when he'd finally collapse into bed hours after her head hit the pillow. Her only indication that he'd even been there at all was the still-warm sheets next to her when she'd roll over in the morning, hoping to steal some time with him before something else called him away.

And that was what those moments had become, too. Theft. Any time at all she was able to snag from him ended up as brief encounters he seemed to oblige her in before giving some excuse and vowing to see her later, that he had to see to something, Iron needed him, and so on.

Somehow, they'd fallen into a rut of a routine again, where Neela's presence appeared to be more tolerated than anything else.

It made things damn difficult when she kept trying to find the right time to talk to him.

There was so much more they needed to share, things she needed to say, truths he didn't yet know, and they'd finally gotten to a point where she thought he might be ready to listen to her . . . But no matter how urgently she wanted to grab the angel, tie him to a chair, and force him to hear what she had to tell him, other things would always command his attention.

I am a spy.

And I am a demon.

Always.

The nuance of everything else mattered very little, even in times when she'd hoped he'd gotten past it.

But the sunlight *did* matter, at least to her. Now that Neela had some exposure to it, she found it mattered very much. Man, did she love the stuff. Loved the heat of it on her skin, the way her cheeks hurt from squinting when she tried to find the sun behind the clouds. Loved the way it chased everyone outside so she could sit quietly in Molly's restaurant and work up a good brood uninterrupted.

Some things, she was coming to realize, were just better in the sun.

Neela speared her fork into her eggs right as the door chimed. The soft gasps behind her was the first clue that the person who'd just walked in was one, a regular, and two, most likely part of the angel's crew.

A small ember of hope struck flint in her chest. Did he know she was there? Had he finally come to see her?

"Neela."

Aaand that ember promptly died on arrival but not before flicking its spark of curiosity northward.

Neela spun on her stool. "Chrome?"

Molly chose that moment to amble through the kitchen door and nearly spilled an entire pot of decaf on her foot when she stopped short. "Holy shit, you shaved! Thank *God*. Drea's been going through my facial moisturizer like crazy. Woman's too polite to tell you that neck carpet of yours was abrading her skin at the rate of most flesh-eating bacteria. Seriously, how much neck play do you two do before moving on to other areas? Actually, you know what?" Molly raised her hand and closed her eyes. "I don't want to know. Just glad to see you're looking more like yourself, and thanks for the new drinking glasses. You didn't have to get me new coffee mugs to go with them, though."

"Yeah, I kinda did. And, uh, thanks," Chrome muttered, then wiped a hand over his clean-shaven face. Neela didn't miss the way he lingered longer than normal at his jawline, checking for overlooked hairs, or the way his newly shaven cheeks showed off the blush that had started to creep up toward his hairline.

"It's nice to see you again," Neela said.

"Same."

"Want to sit down?" Neela offered him the stool next to her.

"Nah, I won't be here long. I came to give you a ride."

"A ride? I don't need to go anywhere just yet. I was going to hang out a bit longer, maybe see if Molly needed help with anything."

"Oh, I'm good! Totally good. A thousand million times good. Have fun!" Molly smiled and twirled her aproned ass back into the kitchen. What the hell was that about?

Chrome nodded toward her food and the sole remaining toast crust. "You finished?"

"Um. Yes . . . but—"

"There's someone who asked me to bring you to him."

Neela's stomach bottomed out. Only one person would make that kind of request of Chrome, and only if they'd finally—

"I can see the wheels spinning, and yeah, Rhode and I talked. Worked things out. He made me make sense of a few things, and I helped him make sense of a few others."

Neela shook her head, as much to shake away the emotion as to portray her disbelief. "You guys are really okay? He told you everything?"

Chrome shrugged. "Okay is kind of a baseline marker for what we are. I predict there are a couple of dude-bonding sweat sessions in our future, because I don't think I'll be able to fully hear some of the details he still needs to share with me unless I expend a shit ton of energy so I'm not tempted to blow up a mountain, but yeah, for now, we're good. And speaking of good," he said, swiping a cinnamon crumb muffin from under the cloche on the counter, "your boy's only got another twenty minutes in him, max, before he starts lighting up my phone asking me if you're okay, so if you want to see him, we better get a move on. I can't fly you where we're going, and the traffic downtown is shit. A few snowflakes and the tourists in this town forget about the all-wheel drive they paid extra for or how to use it."

Neela swiped the last bit of toast, popped it into her mouth, grabbed her coat, and was already out the door before Chrome took his first bite of muffin.

CHAPTER 31

The roof of the private parking garage had turned into as much of a winter wonderland as Neela could imagine. The snowfall had gone from a dusting to slightly more serious in under an hour, with a solid two inches already coating the pavement. All the levels below were crammed full of self-important cars in compact spaces, while the roof was unapologetically barren.

Barren save for Rhode, who stood in front of a silver luxury-class SUV, complete with temporary tags and extra shine on the tires.

But the brightest shine was coming off the angel who leaned against it. With his woolen trench coat's collar popped, fists in his pockets, and blazing eyes on Neela, he looked like a man of many secrets, as well as a man of many regrets.

"Call me if he's an asshole," Chrome shouted from the window.

"Um, okay," Neela murmured absentmindedly while Rhode just nodded to Chrome in a manner that simultaneously said *Thanks* and *Really?*

And then they were alone. Nothing between them except for

several dozen feet worth of snow-covered asphalt and even more unspoken secrets.

"Hi," she said, uncertain how to proceed. "So, what's this—"

The snow swirled around her in a flurry of confusion. Rhode's wings arced to the sides as he half flew, half ran toward her. She was yanked up against his chest and absorbing his kiss before the next word even had time to form in her throat.

There was a consuming comfort to being wrapped in his warmth again, as if his touch was the only one capable of chasing away the permanent chill that had followed her around her whole life. And when he opened his coat and held her closer to him with both wool and wings, he claimed the part of her that had always yearned to be truly declared by another.

When the kiss broke, it was with a promise of reckoning, and she truly had no earthly idea which Rhode would speak to her next. The chilly, business-like seraph who looked at her as a means to an end? The sardonic, pained seraph who resented her for the hand she'd had in his torment by virtue of who she was? Or the wicked and wonderful seraph who, in precious private moments, called her his and prized her as one of his family?

Neela wasn't entirely sure she was ready for the whiplash, but she was most definitely ready for him, and if he thought he was going to call her out there to freeze her butt off, kiss her senseless, and pretend what they shared was only surface level, then he had another thing—

"Why did I ever think I could keep myself away from you?" he breathed against her mouth before stealing another soft kiss.

"Because men are dumb," she murmured against his chest. "At least according to mortal TV."

He huffed out a small laugh. "Mortals are dumb, but they have the benefit of occasionally dying before they're hit with the consequences of their actions. It's a bit different when you're an immortal and time is just another length of rope with which to—"

Neela leaned back and put her fingers over his mouth. "Can we just not go there with the death analogies?"

Rhode kissed her fingers and curled them close to his chest. "Agreed. But I'd like to ask you something as well."

"Shoot."

"Will you forgive me?"

Neela blinked. "There's nothing to forgive."

"No, let me finish. I *must* say this." He took a deep breath and looked back at the car a moment before giving her his full attention. "Chrome helped me buy that. It's my first purchase as a citizen of the modern world. I meant to surprise you with it."

"So that's where you were this week, with Chrome. That's wonderful."

Then his gaze darkened and took on that intense look she'd seen from him too often. "It's all because of you."

"Me?"

Rhode's wings shimmered away as he escorted her toward the vehicle. "You made me realize that I can never have a future without letting go of the past."

"If anyone had a damn good reason for not letting go of their past, it'd be you."

"No, hear me." Then he gentled his tone. "Please. I was using what had been done to me as an excuse and was content to allow my fury to burn hot enough to propel me into whatever future I never expected to live long enough to have. Until you came along and made me realize that hot air only lasts for so long."

Neela shook her head, a bit overwhelmed at his admission. "I didn't do anything."

He lifted her chin higher. "Oh, little demon, you know that's not true. And that is *my* fault for making you feel that way." Then he opened the passenger door for her, and the eagerness in his eyes was bright enough to light ten city blocks. "I'd like to share this world with you, to discover it together, if that is what you'd like as well."

She didn't know whether it was the temperature outside or the promise of heat inside, but her butt found that leather in a speed that surprised even herself. Then he climbed in the driver's seat beside her and closed the door. His hands found hers again, and she remembered how much she missed this. How much she missed *him*.

The smooth plastic shell hitting her palm was a surprise.

"What's this?"

"Your key."

"*My* key?"

But he was serious. Dead serious. "This vehicle is yours. Not mine. If we're going to figure this living-life-aboveground thing out together, then I need you right here with me, learning and driving and hopefully *not* skidding out, as I may have almost done on the way over here." A gentle tease lifted the corner of his lips, and it made her heart swell.

"You're really doing this. You're not kidding, are you? This is really mine?"

Rhode nodded. "Paperwork's in the glove box. Permanent plates will be available in a few weeks. This private garage is one of many places you can park. Bronze actually owns the property, along with several storage units for his bikes. You need oil changes, tire rotations, or anything so much as a car wash, you let me know and I'll take care of it. But nothing would make me so happy as to figure this thing out together, not as partners or roommates but as soul bonds. *True* soul bonds."

Neela's throat tightened with a pang that threatened to warn her off what she still needed to do, what she needed to tell him. Her lip quivered beneath the weight of his confession, though, of what the small key fob in her hand not only symbolized but the future it would steer her toward.

A future with Rhode in it, with the angels, the mates, a home, all of it wrapped up neatly beneath the blanket of only her second snowfall ever. And once they finally defeated Cyro and reclaimed the relic, they'd have time to talk about what was to come. Crawling before walking. Parking before racing.

For the first time in her existence, time didn't seem like such a somber sentence, not with Rhode by her side to hold her hand should she stumble.

We have time. He's giving me time and asking for it in return.

It was a promise she swore she wouldn't waste. Later, she'd sit him down, hold *his* hands, and speak the truth her heart needed to tell him. Lift the final weight so they could both soar.

Until then, she'd seize every moment with this angel.

So she chucked the key fob into the console, threw her arms around him, and captured his lips in a searing kiss.

NEELA'S WEIGHT in his arms was a comfort his body had begged for. He hadn't known the joys of such tight confines as the front seats of cars until he'd crawled in next to her and was hit with the concentrated scent of hyssop and earthly vitality. It was *her* scent. A smell that would forever be etched onto his skin and scored into his soul as uniquely hers. It enveloped every part of the car, blanketing his senses and driving him mad. The heat blowing from the vents didn't help, either. All it did was tease the ends of her hair, offering up her charms like the distracting scarf of a belly dancer.

The entire scenario was a game he'd never learned to play, and he was gambling with something far more precious than money.

Many times, desperation had threatened to get the better of him, but he'd always been able to, if not outsmart, at least outlast it. When it came to Neela, however, he had taken an undue risk, and now that he'd finally gotten his head out of the sand and secured it in the direction of what mattered most, he was worried he might have been too late.

But then his arms were around her again, and he was fervently sipping from her mouth, every logical thought casting itself off to the dancing snowflakes beyond the windows.

The heat of the soul bond flared to life beneath his skin, and the fury of it forced a groan into her mouth.

"You know," she said, breathless, "remind me to thank Chrome for the extra leg room."

Rhode unzipped her coat as she helped him shuck out of his. "Remind me to show you what happens when you mention another man's name while I have my hands on you."

"Oh, fine. Very well." Neela leaned back, feigning annoyance with an exasperation that refused to meet her eyes.

He took the opening for what it was and quickly scooped her onto his lap, yelps and all. Her weight was the blanket his soul would never grow tired of. Large thighs filled his palms as he slid her impossibly closer against him, until his straining cock begged to close the few inches separating them. She wore an orange-and-black plaid knee-length skirt that tied at the waist and would have been shreds on the floor if another idea hadn't occurred to him first.

"I want to see you come apart in this car, little demon. Can you do that for me?"

Neela's breaths were thick and heated and pulled her delicious breasts higher to the edge of her scoop-neck sweater. "That doesn't sound like that big of an ask," she said, undoing the buttons of his silk shirt.

"Hold a moment," he said, offering a delicate kiss to the tops of her breasts while he stilled her questing fingers. "I want something first."

Her sly eyebrow lifted. "Yes?"

But the realization soon lit her face when his fingers traced a map of salvation up the inside of her thigh. He held her against him as she squirmed and writhed, but he refused to let her free, no matter how many times she pouted that damn lower lip and tried to shimmy around his arms.

When he found the barrier of fabric guarding his treasure, he slipped one finger beneath it and moaned when it came away slick and weeping.

Then he froze when her hands caged his face and those arresting gold eyes bore into him. "Together," she breathed.

It was the word that course-corrected his journey onto a path he always needed to follow. With her slim eyebrows raised and that hopeful smile lighting her features, searching for the same in his, he somehow knew this was different.

They found each other's mouths, not with the ravenous pace of earlier but with the gentle rhythm they'd fall into when they were alone in bed and time was inconsequential. Hours were measured in happiness and hushed breaths instead of their proximity to the approaching sun.

So he slowed his pace. Slowed and savored it, letting her free his arousal while he slid her underwear to the side. Neela sank down on him, and he hissed against her mouth. The prior urgency of harried lovers ebbed away and was replaced by the gentle support of one who'd never let her go. The sensation was unlike anything he'd ever felt before. They kissed as they rocked, moving their tongues in time to the erotic pulls of their bodies, and he, again, saw the genius of their confines. There was no room for questions, no room for elaborate foreplay. There was only room for them and what each could call out of the other while cradling them close.

It was enough to make his chest hurt and his soul cry with the beauty of it all.

Neela quickened her pace, and Rhode encouraged her higher with one hand on her backside while the other cradled her head lest she bump it on the low ceiling. Their kisses grew sloppier, their clothes more wrinkled. Neela's sweater had fallen low enough to reveal more of the mounded breasts he would close his eyes and dream about long after she'd left him for the day.

"Fuck, Neela," he groaned, touching his forehead to hers. "Soon, little demon. I fear it'll be too soon." Rhode's balls tightened farther, and he began to lift up into her, chasing the tempo of her rising gasps and quivering thighs.

When Neela didn't say anything, he pulled back to look at her and nearly came undone. Pleasure painted her features into the shining portrait of the woman who'd have his heart forever. Heart, body, soul, whatever she wanted, it was hers. *He* was hers, while the rest of the world could fall away beyond the SUV's foggy windows and the sleepy snowstorm swirling around them.

The realization punched through the base of his spine, and they both cried out as he released into her tightening core. Ripple after ripple sent tremors along the landscapes of both their skins. There was no beginning or end for either of them anymore. What was had finally been put to bed, and what they were would carry him on for as many years as the mages gave him.

When Neela collapsed against him, sated and adding her exhausted breaths to the heated cabin air, he held her more tightly against his chest.

Soul to soul.

Heart to heart.

So close that neither of their pasts could ever pry them apart again.

And come tomorrow, when they finally lured Cyro out of whatever hole he'd been hiding in, Rhode would make damn sure of it.

Neela couldn't figure out whether the stress headache currently digging its talons into her temples was due to cramming her hair into the knit hat she'd been encouraged to wear or due to the reason she had to wear the thing in the first place. The hood to her white puffer coat was calling her name, its faux-fur trim hanging off her shoulders in a mournful beggar's pose as she itched to throw it over her head.

But the hood, however preferable for her comfort, wouldn't have made her the identifiable target she needed to be. She could hardly find fault in the argument, especially as she was crowded among the far too many joyful kids and their huddled-together parents beneath the pseudo-snowstorm-turned-preemptive-snow-day. All over a few inches of snow that, according to Chrome, any decent set of snow tires could have handled.

And she'd thought New Englanders weren't so scared away by the white stuff that school districts had to call a snow day the night before.

Tourist towns were a different breed, apparently.

The sudden school closures had turned into the perfect opportunity, however, to try and draw Cyro out of hiding. The municipal park complex in Aurora was a massive space that housed everything from hiking trails to a dozen sports fields to playgrounds and, most delightedly for the kiddos, the most kick-ass hill that sported the additional benefit of being well-lit at night due to its proximity to the high school soccer team's practice field. It doubly served as the perfect spot for parents to go and sit on nearby bleachers while their kids went sledding and the adults got to have precious private moments with their travel mugs full of hot toddies—or coffee, if anyone inquired as to what was actually in the tumblers.

Bonus points for the town's rec workers, who figured out how to blast music through the speakers to mark the occasion of Aurora's first snow day of the season (which, again, hadn't actually happened yet).

The employees had no idea they were also scoring the soundtrack to the demon ruler's potential arrival on stage, otherwise known as Neela's personal panic attack.

No matter how many conversations she'd had with the sentinels or how many times Rhode had held her hands and assured her that no harm would come to any of the mortals on the field, she had a hard time absorbing the potential outcome. She was nothing if not a *seeing is believing* type of person. Otherwise, who the hell would decide to grow a damn greenhouse underground if they hadn't seen it already on YouTube?

Sane people wouldn't. Only desperate people.

So, she'd needed some convincing on that front even though the logic, however much of a high-priced gamble it seemed, made sense. The more public the area, the less possibility that things could erupt into a battle that would head south real fast. Cyro wanted the general population of mortals to know about demons as much as he wanted to give up his quest to destroy the Empyrean.

It was a safety-in-numbers game, which meant Neela's most identifiable feature, her hair, had to be visible enough for the charmers to find her but also be hidden enough to blend in.

All that she could get behind, but that had been *before* Rhode had welcomed her into the safety of that brand-new vehicle, plunked the key into her hand, and effectively stitched together all the broken bits inside her. For the first time in her life, she could actually *feel* what it meant to belong to someone, to have someone belong to her. There was a magnetism to it that no Internet video or role-playing game could have ever portrayed the truth of. She realized that now. That sensation was so brilliantly vital, it was a wonder how she ever thought there was safety behind avatars in the first place.

And she was itching to get back to that life. But first, she had to make sure her previous life didn't follow her there.

Neela sat on the cold bleachers and pretended to watch the children play. While her face remained pinned toward the hill, the shadows around the complex drew the bulk of her attention.

All the angels were there, spread out and armed to impossible lengths—lengths she seriously wished they could avoid. While the charmers loved the flare of battle, Cyro loved the flare of a different sort of battle: one with words and far too much exposition to be an efficient use of time. But that was what happened when an immortal ruler had a captive audience and enjoyed the sound of his voice almost as much as the screams of others.

By design, Neela didn't know where any of the angels were located, including Rhode, only that they were closer than she could imagine. Her soul bond had assured her that she'd be out of there as soon as Cyro surfaced.

It's not your fight, little demon. And I'll never allow it to be. Never again.

Rhode had offered her no shortage of assurances that they

had a plan for every possible outcome, with tricks up their sleeves Cyro couldn't possibly know about.

Neela breathed out and momentarily let the cloud of her breath distract her from the mental acrobatics she couldn't seem to keep her mind from.

"It'll be over soon," she whispered to herself as she huddled farther into her coat. "Not much longer."

"I couldn't agree more."

The nearby serpentine voice slithered down the side of her neck and jerked Neela's head to the right. A woman with long blond hair sporting a fashionable lavender fleece ear band and matching winter coat pursed her lips over the rim of a travel mug, but no breath fogged around her. When she inhaled again, she smiled at Neela, and gold irises flashed a different sort of welcome. Hunkered in the shadows at the corner of the bleachers, her tall muscular form began to change shape. Limbs thickened to masculine proportions, and hair shimmered out of sight to reveal the charmer's familiar gold and teal tattoos, along with the two gold bands around his throat.

Elite, not mystic.

Neela schooled her features so the relief wouldn't show. If Cyro sent warrior charmers to claim her, then he still didn't know that magic could harm her there. Just like Rhode suspected.

Neela pinned her shoulders back and prepared to dive into the script she and Rhode had come up with. "I know why you're here, and if Cyro wants—"

"You have no idea what he wants," the elite fired back.

Neela stumbled a moment, surprised by the interruption but not the harshness, then quickly gathered her thoughts again. "What I was saying, asshole, was that if Cyro wants me at all, I'll come willingly."

The charmer's eyes squinted, but that time, he held his tongue.

Yeah, that's right. This is my *playbook we're running. I'm not the wallflower you remember.*

"I'll meet with him and do so without restraint, if that's what he wants, but it can't be here. It's got to be on the other side of the park, away from all these people. No scene on my end if there'll be no scene on his."

"The mortals have changed you," the thing mused. "Someone somewhere made the mistake of letting you think you have any say in what happens to you."

"And someone somewhere doesn't give a shit because you've been ordered to bring me to Cyro." Neela leaned forward. "So you'll do it because while my choices may be limited at the moment, they definitely have an impact on what he'll do to you if you don't deliver. Funny," she said, resting her knuckles under her chin. "I guess that means I'm the one who has a say in what happens to *you*."

The charmer lunged for her, snapping his teeth, but she just put her hand up. "I can't be harmed, remember? So save the aggression for someone who will be impressed by it and let's get this over with."

As Neela was escorted to the far, far, *far* side of the park by the elite and two more charmers who slid out from the crowd to join the party, she kept checking in with her racing heart, giving it all the pep talks needed to keep powering her through whatever bravery it had mistakenly blessed her with.

In no world had she ever stood up for herself against her kind, let alone rap them across the knuckles with her newfound take-no-shit temperament.

Which, unfortunately, also had a time limit. She had, at best, another ten minutes of bravado left in her before the cracks in her facade would start to show, and she'd have no choice but to bow out and let Rhode and the sentinels take over.

And she *really* didn't want to do that. She'd just found her home, her family. Did she want them to think she couldn't pull her own weight, especially with her sire?

She could do this. She had to.

They reached the end of the unused field, which was far enough away from the meat of the park that the music had become a faint suggestion among the snowflakes. There was no one to greet them at first. Just mounds of untrodden snow piling around thick tree trunks.

Then the snow around one of the trees began to shimmer and move, until it was pulled into the tall shape of a man with broad shoulders, no hair, and the sunken face of the person who'd had a starring role in so many of her nightmares.

"Neela." Her name on his lips drew fresh score marks down her skin. "So nice of you to meet me. I've missed you."

She didn't say anything, only nodded her acknowledgment while she frantically scanned the fit of his black three-piece suit for any bulges or asymmetrical folds that might indicate the hidden relic.

"Do you have anything to say for yourself?"

That caught her off guard. "For what?"

"For forsaking the life I gave you in favor of some mortal existence we both know you could never truly survive in."

"I've been surviving just fine." *C'mon, Neela, look! Where is it? Where would he keep it?*

His slacks were freshly pressed and tailored perfectly to his muscular frame, as they always were, with not even the front leg crease out of alignment. The overcoat he wore was open but not particularly bulky. Nothing to indicate stuffed pockets.

"Oh, I highly doubt that. You know, of all the beings ever created on this rock, mortal humans are the least welcoming. Did you know that? And yet, for some reason, they insist other-wise, even going so far as to applaud other species for accepting those not like them into their packs. Those asinine tales of golden retrievers becoming mothers to cheetahs or some abandoned marmoset being adopted by capuchin monkeys and raised as their own. It's always the mammals, mind you, never the sharks or the scorpions. Ever wonder why that is?"

"Couldn't say." Neela squinted against the meager moonlight as Cyro shifted into his usual pacing. She tried to catch a glimpse inside his overcoat, to see whether there was a pocket she'd missed or some sort of necklace.

Nothing. He wore nothing to indicate he had anything on him other than an abundance of arrogance.

Her stomach began twisting into knots. *Please be there. Please.*

"Because *true* predators know that even creatures born from your own body wouldn't hesitate to turn their back on you if it so suited them, let alone ones you adopt as your own." Cyro drew closer to her, and his expression faltered from that familiar haughtiness to an almost stilted sadness. "You were the closest thing to true kin I ever had."

"And you tried to kill me. Like, *a lot.*"

Then his brows drew down, and a mask of quiet fury settled into place. "Do you know what it's like to live in darkness for so long? To be the first of your kind, the *only* of your kind, but relegated to depths only as deep as the shadows would allow? As *they* would allow?" He cast a finger toward the sky, his chest heaving, puffing out to a size that no calm thought ever followed. "And then I created you." He drew his arms out toward her as though she was some prized showpiece. "Born from my body, crafted from my magic, but elementally committed to hijacking the source of the very beings who dared to put creatures like you and me in a box in the first place." A remnant of something flashed in his golden eyes, something so similar to the longing she'd seen on Rhode's face and the faces of everyone she'd met since.

It was the look of hope right before the cold wave of disappointment snuffed it out.

"You were supposed to be the answer to my sentence. The

one being who could infiltrate the Empyrean and dismantle it so you and I and all the other charmers who came after you could finally live freely in a world without light." Then his face fell and, with it, his arms. "I was that golden retriever offering you a life unlike any other, and instead of embracing it, you abandoned me."

A flash of something smooth and white peeked out from his wrist as he lowered his arm, and she sucked in a breath. *The relic! I was right!*

Neela's mind spun as she tugged on her ear and tried to keep him talking. "I wouldn't call it abandonment. You had no use for me. I didn't have any powers. I couldn't do what you wanted."

"I wanted to live!" he screamed at her. "I wanted to live with someone like me, beside me, born *of* me, who could do what I could not. But instead, all you did, day in and day out, was remind me of every single thing *you* could not do. How your existence, the existence *I* gave you, was better suited for anything other than what I could provide for you. A cheetah who preferred the open spaces of the Savannah instead of the canary I needed in the coal mines." His gaze darkened. "But I don't like my pets escaping, no matter how damaged they are, and I have built a far better cage for you than the one you remember. Enough of this nonsense. It's time to return where you belong."

The rope appeared around her neck before Neela had a chance to scream. Cyro pulled *hard,* and the breath from her lungs squeezed out of her in raspy ribbons. A portal flashed behind him, and a dozen or so charmers walked out, each carrying more of those cargo net guns, in addition to several other firearms she didn't recognize.

What she *did* recognize was the relic, white, fang-like, and curving around Cyro's wrist like a crescent-moon bangle.

Neela curled her fingers around the rope and fought for purchase against the smooth nylon fibers, finding no give whatsoever. In front of her, a firing squad of charmers aimed their guns at her and held the funnels of their launchers in stacked positions to ensure maximum coverage, all saying the same message.

If she tried to run, they'd find her.

Cyro tugged on the rope while holding his other hand high and squeezing it into a fist. "Now."

Neela braced for the telltale clicks of triggers, the yank on her neck—

A sharp whine cut through the night, and the rope at her neck went lax. Air rushed into her lungs as she chased the track of the sound. On the ground, a gleaming titanium arrow staked the severed tactical rope to the snow-packed earth.

The sky erupted after that.

Several sets of metallic wings dive-bombed through the snow and let loose a hail of angel fire into the demons charging toward her. The fiery bullets and projectiles lit up the flailing bodies like the grand finale of a fireworks celebration. Those who weren't thrashing from the fire had dropped to the snow, wasting time while they tried to pull out weapons that would work on the angels.

Meanwhile, a certain set of wings had yet to materialize. Neela assessed the arrow at her feet again and smiled. Despite the metal, she'd recognize the fire engulfing the arrowhead anywhere. Its heat was something that would never harm her.

Then Rhode's boots hit the snow at her side. He threw the bow he'd been holding over his back and urgently grabbed her to his chest. "Are you all right?"

"I am now. But Cyro has the relic. It's on his—"

A bolt of green magic speared through the clearing and sliced across the ground where Neela and Rhode stood, spraying snow everywhere and sending them both flying in different directions.

Neela's back hit a tree, and her head scraped against the

frozen bark. When she landed in the snow, she tried to move her body, but it was like dragging her limbs through sand. Once she finally got her knees under her, she managed to sit back and winced.

Crimson drops began to dapple the snow around her knees. Neela's hand flew to the back of her head where her neck met her scalp, and she let out a withered groan. A small patch of bare skin greeted her fingers where hair should be. When she pulled her hand away, blood came with it.

"Now *that* is quite an interesting development."

Neela screamed as Cyro grabbed her by the hair and lifted her to her feet.

In front of her, Rhode sprang up, kamas already in hand, rhodium armor rippling over his tense body. "Fight me. Fight *me*, you asshole! She's not worth it."

The anger in Rhode's voice was expected, but it didn't lessen the blow of his words.

He doesn't mean that. He's trying to fight for you.

Cyro grinned. "You know, it's funny you should bring up the subject of her worth because, while I'm nothing if not a truth-teller, I'm afraid the same can't be said of our dear Neela. You see, it seems she has been telling some tall tales. For instance, I never knew she was so vulnerable aboveground in the mortal lands. My goodness, can you imagine the agita it would have saved me to just have killed her here outright all those years ago? What a missed opportunity." His face twisted into a scowl, but something far more sinister danced in his eyes. "And so, I would be remiss letting another tale go by. Tell me, *Axtar*, do you still think she'll be worth it once you find out that *she* was the one who told me to do the rhodium experimentation on you in the first place?"

CHAPTER 33

I f it hadn't been for the very vital services required to keep Rhode's blood pumping and fire at the ready, his brain would have short-circuited. Just ground everything to a fucking halt because his neural synapses wouldn't have been able to make sense of two very important things: the words Cyro had just spoken or the stricken expression painting Neela's face with hues of abject horror and bitter remorse. The same kind of affliction common among anyone for whom lying was a way of life and not just a misinformed oopsie.

White-hot emotion warred with his rage, and for the first time in his immortal life, all courses of action eluded him. Shame replaced sense and flooded in fiery and furious on the heels of Cyro's bishop moving in for the kill while the bastard still had his hands on Rhode's queen. Around him, the faint sounds of battle faded into the background. Whatever charmers hadn't yet been dispatched were either flailing around at a good clip or were giving a few of the sentinels a halfway decent workout.

But far more of his brothers stood idle around him, with a stiff shock freezing their advances. Everyone waited for whoever was going to make a move next. Meanwhile, Neela kicked a heel out, trying to break free, but Cyro was faster, drawing a knife to her throat before her foot could even return to the ground.

Rhode's bow was in his hands, and a flaming arrow nocked and aimed at Cyro's skull. "I don't miss," he warned.

"Neither do I." Cyro narrowed his eyes and let the challenge permeate the air between them. "You know, I had every intention of killing you outright. I would have found your intelligence master eventually. One thing I know you have experience in is just how true of a concept *eventually* can be for immortals like us. *Eventually*, the pain will stop. *Eventually*, I'll find what I'm looking for. Or, as was the case with you, *eventually*, something will fall into my lap that has the potential to negate the other two. Neela was that eventuality."

Chrome joined Rhode at his side, with his guns serving as effortless extensions of his arms. "You don't need to hear this shit."

Behind Cyro, Titan and Iron flanked the demon ruler's back, while the rest of the angels finished off whichever charmers hadn't bothered to die quickly enough.

Iron swung his mace around in a circle, blue flames lighting the snowy arena like a fire dancer's taunt. "Give her up, asshole."

They were all waiting for Rhode, for any semblance of a sign that he was done chit-chatting because they all had other places to be. Cyro was one concentrated blast of angel fire away from being nothing more than a bad memory. Then they'd have the relic. Neela had already tugged at her earlobe and given the signal of what they'd all been hoping for. That she'd been right and Cyro had been arrogant enough to keep the artifact on his person.

But for the life of him, Rhode couldn't release that arrow. Not yet. He told himself it was because of the knife at Neela's throat and the way her panic made her too much of a liability, even for an expert marksman like him. One outburst or damn muscle twitch and he ran the risk of not being fast enough to kill Cyro before the bastard delivered on his own promise.

Rhode told himself all of those things, but the gnawing pit in his stomach hadn't started to fester until Cyro dangled a carrot of the truth in front of him.

Because Neela's face said it all, even as tears leaked from the corners of her eyes and her brows furrowed into pleading slants. But it wasn't until his gut had started to sour from churned-up bile that he knew.

Whatever Cyro had to say would be the truth, which wasn't just curiosity catnip for a former spy like him but basic intelligence, and the bastard had banked on it.

Rhode found Neela's eyes. "I trust you."

Mages, it was the truth, wasn't it? He *did* trust her, with his life, his brothers, but something about the stricken look on her face sent warning bells clamoring around in his skull.

"Rhode," she said, and the quiver in her voice nearly killed him. "Whatever he says, know that—"

"It will make things far more interesting than they already are," Cyro said. "Just like the idea Neela gave me when I had begun to grow tired of our . . . let's just say, time together."

The muscles at the back of Rhode's neck tightened against the memories that threatened to rise up.

Cyro reinforced his grip on the knife at her neck. "This most recent stint aboveground was hardly the first time she'd tried to escape, just her most successful."

Neela sucked in a sharp breath.

"Oh yes, I knew. That night before the experiments began, one of the mystics responsible for the enchantments on the angel's cell informed me you'd been spending a lot of time there, far more than necessary to just clean and feed the fool. So, I decided to pay you a visit. Do you remember what we talked about?"

"Please. You don't know what you're saying."

"I believe I recall the exchange exactly. I asked why you had taken such a keen interest in our prisoner, and you said you were simply curious. But when I told you that I had grown tired of his treatments and was thinking about changing course, that was when your behavior went from quiet and unassuming to quite concerned. I'd never seen you act in such a way before. So imagine my surprise when I had already retreated halfway down the hall and you came running out after me with an idea you just thought of that might help our progress." Sparks of delight flashed in Cyro's face as his mouth split into a vile smile. "It was *you* who then mentioned rhodium experimentation. What it might do to him, how it would meld with my magic and possibly create an ally of an enemy. *You* were the one to suggest physically altering his makeup, rather than relying on the corrosive metal defenses my mystics had been exhausting. Rhodium had not been a metal on my radar until you rattled off its properties, already well researched, I might add, and why they would change the game for the battle against the angels."

Every *you* was a fresh jagged slice across Rhode's heart, but when he scanned Neela's face for any sign of dissent, there was none. An answering thunder began to build in his ears, doing its level best to block out the pain trying to choke him.

"I was going to *leave* you!" she roared at Cyro, heedless of how close the knife got to her. Then she searched out Rhode's face again. "I had a plan, yes, but my plan was to finally escape *with* you. I was going to take you with me to the mortal lands. I was going to get us both out and save you! But then he found me in my room the night before I was planning to leave, and I panicked, Rhode. I panicked. What if I got caught with you? What would he do to you in retribution for my crime? So I came up with the most awful thing I could think of to revert Cyro's attention. I knew that whatever diversion I thought of had to play to the asshole's own brand of mental and physical warfare. Only then would he forget all about me so I could go back to being the invisible charmer I always was and take you with me when I left. I needed to first get him out of my hair, and that awful idea was the only thing I thought he'd believe."

She looked away, as if to find solace in the snow. "I got the idea from a video game. But it was never supposed to happen. It was too complex and far too outlandish compared to anything he'd tried before. I-I never expected him to call my bluff." Something like remorse softened her features, but Rhode was shaking too hard to make sense of it. "The next morning, I ran to your cell, prepared to get us both out of there, but the experiments had already begun, and I couldn't do anything to stop them or save you."

Rhode's bicep twitched as the bowstring slipped a notch and bit into the valley of his knuckles even harder. Beside him, Chrome had been stunned into silence, just like the others. Iron's mace slowed its rotation until it hung limply by his side.

Without him meaning to, Rhode's armor melted away, as if her very words were the only things corrosive enough to peel back the shell of the very thing she'd created.

For the first time in his life, the truth evaded him.

His head jerked from side to side in disbelief, and he had to lean on his brain to make his body move in ways his mouth could not. Fuck, his throat hurt, the damn thing tensing beneath the emotion that had surged up.

She'd . . . known?

In the distance, the faint tinkling melody of an ice cream truck rolling up to the crowd broke through the cloud of confusion in his mind. It was indistinct, almost an echo, but it was loud enough to catch the immortal ears of everyone there, including Cyro.

Recognition curled the demon ruler's lip before Rhode could understand what was happening. "Neela couldn't save you.

Didn't *want* to save you. Your fate was inevitable, just like the fate of all mortals."

Cyro let go of Neela's hair but kept the knife at her throat. In the span of a blink, the demon ruler conjured an electric orb of green magic in his hand and aimed it at the ice cream truck.

LOOK AT ME. Please look at me, Rhode.

But he didn't. Eyes that had burned white-hot a moment ago had deadened to the point of despair. Even against the bite of Cyro's knife, Neela tried to cast her soul out to him in some way, to convince him that she was telling the truth. However, instead of her mate absorbing the veracity of her words, they just pinged around the frozen tree trunks until they slammed back into her with the echoes of her mistakes.

She had so much to say, so much to explain, but there was no time. She'd foolishly used up that commodity and instantly regretted every opportunity she'd had to tie him to the bed and force him to hear what her heart needed him to know.

Instead, her fucking sire had known and managed to manipulate her yet again.

Neela refused to look at Cyro and tried to find a way to reach Rhode, but when his armor shimmered away, taking the light with it, only darkened disappointment remained across his cold features. Rage had turned to resignation, and his ferocity seemed to peter out along with their shared spark. Questions replaced concerns as her heart shattered into a thousand pieces.

Then the soft jangling call of an ice cream truck hit her ear, and even though it was a good distance away, a new fear took over. An ice cream truck meant lines of kids and parents. Huddled groups of souls en masse.

Easy pickings.

The pressure holding the knife at her throat lessened ever so slightly, and her stomach sank into her heels. Cyro had just connected the same dots she had.

He finally freed her hair, and the blood rushing back to her scalp nearly caused her to pass out. Green light flared over her shoulder, and an orb of magic sat poised in Cyro's palm, aimed at his target.

Shit. He's going to kill those families. He's going to—

Her boot nudged something stuck in the snow. When she looked down, the magic's green hue illuminated Rhode's arrow, the one he'd used to sever the rope around her neck from earlier. The one still infused, albeit dimly, with his angel fire.

The plan punched into her before she had time to analyze it or look for confirmation in all the discerning eyes that now pointedly evaded hers.

Cyro wound his arm back, and the sheen from the relic's smooth surface beneath his sleeve winked its presence under the magic's green glow. The thing was still cuffed around his wrist and peeked out like a forgotten mass-market paperback in a sea of hardcovers.

The arrow was in her hand an instant later. She gripped that thing, pulled down Cyro's wrist, yanked the relic free of his arm, and struck—herself.

The arrowhead sliced cleanly across her forearm, but both she and Cyro roared with the power that poured out of her. The bright light of her soul bond's healing magic forced them to the ground while she gritted her teeth against it, but it was Rhode's fire that had found its mark. Flames leaped from the arrow and connected with Cyro's pant leg. Then combustion did what combustion did. The demon ruler cried out as fire found skin, right as the pulsing energy of Neela's light shot him and his magic into the snowy sky.

Somewhere, someone said her name. Or some version of it. She couldn't be sure because a vibrating wail mingled with the sounds of Cyro's screams. Hands were on her, lifting her, checking her arm, her neck, the back of her head, but she didn't track any of them. She was too focused on the portal above that Cyro had somehow managed to open. A deafening whine and a pop followed, and then the bastard was swallowed up by the night sky.

"Neela!"

That time, her name came through loud and clear, despite the ringing in her ears, but something was off about it.

When she was finally pulled to her feet, she realized why it sounded wrong.

Rhode hadn't spoken it. Chrome, instead, had been the one to check her over and throw her behind his winged back while he scanned for any more surprises.

One by one, the rest of the angels cleared the scene and joined them.

But not Rhode. He was already gone.

CHAPTER 34

A scaly slab of lichen-riddled bark hung off the giant white oak tree as yet another mark of shame against the hundred-foot-tall behemoth. Over the past several weeks that Rhode had come to visit the thing at the North Woods Arboretum, the poor tree hadn't improved much. At least, based on what he knew of trees, which was not a whole lot. The silver-tinged bark looked more flaky than fertile, but judging by the dieback on some of its lower branches, mites or other insects had been having a field day on its insides.

The giant fucking red X spray-painted across its midsection also served as a massive giveaway that this sucker was slated for the chipper.

That was new. Hadn't been there the week before, nor the temporary placard detailing what would be coming into that part of the exhibit come springtime.

Because, of course, the mortals had to wait until the ground thawed before they could remove the tree and replace it with whatever pretty things people loved that didn't need to be sullied by complicated feelings about longevity, perseverance, and acceptance despite appearance that the old tree conjured up.

Never had Rhode sympathized with a plant before or seen so much of himself in how hard the thing was fighting, despite getting constantly kicked between the roots just when one of its struggling branches had managed to show a bit of green for the first time in years.

But efforts didn't matter, only actions, and just like the old oak slated for execution, longevity meant jack shit, as Chrome would say, if cancer decided to join the party.

Rhode fingered the peeling, dying bark and ripped it free of its tether. There wasn't even a faint suggestion of green beneath. Nothing to offer appreciation for him removing the scab so the fresh stuff below could get its fair shot at some sunlight. If there *was* any health left in the thing, the oak had little interest in making him aware of it.

Even the damn tree couldn't trust him with its secrets. What a theme his life had taken on.

Two sets of approaching footsteps crunched through the hard pack of snow behind him. "Do you want to buy her a drink first before you start feeling her up like that?"

Chrome's question was the sandpaper rubdown his skin had been avoiding since Neela had declared not only to his enemies but also his brothers that her trust did not go both ways.

"I wish to be alone," Rhode replied.

"Too bad." Iron's curt exclamation was delivered with the authority of one used to being simultaneously unchallenged and also one who was really, really good when some fool did make the mistake and stepped up to challenge him. Either way, those two words held an expectation that Rhode was *so* not in the mood to debate.

Chrome hinged over at the hips and squinted to read a nearby placard on what Rhode thought was a red maple, but then the sentinel shook his head in surrender when he got to the genus' Latin name and popped a square of peppermint gum into his mouth. "Neela's moving out."

Rhode looked to the sky and clasped his hands behind his back to keep his composure at the mention of her name. "I can see why she would want to."

"Into her own apartment."

Rhode had to pause to check that his spine was still attached to his neck when he whipped his head in Chrome's direction. "What?"

"The den wasn't for her, she said." Chrome held his palms up to stop the questions Rhode had at the ready. "And before you go grilling me for details, I'm telling you right now that I don't have any. I only know it at all because Drea asked me to do a background check on the property management company that runs the apartment complex Neela's interested in. Aside from that, I'm spectacularly out of the loop except for, and I quote, 'when it comes to lifting the heavy shit on move-in day.' Seriously, those two have developed some sort of secret code language that even I can't decipher." The flush of red tingeing his complexion was the only giveaway to how frustrated the angel was over that fact.

To hell with it. Rhode let his shared aggravation come out in the question he'd just been told was pointless to ask. "Why are you letting her leave?"

Chrome scoffed. "I'm a thousand percent certain no one's *letting* her do anything."

"Why do you care?" Ever the astute asshole, Iron was brutally direct and deserving of one of those marksmanship badges the American military gave out to its most lethal snipers.

Rhode dodged the question about as well as he'd been dodging every thought of Neela since she'd revealed, while in his enemy's arms no less, the personal role she'd had in his torture and how she hadn't bothered to share any of that with her soul bond. All the times he'd been with her, around her, fucking *inside* her, and she still kept secrets from him. *About* him.

As a spy, he would have appreciated her ability to hold out on dispelling information if not for the fact that he was at the center of said information.

No, she'd waited to air those particular gems until she had no other choice. Until she'd been exposed and had nowhere else to turn except toward the truth.

"I care that she's well. That's all," he said, schooling the emotion from his features.

The large angel folded his arms over his chest and stared at him blandly. "Bullshit. You're more butthurt over how she ripped the Band-Aid off, rather than why she might have had it on in the first place."

"Escape and evade, Iron. That's what she was about. The rest of it is just a bunch of pretty pictures. Lies. More smoke and mirrors." Neela had proven as much when she'd flung out that sad sack story about wanting to escape with him.

And the worst part of it all was that he'd wanted to believe her, as ludicrous as it sounded. But no matter how many times he tried to picture his steel-backed soul bond sneaking through Cyro's compound to try and save them both from what was coming for them, another image weighed equally hot and heavy in his mind.

One of Neela telling Cyro exactly what he wanted to hear to save herself.

Which was the lie?

Rhode waved the image away. "Look, I appreciate the welfare check, but I prefer to be alone— *Oomph!*" Hard-packed snow found its way into every orifice responsible for getting oxygen to the more vital parts of him. Shaking his head and spitting out the cold stuff, he turned, nostrils flaring, only to lunge behind the dying oak when a snowball the size of a small watermelon careened toward him. "What the fuck, Chrome?" he yelled, peeking his head around the trunk.

But the angel was already bending down, grunting beneath the weight of—goddammit—*another* snowball. Or to be more accurate, a snow boulder.

"You keep saying stupid and hypocritical shit, I'ma keep heaving this white stuff at you with the goal of eventually packing in your backward brain with so much cold that it has no choice but to shut down the hysterics and see things through the eyes of survival."

"Avoiding you two *is* survival!" Rhode threw himself behind the oak again when Iron double-fisted two snowpacks and sent them flying at his head. *Wonderful.* Despite the worst of the snow hitting the tree, there was still plenty of impact to make him grunt and cause his back teeth to clench. When it was clear those two had no intention of giving up, Rhode threw his hands up and spit out words of surrender. "All right already. Enough! I get it, okay? I get it."

When Rhode finally came out from behind the tree, arms behind his head like some hostage, it was to the soured and thoroughly pissed-off expressions of two sentinels who clearly would have had no problem burying him beneath the snow just so they could come out on top.

Mages, he was so tired of this. Tired of questioning everyone's intentions, including his own. For once in his life, he'd happily carve out key organs just to be told the truth without coercion or tricks.

What a lousy spy he'd become, expecting the truth so easily from others while being too exhausted to serve it up himself. Irony was the karmic bitter pill that was constantly getting shoved down his throat, and he'd never quite developed a taste for the stuff.

Rhode wasn't entirely surprised that Chrome was the first to step forward, hands blessedly empty of snowballs, thank the mages.

"Since we're on the subject of survival, let's pick at that scab for a bit. Here's a newsflash for ya: you *can't* survive without your soul bond. Period. End of story." Then the angel jabbed a blunt finger at Rhode's chest. "You, more than anyone, know how important secrets are to survival. I wouldn't have branded you as my seraphim commander if you didn't know that truth."

Iron cracked a jaw and grunted his agreement. "And if it wasn't for you and your secrets, Rhode, Chrome might not be here. Hell, none of us might even be here if you'd been one breath weaker." Dark sincerity floated in the shadows of the sentinel's mismatched eyes, conjuring up memories and alternatives none of them wanted to contemplate. "But you weren't. And neither was Neela."

Aaand there they were again. Back at the beginning of the very ride that had made him so goddamn nauseous that it'd seemed safer to stick to the carnival games than to go anywhere near the subject and admit how chickenshit he was.

But coward or no, some things still hadn't changed.

"She lied to me."

"To save herself. To save *you*," Chrome pointed out.

"But that's just it. I have no idea what's truth or fiction. Do I believe that Cyro's own get had a plan to rescue me all along? That she merely got caught and *that* was why I had to face the consequences of her farce-turned-reality? Or was it all part of a plan to finally win favor in the eyes of the one being who never returned it? For weeks, I have come here and spun all sorts of stories and scenarios of what could have been, what she may have known and when. The web of my mind is so tangled with possibilities, and to hear more lies from her would completely—"

"Does it matter?" Iron asked, serious as a heart attack.

The gears in Rhode's mind ground to a halt, because in no

way had the angel just asked that question. "Does. It. *Matter?* How the hell can you even ask me that?"

"How the hell did any of us get to a point where you'd make me ask it?"

At a loss for sense and next steps that didn't involve stabbing his kama into Iron's ear canal, all he could do was shake his head in disbelief.

"Let me clarify things, because, for the most part, we can give you the benefit of the doubt as to why you don't have your head screwed on straight. But the statute of limitations on said benefit expired, oh, I don't know, the minute your soul bond said she was about to sign a lease on an apartment that had nothing to do with you."

"Careful," Rhode ground out.

"We've all had secrets," Iron said, impressing upon him the full weight of Rhode's position. "The *why* of them was never as important as the execution, because at the end of the day, we always trusted each other and knew that whatever words we had to say were always said in service of the Empyrean. What came out of our mouths didn't matter. Betrayal doesn't come from words. It comes from actions. So I'll ask you again, does anything Neela said when Cyro's blade was at her throat actually fucking matter?"

Rhode's chest pumped air through his lungs at jet-engine speeds. For the first time in too many weeks, he sifted through memories, not of that snowy evening at the park but of every other moment he'd shared with Neela. The day he found her, tangled and frantic beneath a charmer's cargo net. The evening she found *him* at the animal shelter and took exactly zero of his brooding bullshit. The intoxicating joy on her face as she flitted from tree to tree in this very arboretum.

The photo booth where all she wanted was a memento to take home, and she gave him one his mouth had since memorized.

He tried damn hard to find the kernels of betrayal, the tell-tale signs of off-color questions or coming and going at odd hours.

And then shame, hot and defacing, rose up in his gut when he found none.

"Holy shit." Rhode stumbled back against the nearest tree trunk both wide and alive enough to support him as the reality of the past few weeks walloped him with the steel-toed end of his size-fifteen boot.

He had exhibited all those things. The accusatory javelins he'd constantly heaved at her. The anger. Pawning her off on other people. Downright abandoning her, leaving her alone at every occasion from meals with his family to this very arboretum.

And what had she done in retribution?

Comforted him. Sought him out when the warrior in him wanted to be alone while the prisoner of war inside his head screamed for companionship. Warmed his bed even though he'd given her very few reasons to return to it.

Then his mind stopped whirling long enough to break down on the exit ramp of their earlier conversation. He'd given her very few reasons to return *period*. So she wasn't.

"I've been such a fucking asshole."

Iron nodded. "Yup."

"And she's leaving," he breathed out, hating the panic that clutched his heart.

"Yeah," Chrome replied, leaning forward on his hips and smiling his trademark shit-eating grin. "So what are you going to do about it?"

Rhode's wings were out and connecting with the nearest thermal before the sentinels' booming laughs shook any more snow from the trees.

CHAPTER 35

Five minutes inside the apartment and already Neela had come to actively despise the color beige. It shouldn't have been that surprising. If such a neutral snoozefest of a color had actually existed on any mortal color wheel, beige was about as opposite as one could get from the preferred neon green and hot pink of her favorite twinkle lights.

Which, she was disheartened to realize, she'd left in the angels' den, because being the only female charmer didn't magically gift her Amazonian height.

Yet another reason on her smorgasbord of arguments to leave.

Rhode had been the one to put the lights up in their—correction, *his*—living quarters, and since he'd actively avoided everything having to do with her and despite many precarious chair balancing acts on her part, she could never quite reach the damn things.

Sure, she could have bugged one of the other angels for help, but there was something about inviting another man into that space that felt like an even bigger betrayal than the one she'd already committed. It didn't improve matters that the space had never been hers to begin with.

The apartment she stood in the middle of had a similar thing going for it. Though far larger than her suite of rooms in Cyro's hideaway, this was also about to be paid for with money that was not her own. The idea left her about as comfortable as a boob in a mammogram machine, but it wasn't like she had a lot of options, and dammit, Drea and the others knew it, too. So when she'd first floated the idea to everyone over breakfast that she might want to try living on her own for a while, Tung was at the ready with the cash hookup.

While taking the handout wasn't exactly fun, it had been necessary. What *hadn't* been necessary were the pitying glances and soft nods of support that were made oh-so-heavier by the uncertainty lingering around her.

In one desperate fell swoop, she'd simultaneously planted every questionable doubt into the only people who'd ever truly cared for her and also delivered the one thing that was a game changer in their quest to get home: the relic.

So, yeah, the appreciation was there, and she hadn't survived that long without knowing she needed to ride that gratitude wave for however long the crest stayed above the surface, but the distrust was there as well. Of course it was. What else would have kept Rhode away from his family for so long? And did she blame him?

Neela set her bag, which contained the sum total of every piece of clothing she only sort of owned, down on the gray low-pile carpet, rooted around for the tape measure, and started outlining what her future would look like etched in graphite measurements and leveled markings. Soon, she'd gone through every inch of the place, sketching out the bones of what her new life would eventually fill in. The place wasn't much. Two bedrooms, a living room connected to a simple dining area, and a standard galley kitchen were all that stood between her and her bedraggled mess of poor choices that refused to give her conscience any moment of peace.

Distractions were one thing, but efficiency, on the other hand, was something else entirely. If she could just mentally picture everything around her filled in, all her shelves, hanging plants, and gauzy curtains, and work at it like a fiend, it would almost—*almost*—take the sting out of the soul-deep throb that refused to go away when she thought of the space without him.

Rhode.

The one person she'd tried so hard to reach was also the one person who had mastered the art of always stepping out of that reach.

Until then, Neela's focus had been doing the lion's share of the lifting, holding her final intact mental fragments by the tits and forcing them into service to measure out the small bathroom's window size. She was doing semi-okay until she walked by the mirror above the pedestal sink.

Instead of her reflection, all Neela could see was Rhode's face. The memories of his squared-off jaw tensing as if he had just chewed on a nail. His deeply dark eyes flashing various shades of disapproval and disgust. Firm lips that had devoured her with passion she'd never thought possible slanted in an angry slash of hurt.

When her mind was in a reasoning mood, it would unhelpfully point out the number of times she'd tried to tell him about how she'd hoped to save him from his torment, from both of their torments . . . along with the number of times she'd shit the bed on that particular goal thanks to Cyro's little public revelation.

The resulting picture was as ugly as the festering wound twisting her heart into some petrified mass that even the most astute mortal paleontologist would have a hard time identifying as belonging to a hominid.

Tearing her gaze away from the mental image of Rhode that

always followed her around regardless of her will to leave it behind, she was equal parts annoyed and grateful when she realized she'd left the paint chips in the car.

Because, despite every cleanser she'd tried, she hadn't managed to buff away the scent of Rhode from the leather.

"Well, that's surely going to change very soon." On heavy limbs, Neela walked out the front door of the garden apartment and almost had to pinwheel her arms to keep from eating pavement.

Rhode stood in the middle of the parking lot with his hands in the pockets of his slacks and his broad chest standing between her and her car. A look of stony resolve was carved into not only his expression but the set of his shoulders as well. He was enormous, his silk shirt immaculate, and wore a quiet rage she'd only ever seen on the mortal Vikings from her video games. The sight of him forced goose bumps to emerge in places she didn't think possible and froze every muscle in her body, including the one at the center of her chest responsible for keeping air in her lungs and her body upright. If she'd had any ounce of decency or self-preservation, she'd have started spewing the apology she'd had saved on her lips from the very moment Cyro was blasted into the sky.

But all she could do was absorb the fierce beauty that she'd worried she'd never see again. Rich deep eyes, a wide brow, a chiseled chin that always had the perfect amount of rasp to it when he'd drag it across her delicate skin.

"What are you doing here?" she managed to say, though how she had trusted her voice to get the words out was beyond her.

"I think we need to have a conversation."

Her heart sank down to her heels. And there it was. The reckoning he expected from her, which, going by his stern demeanor, was to be delivered with no small amount of flourish and groveling on her part.

She could grovel. If that was what she needed to do to get him to finally listen to her, then that was what she'd do.

"I don't know where to begin, honestly." Neela took a tentative step closer and wrung her hands beneath her chin. "For so damn long, I've had the words at the ready. But now that you're here, I'm terrified that they won't be enough, that they won't satisfy you." She took a deep bracing breath and closed her eyes, willing every ounce of remorse and compassion into the explanation she prayed he'd accept. "Rhode—"

"The light suits you here."

Her eyes flew open, but before she could inquire further, she was stopped by the seraph's monotonous pacing across the pavement, which was only broken up by the occasional glance back toward where her apartment was.

"Eastwardly facing windows, attached garage, security cameras evenly spaced throughout the perimeter. The property management company is pretty good at selecting tenants as well, according to Chrome's background check. No history of tenant evictions or small claims suits. It's a small property, ten units. Easy to keep on top of. Employs regular lawn maintenance and snow removal contractors, all with equally clean records and up-to-date full insurance. Maintains an average tenancy of five years and has only ever raised rents to keep in line with municipal tax increases. They even get the building power washed and gutters cleaned on a regular cycle, which is practically unheard of in most mortal housing developments these days."

Neela's mind spun at the speed he paced in front of her. "What the hell are you talking about?"

"I'm saying your instincts about this place are spot-on. It's perfect, and that doesn't surprise me. Your instincts are always perfect."

Whatever native magnetism Rhode had exuded earlier to freeze her in place had slowly begun to unstitch itself from her limbs. Her brows made quick work of their newfound freedom and immediately shot to her hairline while she searched for words beneath a veil of confusion. On impulse, phrases like *let me explain* and *I'm sorry* came to the forefront, but every time they were loaded into the rocket of her mouth, poised to fly, Rhode's dark and twitchy frame passed across her nose like some courtroom prosecutor delivering closing remarks right before the jury was about to break for lunch.

"I remember you," he said emphatically to the painted lines in the parking lot that resembled her not in the slightest. "Maybe not fully, not in the way I should have, but my *soul* remembered you."

Neela shook her head. "You're not making sense."

"That's exactly it," he exclaimed, waving his hands in the air, trying to plead his case to a jury of pigeons who'd stopped to peck at a discarded muffin wrapper. "When Cyro had his knife to your throat, I didn't see red. I saw flames. I saw the mass destruction of everything around us for miles. I saw who I needed to kill, what I needed to sacrifice, how much damage I could sustain and still fight to get you free. I saw body counts and centuries-old trees buried beneath the snow mounds. There was no logic to it, only training. And when you hissed at him and that blade pressed farther against the delicate column of your throat, I lost my fucking mind. All I could think about was how soon I could slice that bastard's arms off and get you in mine. So when you started speaking, any semblance of my rational brain had been demoted to reserve status at best."

Somewhere in the back of her mind, a warning went off. A caution against interrupting whatever outpouring Rhode was coming to terms with, despite the torrent of things she'd held inside for weeks on end.

Finally, his pacing ceased, and he grabbed up her hands in a desperate gesture of acceptance. "I should have trusted your instincts. I should have known that under no circumstances would you have done the things you had, said what you did, if there were any other options available. I didn't believe you then, but my disbelief wasn't born of mistrust and hatred of *you* but of Cyro and every sick fuck who delighted in the torture of others."

All the taught muscles in her middle slowly untangled from her vital organs, allowing her to take the first full breath in weeks. And once the seal had been broken on that blockage, she'd finally been able to breathe him in. *Really* breathe him in, into her lungs, cells, and every aching part of her that had been starved for so long. But she stalled out that inhale in favor of gripping the sides of his face so she could immediately tell her truth. "You have to know that I never meant to hurt you. I never meant—"

"I love you."

Neela paused, needing all the time available for her brainwaves to fall over themselves untangling those three little words.

"You can't love me. You don't even like me that much."

"I love you," he repeated more insistently.

"No, you don't. You *can't*. You can hardly stand to be in the same room with me. I've had more breakfasts with members of your family without you present than with you there. I've had cooking lessons from Steel, gone on shopping trips with Molly and Drea where Brass accompanied us, and even been taught by Iron where best to stab a dagger into a man for maximum takedown with minimum thrust. Since I've been at the den, I've slept in your bed more times than you have, except for the few occasions when we'd both been so strung out and exhausted that we couldn't keep our hands off each other."

"More than a few times," he amended, and damn if her heart and other heated parts of her didn't remember every single one of those times.

Neela closed her eyes and sought out the strength she

needed to paint the true picture of what life had been like for her from the time he'd first found her in that mechanic's parking lot to this one. But the energy just wasn't there. How could it be? She'd spent so much time analyzing every misstep she'd made when it came to him, and now that he was here, touching her like *he'd* been in the wrong, she just had nothing left in the tank to fight with.

"I love you," he said again, rubbing soothing circles into the fleshy pads between her thumbs and index fingers. "I was so eternally wrong about everything. I let preconceived notions of who you were get in the way of what, deep down, essential parts of me knew you to truly be. My soul has been crying out for you since we both shared the same air in that dank cell, and I had no idea who you were or whether the soothing presence I felt was even real. My entire being screamed for you across the whispered inches that separated us then, and it hasn't shut up since."

As if reclaiming some of those lost inches, he brought her gathered knuckles to his lips and gently pressed his insistence into them. "You gave me back my time, and now it's my turn to give you back yours, because I can't spend another fucking second walking around this mortal coil like a mindless zombie hoping I'll find answers any place except where I've been afraid to look. *You're* my answer, Neela. You've shown me how to bask in the sunlight when you've only known it through others' experiences. You've cradled and nurtured lives that never had the capability of thanking you but are all the better for your undying care and love. And *I* want to return that love to you. It's so far past time someone showed you any scrap of the care you deserve, and I can't live another day knowing that you and I both have an entire lifecycle of a star's worth of time ahead of us and that we might spend it apart because I couldn't summon the stones to trust you."

Neela sniffed away the sharp prickle that was always the precursor to far wetter and messier things, but then Rhode cradled her face and inched his thumbs higher beneath the creases of her eyes, as if anxiously waiting for the first opportunity to care for her, starting with tending to the tears he'd caused.

"Are you being serious? Or is this another whiplash moment that I'll have to figure out how to endure on my own once you leave me again?"

"The only way I'm leaving is by following you wherever you intend to explore. I love you. I'll say it as many times as I need to for you to believe me."

Slowly, the rust caging her heart had begun to peel away, leaving that dead organ free to pump as much joy into her body as she could stomach. Which was, like, a lot. But then another sobering reality dampened the moment. "I can't be with you in the den, Rhode. It's too dark, too much like what I've known and dreaded. I want sunlight and stars and green grass. But I can't take you away from your family. I won't do that to you."

"You're not taking me away from anything. You're *giving* me everything. I could live under a park bench and sleep like the dead knowing you sat above me hours earlier."

Neela snorted. "You're being ridiculous."

"Try me."

And then she did. All of it. She tried on every single word for size and came away wrapped in the coziest embrace of comfort and adoration she'd ever experienced. It made her heart swell and her defenses soften.

"I love you, Rhode," she said, treasuring how those words felt on her tongue. "I— Oh my God, I left him in the car!"

Neela dashed around Rhode, not even sparing a moment to enjoy how adorable he looked with his features twisted in confusion, and bolted to the back of her SUV. A click of the key fob later, the hatch was up, and a giant Anatolian Shepherd leaped out of the vehicle, planting three paws solidly on the ground. The whole sit-stay routine lasted for the span of a good full-body shake before the dog was angling for Rhode and jumping up, licking the face of the angel she adored more than she ever thought possible.

"What-what is this? How? Easy, Lucky, easy! Oh God, he licked my teeth." Rolling laughs bellowed out of Rhode at such an abnormal pitch she wondered whether she'd get her first noise complaint before she'd even officially moved in.

"His name's Cerberus now. Officially adopted this morning and my new permanent roommate. Though, to be honest, I was hoping he could be your permanent roommate as well. That's what I had in mind, at least, when I adopted him, even if you and I didn't—"

Rhode swept her into his arms and seared his mouth to hers in a kiss so fraught with emotion that no words could ever have a chance of conveying the depths of his passion. Slowly, brick by brick, his lips punched out the dark windows of her past and let the light pour in with a high-beam's worth of abundance. It was in every grip of her waist, every gentle tug of her hair. The man's body spoke of promised eternities in the light and moved with a dance that they had their entire lifetimes to learn.

She'd finally found her sun-filled eternity and no amount of darkness could ever claim their souls again. Because darkness only lurked where one let it, and she was determined to allow as much light in as possible.

Rhode's possessive grip around her waist tugged at her soul's desire. "We're a true family now, little demon, and I couldn't be happier because you've always had my whole heart."

A lick on one cheek and a kiss on the other sealed the deal.

She was finally home.

EPILOGUE

One Month Later

The deep loamy soil beneath Rhode's boots had begun to finally soften as winter took its slow and final march out of the area. He couldn't say he was sad to see it go. The plans he'd been kicking around were somewhat seasonally dependent, which was why their current trip to Aurora's Landscaping and Garden Supply Center had been pushed off by a few weeks.

The visit, when he'd suggested it to Neela, had been met with the same amount of exuberance if he'd just told her he'd scored tickets to New York Comic Con, complete with celebrity meet and greets. Plump cheeks, achingly gorgeous smile, strong legs bouncing from toe to toe, and the flush dappling her alabaster skin that he mentally challenged himself to recreate on other parts of her later. Neela's joy had been a balm to his thawing soul, and when opening day arrived for the town's plant mecca, her vehicle was the first one in the parking lot.

"Ooh, what do you think of these?" Neela snatched up one of three small earthen pots that held another mound of soil with a green stem shooting out of it.

Rhode leaned forward and squinted at the thing. "What is it?"

"Orange butterfly milkweed. I'm thinking of making a butterfly garden for the monarch butterflies. Did you know that the eastern monarch butterfly population is in the shitter? Down fifty-nine percent in central Mexico due to habitat loss. If I could build out even a small patch of garden that'll attract them, maybe they'll call it home this summer and it'll help grow their local numbers a tad. I know we're not in Mexico, but every little bit helps, right?"

The fact that this woman had not only researched declining butterfly populations in parts of North America where *she did not live* but enacted a plan to save them regardless was enough to make him consider tattooing her name across his heart just so he'd always be able to guard her eternal kindness.

Rhode leaned over Neela's shoulder, picked up two more of those pots that looked identical to all the other pots but what the hell did he know, and put them in their shopping cart. The sign above the planters offered up a variety of *Monarch Munchies*, according to the pastel chalked floral script, but he'd have to take their word for it.

Neela rose up on her toes and kissed the edge of his jaw. "I love you." Then she bent down to a lower shelf he hadn't seen and put several more pots in the cart. "We're also getting the grayleaf goldenrod and the smooth blue aster. The aster won't start blooming until August, while the others start in June, but it'll last a bit longer into October. Between all the plants, that should give the butterflies most of the summer and fall seasons to enjoy themselves." Then her eyes drifted around his shoulder and took on a liquid sheen. "Oh my God, they have winterberry shrubs! Those will be perfect for the soggier land near the property's creek. And they're partial shade fiends, too, so it should work out great!"

Rhode aimed the cart toward whatever bush thing would be coming home with them next and knew he didn't have to look any further to know he'd made the right decision.

While the apartment Neela had originally chosen was certainly a wonderful place for her, the fact that she wouldn't have any land to work, grow, and fill with all the living things she had yet to care for made his heart physically hurt. And while Cerberus would have been the perfect apartment dog, contrary to popular belief owing to his size, it just wasn't fair to either of them. The dimensions of the cage didn't matter as long as someone else owned it. So when he'd floated the idea to her about buying a plot of land and building out their own space instead, he'd barely had time to catch her before she lofted herself into his arms and tackled him to the bed in squealing glee.

The weeks had been somewhat of a whirlwind after that, what with him recruiting the other sentinels to help him scout out the perfect property, buy it for pennies on the dollar—because who the hell wanted to buy frozen, undeveloped, and partially forested land in the middle of a New England winter? —and start getting some architectural and utility sketches mapped out. It'd still be many months before they could officially break ground on the project, but that didn't stop Neela from taking care of the flora along the property's perimeter. She called it her therapy, and her happiness was his everything.

Surprisingly, Iron had been the most helpful, especially when it came to scouting out the ideal location. Unfortunately, his help also came with a boatload of frustrated grunts and aggravated murmurs that made working with the angel more of a bitchfest than a build meeting.

But it wasn't like Rhode couldn't understand why.

"There's a piece missing," Iron had explained with a soul-deep weariness Rhode wished he couldn't relate to. "The relic is mostly intact, but a part of it got chipped. I suspect it happened when Neela swiped it off Cyro's wrist, judging by where the break is. It's not a huge piece. We hardly noticed it at first. But it's enough to make me worried that the juice this thing's holding might not be sufficient to get us home."

Then there were the unspoken worries about what sort of juice they were all hoping the relic still had in the first place. So much was riding on little more than estimation, supposition, and triangulated theories that there was so little left to throw into the hope bucket at times.

But that hadn't been the only thing that had chased Iron into the role of Rhode and Neela's foreman.

He'd been having dreams. Or *the* dream, as Iron had put it. One single recurring dream he refused to give details about except that it involved a woman. But whenever Rhode tried to delicately pick at that scab, knowing full well just how miserable it was to unlock something just to satisfy the curiosity of others, he treaded *really* fucking carefully. After he was met with silence the second time, Rhode gave up.

If Iron wanted to talk about it, he would. And if he wanted to throw himself into a project that kept his mind on things that were easier to solve, Rhode had no problem giving him the outlet to do so.

While Rhode rested his forearms on the handle of the cart and waited for Neela to inspect an eastern prickly pear plant, which, according to the lecture she'd just given him, was the only native cactus in New Hampshire, an elderly gentleman hobbled into the aisle across from him. Dapper as ever, with a navy sweater, gray-and-red flat cap, and cane that looked handmade, the man extended his elbow to the woman next to him—his wife, presumably—who accepted it instinctively. She then clutched the two halves of her sweater tighter against her throat and stood a bit taller as she lifted her glasses to read one of the tags beneath a watering can on the higher shelf. When her sandalwood orthopedic shoes got a bit too wobbly for the man's liking, he set his cane aside and cupped her elbow with both hands, guiding her steadily the few extra inches to read what she needed to. Once satisfied and stationary again, she looked up at the man and smiled, shrinking her watery eyes into tiny slits behind her large thick cat-eye glasses. And wouldn't you know, that man, who Rhode guessed had to have been pushing the better part of his eighties, summoned whatever strength his brittle bones could still squeeze out, reached up, and snagged her selection down from the shelf.

The quivering joy on her face was a memory Rhode promised to play on repeat whenever the years ahead of him got too heavy with expectation.

The man carefully placed the teal watering can in the shopping basket at his elbow and continued escorting his wife around the store. The look of unabashed adoration on his face filled out every wrinkle, somehow giving him a vitality far younger than his years. When he brushed past Rhode, the man dipped his head slightly, then gestured toward Rhode's shopping cart and said, "Just keep pushing and you'll be all right."

And he would be. The realization left him dazzled, delirious, and damn determined to care for Neela in whatever way she needed him to.

It was another promise he swore to himself and one that had been immediately etched onto his soul as fiercely as Neela's name had been.

She was a part of his family, and family came first. Always.

FOR UNTOLD EONS, Iron has been the dark horse of the fallen angel sentinels. With a haunted past that plagues his future, he keeps his eyes on the prize: returning to the Empyrean. But when heated dreams finally show him his ticket home, the mate they reveal is single, pregnant, and prefers solitude to the support she very much needs. Find out what happens when the last of the sentinels must face an impossible choice: save his soul bond, or save the world. Start reading *Angel's Smoke!*

CAN WE KEEP IN TOUCH? Are you curious to see what happens when Neela plans a birthday party for Cerberus, complete with a K-9 agility course, but Rhode and Chrome think they can each master the course better than the other? It's a battle of brotherly love and Empyrean egos. Claim your BONUS EPILOGUE when you sign up to my newsletter to see how what should have been a fun romp for the dog turns into a sentinel strength and agility competition that would shame even the Greek gods themselves. Enjoy!

THANK you so much for reading *Angel's Vengeance!* If you loved seeing Rhode and Neela's relationship grow, let your friends know. Help other readers fall in love with this couple, and all those hunky angels, by leaving a review.

SCAN THE QR code to start reading *Angel's Smoke* and the BONUS EPILOGUE today!

ACKNOWLEDGMENTS

Rhode's story was a book I wasn't sure I had it in me to write. When the idea came to me of another fallen angel who was somehow floating out there, alone and abandoned, it felt so *heavy,* but was something I couldn't shake.

Thank you to Cynthia St. Aubin and Ben for being the cheerleaders I needed to push through the scarier parts of telling this story, and for convincing me to keep going so Rhode and Neela could find their happily ever afters. Theirs were particularly sweet and ever-so needed.

Here's to doing the hard things!

ABOUT THE AUTHOR

Aimee Robinson is a lover of romance novels in all forms. Her absolute favorites, though, are the ones that offer a little bit of something *extra*: time travel, guardian angels, good old-fashioned meddlesome grandmothers with a supernatural secret to hide, you name it.

She believes romance novels should transport you from the humdrum to the swoonworthy, preferably while being curled up on the couch with chocolate and tea (or a martini . . . or both!). Aimee's overactive imagination lends itself to fun tales with emotional adventures, sexy snark, and happily ever afters.

When not writing or reading, Aimee enjoys spending time with her husband and keeping up with her two young sons.